Praise for Adriana Locke

"Adriana Locke creates magic with unforgettable romances and captivating characters. She's a go-to author if I want to escape into a great read."

—*New York Times* bestselling author S. L. Scott

"Adriana Locke writes the most delicious heroes and sassy heroines who bring them to their knees. Her books are funny, raw, and heartfelt. She also has a great smile, but that's beside the point."

—*USA Today* bestselling author L. J. Shen

"No one does blue-collar, small-town, 'everyman' (and woman!) romance like Adriana Locke. She masterfully creates truly epic love stories for characters who could be your neighbor, your best friend—you! Each one is more addictive and heart-stoppingly romantic than the last."

—*USA Today* bestselling author Kennedy Ryan

"Adriana's sharp prose, witty dialogue, and flawless blend of humor and steam meld together to create unputdownable, up-all-night reads!"

—*Wall Street Journal* bestselling author Winter Renshaw

BETWEEN NOW AND FOREVER

OTHER TITLES BY ADRIANA LOCKE

The Exception Series

The Exception
The Perception

Landry Family Series

Sway
Swing
Switch
Swear
Swink
Sweet

The Gibson Boys Series

Crank
Craft
Cross (a novella)
Crave
Crazy

Dogwood Lane Series

Tumble

Tangle

Trouble

Carmichael Family Series

Flirt

Fling

Fluke

Flaunt

Flame

Stand-Alone Novels

Sacrifice

Wherever It Leads

Written in the Scars

Lucky Number Eleven

Like You Love Me

The Sweet Spot

Nothing But It All

The Marshall Family Series

More Than I Could

This Much Is True

The Brewer Family Series

The Proposal

Landry Family Security Series

Pulse

BETWEEN NOW AND FOREVER

ADRIANA LOCKE

This is a work of fiction. Names, characters, organizations, places, events, and incidents are either products of the author's imagination or are used fictitiously. Otherwise, any resemblance to actual persons, living or dead, is purely coincidental.

Published by Montlake, Seattle

www.apub.com

ISBN-13: 9781662512445 (paperback)
ISBN-13: 9781662512452 (digital)

Cover design by Letitia Hasser
Cover photography by Regina Wamba of ReginaWamba.com

Printed in the United States of America

To my sons, who are, without a doubt, my best work.
You can never imagine how much I love you.

CHAPTER ONE

Gabrielle

"Be careful. You never know which way that pickle's gonna squirt, Gabs."

My laughter fills the small kitchen. The sound cuts through the dust particles dancing in the sunlight, adding another layer of magic to the room. As much as my cousin Cricket tries to remain steadfast, the corners of her lips lift.

"Get your mind out of the gutter," she says, removing her latex gloves. The rubber squeaks as it slides off her fingertips. "Why do you have to make everything so dirty?"

"*Oh, come on.* You're the one talking about phallic-shaped items squirting. *You* went there. Not me."

Cricket huffs, her perfect bright-red curls bouncing at her shoulders. "Fine. I'll put it another, more straightforward way: you can't always predict the outcome of home improvement projects, Gabby. It may look like a simple drywall patch. But the next thing you know, you find termites and have to call a contractor to rebuild the walls." She lifts a brow, eyeing me carefully, like her mother, my aunt Diane, used to do when I was a little girl. "Just . . . *go slowly*. Don't jump into a bunch of projects at once."

I wipe my forehead with the back of my hand. *She's probably thinking about the grid incident.*

"*Yes,"* she says. "This has everything to do with you single-handedly bringing down the electric grid for half a city block."

"That's *so* unfair. How was I to know you can't hook outside lights to the main electric line coming into your house? Doesn't that seem, I don't know, like *the point*?"

She tosses the gloves into the trash bin. "What about when you hooked water pipes to the drainpipes under the sink in some half-cocked plumbing project?"

"Forgive me for not knowing that not all those pipes . . . piped."

"Only you, Gabs. Only you."

"Don't you have better things to do than catalog all my do-it-yourself adventures?" I ask, putting a hand on my hip.

Cricket laughs. "Yes, actually, I do. But when you choose to call me every time you're standing next to an emergency vehicle, the EMT tending to the results of your *do-it-yourself adventures*, it makes them hard to forget."

"I don't recall hearing you complain when the fire chief asked if you were single."

Her cheeks flush as she waves a hand through the air. "Oh, don't start with that. He only saw me through FaceTime. Besides, the man was nothing short of a baby. His idea of a night out probably came with a curfew."

I lean against the cabinets and smile, watching her collect what's left of the cardboard boxes scattered around the room.

Despite travel fatigue, strongly scented cleaning supplies, and a lack of appropriate caffeine levels, it feels good to be *home.*

Waking up the last two mornings in the small, sleepy town where I grew up has been a balm to my soul. Pine trees scent the air. The sun is brighter—*warmer*—on my face each morning. Having family and neighbors stop by to say hello has been wonderful.

It's everything I hoped it would be. *Everything I needed it to be.*

"There," Cricket says, surveying our handiwork with satisfaction. "I think that's the last box. Is there anything else in the garage?"

"Nope. Your micromanaging talents ensured that my new house was cleaned from top to bottom, and all our possessions were put away."

"In just three days, despite your insistence that it would take at least fourteen." She rests her hip against the wooden table I've had longer than my children. "How does it feel to be settled in and ready for your new life in Alden?"

The sun chooses this moment to peek out from behind the clouds and shine into the kitchen.

Despite a pinched nerve in my shoulder from the fourteen-hour drive from Boston to Ohio, fatigue deep in my bones, and the deflating effect of being on the other side of an adrenaline rush, I'm cautiously optimistic about the future. It's been years since I've felt so confident, so sure that I'm making the right decision. But admitting that out loud feels like inviting the universe to prove me wrong. So I tiptoe right around her question.

"It feels like my new life in Alden is calling for a hot bubble bath and a bottle of something red," I say, hopping onto the counter.

"That sounds delightful. Peter will be home shortly, and I need to start dinner. Would you and the boys like to come over? I'm fixing herb-crusted chicken and potatoes like Grandma used to make. Remember them? She'd smother them in cheese."

My stomach rumbles, and my heart warms at the memory. "That sounds incredible, but we ate at your house last night. We need to eat at home and start new routines."

"But what will you have? You haven't gone to the grocery store yet."

"We'll order a pizza or something. Does Thompson's in Logan still deliver in Alden?"

"Yes, but will the boys want pizza for dinner?" She's slightly horrified. "Didn't you feed them that for lunch?"

I laugh. "They're fourteen and seven. I'm pretty sure they'd eat pizza for every meal and be happy."

"Give them a month, and I'll have them requesting vegetables with their meals like Kyle."

"Cricket, your son is an anomaly."

She grins smugly. "Maybe so. But I'll do my best to get Dylan and Carter on the anomaly train with him."

"Good luck with that."

She scurries around the kitchen, tidying up a few areas. I appreciate her attention to her work—truly. But the house will never be this clean or organized again. Whatever code in her DNA is responsible for her domestic abilities, I didn't get it in mine.

Cricket and I have always been opposites. Growing up, she played with baby dolls while I canvassed the town, trying to find enough kids to form a kickball game. In high school, she was the homecoming queen. I had a spare key to the school gym. She was tall with a perfect smile and her mother's good sensibilities. I was barely five foot one, flirting with scoliosis, and harboring my mother's propensity to daydream.

Despite our differences, we were always great friends. I'd never seen her cry as hard as she did when I left town for college. She begged me to stay and commute to a university closer to home. I might have done that if the only scholarship I was offered wasn't over two hours away. And unlike her parents, my single mother couldn't pitch in on tuition.

"Is that your doorbell?" Cricket strains to hear the faint echo ringing through the house. "It sounds like a sick cat."

I listen, making a sour face. "It does sound doorbell-y in a tortured, haunted way."

"We need to have someone fix that," she says, heading into the foyer. "*But not you.* That could be an electrical issue, so hands off."

I roll my eyes and slide from the counter. My feet hit the floor as the door opens and shuts.

"Gabby, this is Della Kendrick," Cricket says, returning to the kitchen with a gorgeous blond woman at her side. "She's lived in Alden for a couple of years. Her house is the green one across the street."

Della gives me a warm smile that reaches her blue eyes. "I'm sorry I haven't come to say hello. And I'm sorry I don't have a plate of cookies or whatever you bring to new neighbors." She pauses, grinning mischievously. "Although, if I made the cookies, you probably shouldn't eat them."

We all laugh.

"You grew up here, right?" Della asks.

"I did. I left for college, met a boy, and never returned," I say.

"Until now," Cricket chimes in. "She's back with two boys of her own. Dylan is fourteen, and Carter is seven."

"Well, I don't know what Alden was like back then," Della says to me. "But it's a nice little town now. Our street is pretty quiet. Kyle's truck is the loudest thing on Bittersweet Court."

Cricket grimaces. "That thing is an embarrassment. I have no idea why he thinks having his truck announce his arrival from a block over is an achievement."

"If that's the worst thing he does, *take it.*" A pain fires through my shoulder at the mention of teenage behavior. "Dylan has been giving me a run for my money. I'm hoping life here will slow him down a little. I'd love to see him enjoying the simple things, like Betty Lou's Diner for burgers and riding bikes around town like we did growing up."

Della raises a perfectly manicured brow. "Cricket rode a bike?"

"Me?" my cousin asks, offended. "Oh, heavens no. The only time I rode a bike ended in stitches. After that unfortunate incident, I stayed home while Gabby rode around with her more thrill-seeking friends."

"Gabby, you'll be unsurprised to discover that Cricket is still uncool," Della says, just before getting an elbow jabbed into her side. She laughs. "I mean it with love."

"I don't know what you're talking about," Cricket says, straightening her cardigan. "I'm fun."

"Oh, come on," Della says, rolling her eyes. "I called you last week to see if you wanted to go out for lunch, and you were ironing your drapes."

"Yes, and they're lovely."

Della looks at me. "See what I mean? Tell me you're fun, Gabrielle. I need a fun friend."

"You'll be happy to know that my to-do list includes three things: keeping my children alive, keeping them out of the juvenile hall, and having more fun. In that order."

Cricket leads us to the foyer. "Please compare definitions of *good time* before leaving home with Della. I watched two men do the walk of shame out of her house a month ago." She turns her attention to her friend. *"At the same time."*

Della's smile is wicked. "If you think that's shameful, you should've seen what happened a few hours before."

I sigh, opening the door for them. "I'm in the middle of the longest dry spell known to man, so no judgment here. Get it."

"Dry spell?" Della asks. "I can fix. I'll get your number from Cricket and then call you this week. We'll make plans."

A shiny black sports car honks as it rolls down the street. Cricket's husband, Peter, waves from the driver's seat.

"Of course he's home early tonight," Cricket mutters. "I haven't started dinner yet."

"You better get going," I say. "I want to bathe before the boys return from the rec center."

Cricket starts down the steps with Della at her side. "I mean it, Gabby. No new projects until we talk."

"Settle down," I say, leaning on a porch column. "I'm just trimming some hedges, painting the front door, and maybe reinforcing the rail around the back of the house before it's fully rotted."

"That sounds fine and good, but I know you," Cricket says over her shoulder. "You'll be on a ladder trying to reroof the place in a week, and I'll have to visit you in the hospital to remind you of this conversation."

"Make sure you bring oatmeal scotchies. They'll help me heal."

Cricket shakes her head and picks up her pace toward her house. Della gives me a final wave before jogging across the street.

I return inside and listen to absolute quiet. No car alarms blare, and no sirens wail in the distance. The neighbors aren't shouting at each other from the backyard. It's silent.

And it's amazing.

I take the steps two at a time, peeling my shirt over my head as I go. The promise of a hot bath, a quiet house, and knowing the boys are with Kyle and not being heathens running in the streets is nearly more than I can take. I strip off my clothes—wishing I'd poured a glass of wine—and fill the tub.

It's been a long time since I could take a bath before midnight. In Boston, I was racing home from work to make dinner, chasing after the kids, and then dealing with whatever fallout the day delivered. By the time I cleaned up our meal, fought with Dylan over his homework, and argued with Carter over video games, the day was expiring.

A bath in the early evening is nothing short of a luxury.

"Oh, what the hell," I say, sprinkling the eucalyptus bath salts I reserve for special occasions into the water. Then I turn to grab my phone before climbing in, only to find it missing. *"Crap."*

Sighing, I wrap myself in a towel, turn off the tap, and hurry back down to the kitchen. I immediately spot my phone next to the toaster. I reach for it, but . . . *"Holy shit,"* I whisper, leaning closer to the window to get a better look. *"Who the heck is this?"*

My mouth is agape.

A man stands in front of a large pickup truck at the house next door. He turns away, giving me a clear shot of him from behind.

Broad shoulders, filling out a red-and-black flannel. Denim covers his long legs and highlights his muscled build. He moves with a confidence that is *so* attractive.

I pull the side of the curtain out of the way and lean even closer for a better view.

He turns toward me, giving me an amazing line of sight to his abs through the front of his unbuttoned shirt.

Pronounced brow. Deep-set eyes. Full lips. A headful of dark hair that's a touch too long. Stubble covers his jawline, as if he forgot to shave for a day or two. It is *delicious.*

I can't look away. I should—I know I should. The smart, neighborly thing would be to grab my phone and return to my bathtub, giving him privacy. But I'm only human, and he's downright gorgeous.

It's as if something's connecting us, refusing to let go.

"And to think that I bought this house without anyone mentioning the view as a selling point," I mumble, craning my neck as he moves toward the back of his truck. No matter how hard I lean against the sink, how sharply the counter bites into my stomach, I can't see him.

My heartbeat strums steadily as shots of adrenaline hit my bloodstream. *What do I do now?*

The doorknob shines in the sunlight, beckoning me to grab it and twist.

I shouldn't. I have a bath waiting for me, a quiet house, and a clean slate with the neighborhood. But as I consider heading upstairs, the pull toward the back deck grows stronger.

It's been a long time since I've felt this tiny thrill of attraction. I've been too busy with life, the kids, and responsibilities to be present in my own world. But I'm here, and the flannel-wearing stud is right there. *Would it be that terrible to give in and just enjoy being a woman looking at a fine male specimen for a minute?*

Can't I have just this one thing?

It's ridiculous—and I mentally rebuke myself the whole time—but I open the back door.

The wood is rough against my bare feet; the sun is warm on my shoulders. I tuck my towel tighter around me and shuffle to the edge of the porch.

Soft country music drifts across the yard, pierced by the ping of tools against metal.

I lean against the rail and pretend to inspect the oversize lilac bushes growing alongside my house. My fingers slip over a heart-shaped leaf as my gaze slips over his driveway. The music fades against my pounding heart as I wait for him to come back into view.

"Where did you go?" I whisper into the breeze. "Come on. Come back to Mama."

He rounds the other side of the truck. His sudden appearance catches me off guard, and whatever cool, calm, and collected front I thought I'd be able to pull off doesn't happen.

He looks up. Our gazes snap together.

I heave a breath.

His stare is potent . . . *intentional.* The intensity is so strong that I flinch. He watches me as unabashedly as I was watching him, as if to say, *"I saw you, nosy lady."*

Get in the house, Gabs.

I drop the leaf and pull away, ready to retreat safely behind my door. But as I step back, a piece of fabric gets snagged by the rail. I whip around to prevent the towel from pulling away.

The tug was too much. It's too late.

There's a snap.

Then a crack.

There's a lot of light on a lot of places it shouldn't be.

"Ah!"

My panicked shriek breaks through the backyard as I topple, bracing for impact.

Oof.

Stems stick into my back and legs. Small branches poke me in uncomfortable places. There's a joke to be made about the stiff shaft poking between my legs, but the flower dusting against my left breast is distracting.

I scramble to pull the towel across my front and catch my breath.

You're right, Cricket. I wince. *Only me.*

CHAPTER TWO

Gabrielle

It takes a whole two seconds to remember the prickliest piece of this situation: *him.*

He saw me. There's no chance in the world the hunky neighbor didn't just witness that ungraceful splash into the flowers. And if he has any manners at all, he's on his way to ensure I'm not hurt.

I glance down at the askew towel.

The only thing hurt is my ego.

I tug the fabric to cover my essential bits. Funnily enough, I imagined removing layers of clothes in front of him just a few moments ago. *Oh, the irony.*

My breathing is hard and loud. I wiggle against the leaves in a futile attempt to be modest—to hide everything hidable, but all it does is make it difficult to listen for footsteps.

I have to get out of here. How can I get through the foliage without . . . "Eek!"

A set of warm hazel eyes peers at me from above.

My hand flattens against my chest, as if the pressure will stop my heart from rattling against my rib cage. The other squeezes the towel at my hip in a death grip.

He's even more handsome up close.

Sunlight hits the side of his cheek, casting shadows across his high cheekbones. His eyes twinkle. His full lips are pressed together as he takes me in, as if he can't decide whether to laugh or to be concerned.

"Um . . . *hi*," I say, although it sounds more like a question than a greeting. I flash him a weak smile. "Guess you saw that, huh?"

"It was a little hard to miss."

"In my head, I had all of my personal parts covered and landed with the grace of a ballerina. That's what you saw, too, right?"

I hold my breath while he runs a large hand over his jaw.

"Yeah," he says, dropping his hand to his side. "You were practically an Olympian."

"Ugh. Couldn't you just have lied to me?"

He balks. "What do you mean?"

"You could've just said, *'Absolutely.'* Or, *'It happened so fast I don't remember what you looked like.'*" I sigh, nestling my head against the leaves. "But you had to take it too far. Now I know you're lying."

"But didn't you just ask me why I couldn't have just lied to you?"

"Never mind," I say, groaning. "Guess I might as well introduce myself. I'm Gabrielle Solomon. It's nice to meet you . . . sort of."

He nods, wearing a confused, maybe even startled, look. A lock of tobacco-colored hair falls across his forehead.

The air is filled with the scent of his cologne. It's spicy and woody with notes of oud, something I can pick out thanks to my job at a department store fragrance counter in college. A hint of citrus comes from nowhere, finishing the scent with a sweet kiss.

I pause, giving him space to introduce himself. But it becomes apparent rather quickly that I can wait all day. He's not saying anything more.

My brows pull together. "A nod? That's it?"

"What do you want me to say?"

"What do you mean?"

"Again, *what do you want me to say?*"

"I don't know. Hello? Introduce yourself. Ask if I'm hurt?" I frown. "You know, you're really botching an opportunity to be a hero."

He smirks. "That would imply that I wanted to be one."

It's not *just* the smirk that liquefies my insides. It's the smirk, combined with his confident and slightly detached tone, that obliterates my ability to respond.

I've had a penchant for the cocky, broody type since elementary school. Levi Kellan sat beside me in class. He rarely looked my way and always had his face stuck in a book. He was casually cool, even as a fifth grader. I was in love.

Levi broke my heart in eighth grade by telling my best friend he was *unavailable* when she asked if he liked me. He didn't say he wasn't interested, nor did he have a girlfriend. He was just mysteriously *unavailable*.

That should've been it for me. The confusion—*What does 'unavailable' even mean?*—should've been a turnoff. Instead, I still dream about self-assured men who are just out of reach. I'm drawn to the ones who keep a part of themselves locked away. They're a treasure chest of surprises.

I gaze up at my neighbor and blush. *I bet he's full of surprises.*

He reaches toward me. I brace for his hand to contact my skin. The anticipation alone nearly lifts me off the flowers to brush against his body quicker. But instead of offering me his palm or checking me for injuries, he grabs the edge of the broken railing and pulls.

Oof.

The piece of wood falls into his grasp with little effort.

"It looks like this whole thing needs to be replaced," he says, inspecting the plank and pointedly ignoring my barely covered body beneath him. "This is rotted."

I release the air in my lungs, annoyed. "It's on my list."

"List of what?"

"Things to fix." I move my hip off a sharp stalk. "I need to paint and to fix the kitchen drain. Stop the toilet upstairs from running. The doorbell sounds like a wounded animal. And now the railing is trash."

"Didn't your home inspection point all of this out?"

"I'm sure it would've."

His brows shoot to the sky. "'Would've'?"

"I didn't have one."

"You bought a house without having it inspected?" He shifts his weight. "Tell me you're kidding."

"Careful. This is starting to sound an awful lot like hero language. Just saying."

He rolls his eyes.

"Look, I'm starting to itch," I say, scratching my shoulder. "So either lend a hand like the gentleman you haven't proven yourself to be or return to your truck and don't watch my Olympic-worthy routine getting out of here."

He tosses the wood onto the porch. "You have a plan, then?"

"My plan to get out of here?"

"No, your plan to fix the railing." He huffs a breath, exasperation thick in his tone. "*Yes*, your plan to get out of the bush."

I narrow my eyes at him before glancing at my surroundings.

The lilacs must be as old as the house because flowers don't grow this thick overnight. I'm tucked so deeply into the center of the plants that I don't think he—*whatever his name is*—would've seen me if he hadn't watched me fall.

Except he did see me, and now I need to get out of here with my dignity intact.

What's left of it, anyway.

"I'm going to"—*I have no clue*—"just climb out next to the house."

I bring my gaze back to his. His eyes steal my breath.

Gold rings hug the irises, blending into a mossy-green hue. The green deepens until it shifts into a chocolate-brown color that lines the outer edge. They're beautiful.

"I need to get back to my truck," he says. "But I also need to know you got out of there without breaking your damn neck."

His voice is gruff, and the edges of the words are sharp. But as he looks down at me, there's a warmth in his eyes and a hint of disingenuousness in his tone that he can't entirely hide.

I lift a brow in a silent challenge.

The corner of his mouth *slightly, only barely* tugs toward the sky. *And I melt.*

"There it is again," I say.

He hums.

"Hero talk." I grin. "You can't help it, can you?"

I want to mess with him more, but my skin is starting to itch again. The scratches from the fall burn, and I know the scrapes down my legs exist by the warmth on my calves. I need to get to my feet and into a bath. But I need him to leave so he doesn't see anything he hasn't already.

"Can I ask you a question?" I ask.

"What?"

"Did you . . ." I reconsider my words. "What all did you see when I fell?"

He braces himself, rolling his tongue around his mouth. Then he grins. "It was a blur."

I study him, carefully surveying his reaction for any sign of mendacity. Lucky for him, I can't tell.

"Good boy." I press my towel to my chest. "Go back to your truck. I'll be fine."

His head tilts to the side, and he holds his palms to the sky as if to say, *"What the hell?"*

"I mean it," I say. "Go. I can't get up with you watching."

He starts to speak but catches himself just before the words leave his tongue. Instead, he shrugs. "Good luck."

I wait until he turns away and the lilacs are taller than his departing head before beginning my careful extraction.

Getting upright is harder than I anticipated, and keeping the towel covering my crotch and boobs is even more challenging. I find two thick pieces of vegetation on which to place my feet and then try to move forward.

Branches and light-purple flowers smack my face, and I sputter against the taste of them on my lips.

I move again, ensuring one foot is stable before picking up the next. Just as I'm about to grab a stem to help propel me forward, the sound of my nightmares—the only thing in the world I'm afraid of—whispers *and rattles* from the left.

My heart skips a beat as I yank my hand back. I'm not sure whether to run or to freeze. *Do I move slowly or in one fast motion?*

Sweat dots my skin. My breaths are ragged. The hairs on the back of my neck stand on end, and I think I might faint.

I'm too scared to look where the sound is coming from, and I don't really need to. *There's only one thing that hisses.*

My scream comes softly at first. Then every ounce of air in my lungs increases the volume of my audible fear. Chills race one after another down my spine as I imagine the proximity of a snake—of the scaly, beady-eyed, legless creature from the depths of hell—to my naked body.

I'm going to be sick.

"Gabrielle." The neighbor's voice finds me just before I spot him. "Gabrielle, what is the matter now?"

He jogs toward me. This time, he's easy to read. Concern—plain and simple.

"Snake," I say, the one syllable stretched into three.

"Where?"

"I don't know. I can only hear it. It's hissing."

He reaches me in record time, and the relief that washes through me is unmatched.

"Is it on your left, or right?" he asks calmly.

"Left. I think." I start to look but swing my eyes back to him instead. "What do I do? I'm afraid to move."

"You're going to be okay. I got you. Just stay still."

He parts the vegetation and inspects the area. I squeeze my thighs so I don't pee.

"There it is," he says, as the hissing grows louder. "It's just a big bull snake. It wants less to do with you than you do him."

"I beg to differ." Tears cloud my vision. "Please, help me. I'm gonna puke."

He stands inches in front of me. The soft, yet strong smile he displays for my benefit causes a tear to trickle down my face.

His smile softens further. "Hey, I said I got you."

"Then get me."

"Okay. Your buddy over there is pissed. I will get between the two of you and lift you up in case he wants to strike."

I whine, my legs wobbling. "Okay."

He wraps his hands around my waist. The towel is crooked and barely covers my chest and thighs. His fingers dip into the fabric in the front and my bare skin in the back.

All non-life-supporting functions come to a screeching halt.

He positions himself between me and the snake—*please don't get bitten*—and all I can concentrate on is how rough the pads of his fingers are against my hips. They're fire—little bolts of heat that permeate the barriers between us and ignite a storm inside me.

He lifts me up and half over and half through the bush in one swift move.

"Oh, my gosh," I say, sucking in a lungful of air. The thought of the snake lingering close by brings on a full-body shiver. "I'm going to have to sell my house now."

He chuckles, pulling me against him.

His body is long and hard as I slide down his torso to the ground. As soon as my feet touch the earth, he digs his fingers deeper in my skin.

"Don't move," he says, holding my gaze.

"Why?"

He shrugs out of his flannel, exposing his wide, tanned shoulders.

My God.

He reaches behind me, and the soft fabric of his shirt touches my . . . bare ass.

Oh. *Oh!*

My eyes go wide as I remember that there are undoubtedly parts of me exposed to the world.

"Hold the towel against your front," he says. Once I'm covered, he steps back and ties his shirt around my waist. He cinches it tightly at my belly button. "There you go. That'll keep you covered until you get inside."

I skim his solid chest, chiseled abdomen, and the hint of a happy trail leading into his jeans as discreetly as I can. But when I raise my attention to his face, his shit-eating grin tells me it wasn't discreet at all.

"Thank you," I say, patting the top of my head with one hand. I pluck a flower out of my hair and toss it on the ground. "I don't know what I would've done without you."

"As soon as you stopped screaming, you would've walked out of there."

"I didn't scream."

"You screamed."

"I don't scream."

His lips twist to hide a smile. "Good to know."

Oof. I walked right into that one without realizing it. *Change the subject.*

"Can I at least get your name since you just saved my life?" I ask.

"Jay."

"Okay, Jay." I smile. "Thank you for being nothing short of amazing."

"You're welcome. I'll see if I can catch the snake once you're inside."

I glance over my shoulder. "Please find it."

"I'll try."

We face one another as if there's more to say. But the fact is, there's not. I've humiliated myself *twice* in front of him. I've said enough. And God knows I've done too much.

He runs a hand over his chin. "You better go."

"Yeah." I take a deep breath, not wanting to walk away from him . . . but knowing I must. "I'll bring your shirt over after I wash it."

"Whatever."

The browns in his irises overtake the green, then the gold. The color changes right before my eyes. And with the progression comes a shift in Jay back to the standoffish stranger he was when he arrived.

"Thanks again," I say, giving him a half smile.

He nods and then turns away.

I clutch the towel to my chest and take myself—and my failed dignity—back inside.

Maybe I'll have two glasses of wine with my bath.

CHAPTER THREE

JAY

Sorry about that." Taylor holds a serving tray in one hand and a drink pitcher in the other. What appears to be a ketchup stain marks her university sweatshirt. "Things get nuts when the Alden Social Club comes in on Friday nights."

My buddy Lark tosses his napkin on the table. "I hope when I'm retired, my wild Friday nights don't include a fish sandwich at Betty Lou's Diner."

"What are you talking about?" I say, laughing. "It's Friday night. You're here." I point at his plate. "And you just finished a—"

"Fish sandwich," he says, shaking his head. "Damn it."

I laugh, raising my pop to my lips and taking a drink.

Betty Lou's Diner, the preeminent eatery in Alden—and the only one open after four—is bustling. All thirteen tables and five stools at the counter have been occupied since Lark and I arrived an hour ago, and Taylor, Betty Lou's granddaughter, hasn't stopped moving.

I wandered into the diner on my first day in town nearly four years ago. It had a bright-green wreath on the door and a welcome sign that felt like an invitation to enter. And since I knew no one in town and had nowhere to go besides back to my rental to unpack, I figured I'd give it a shot.

It's been an almost daily occurrence ever since.

"What about you, Jay?" Taylor asks. "Do you need anything else?"

I set my glass down. "No. I'm good."

"Grandma made coconut cream pie," Taylor says, taunting me with my favorite dessert. "I know you're dying for a piece."

Not even Betty Lou's pie will satisfy my craving tonight, Taylor.

My mind takes the opportunity to replay the day's events. *More like the day's highlight reel.*

Smooth, freckled skin. Bright-green eyes. A dip at the small of her back that fits my hand perfectly.

Now, that *sounds delicious.*

"I'm good," I say. "That extra potato salad you brought filled me up."

"But did it butter you up?"

Lark chuckles, watching the weekly volley between me and Taylor.

"No," I say.

"Come on, Jay," she says, the words a plea. "You'd love her. She's so pretty and smart, and she teaches—"

"No, Taylor." I laugh. "I'm not going to date your boyfriend's mom."

She huffs. "You're letting all of that"—she sets the pitcher down and waves her hand up and down me like a game show hostess—"go to waste."

"How do you know what I'm letting go to waste?"

"You can't be doing anything too fantastic because you're in here every damn night."

"Touché."

She rolls her eyes.

The food and company are both good. Why go anywhere else?

"We'll take the check whenever you get a minute," Lark says, smiling.

"Will do." She swipes the pitcher back up and looks at me out of the corner of her eye. "But I'm charging you for double the potato salad."

"It's a small price to pay for avoiding a date."

She loads our empty plates—and the mayonnaise bottle that Lark can't eat without—onto her tray. "Do you dream of being alone for the rest of your life? Who hurt you?"

It's a joke. I know Taylor. She's a sweetheart. If she had any idea of how on point her question really was, she'd shit.

"He has mommy issues," Lark says, winking at me.

"It's more like the idea of not having anyone else's problems to manage, or feelings to consider, or crap to move on the bathroom counter so I can brush my teeth in the mornings sounds like heaven," I say.

Taylor makes a face at me, expressing her exasperation, and then scurries toward the kitchen.

The day's final rays of sunlight filter through the windows, bathing the dining room in a warm, muted glow. Familiar scents and friendly voices fill the air, creating a relaxing, homelike ambiance that attracts as many patrons as the food. As much as I love the fish on Friday nights and the homemade soups for which Betty Lou is regionally famous, it's the vibe that brings me back.

I yawn, stretching my legs out in front of me.

"How did the walk-through with Weatherspoon go today?" Lark asks, rolling his straw wrapper into a tiny ball. "Did he sign off on the house, or was he a dick?"

"Well, he's always a dick . . ."

Lark chuckles.

"He signed off. I think he would've kept us there indefinitely, spinning our wheels, thanks to his pissing match with the inspector." I roll my head side to side to keep tension from settling in the back of my neck. "But the owner happened to come by the house—pure happenstance—and gushed over how much she loved the woodwork. I think that helped get us out of there."

"Probably. What are you working on next?"

"We're starting on a farmhouse out by Fell's Creek. It's not a huge job. We're renovating what's there and adding a sunroom on the south side. It's good money for what it is."

"That's how we like it."

I grin. "That's how we like it."

"You know what else we like?"

"What's that?"

A slow, mischievous smile splits his cheeks. It's his feral smile, and enough to strike fear in a mere mortal. But I've known Lark long enough to know not to be scared. Just wary.

"We like five foot one, maybe five two, dark-blond or light-brown-haired women who are wrapped in a towel in the middle of the yard and look at us like we're the man of their dreams."

I sigh, tilting my chin toward the ceiling. That was *not* how Gabrielle looked at me. *Damn it.*

Somehow, the idea that someone saw the snake debacle a few hours ago didn't cross my mind. But it should've.

And I should've known the news would make its way to Lark.

Nothing about what happened should make this conversation awkward. Aside from Gabrielle being beyond beautiful and knowing how she feels in my arms being impossible to wipe from my memory—especially after not having a woman in them except for superficial encounters—our interaction was *a thing that happened.* Maybe it's a story brought up over beers or a laugh to be had when I see a snake going forward, but it wasn't a big deal.

So why does it feel like one?

"I've waited the entire meal for you to bring this up," he says, smirking. "It's funny that you didn't."

"Is it? Because I'm sure you had things happen today that you haven't told me."

"Trust me, my man. If I had an angel fall from heaven and land in my arms—"

"Shut the fuck up." I chuckle in disbelief.

He leans forward, resting his elbows on the table. "See, if you would've brought it up, I wouldn't have thought anything about it. But . . . you didn't. And that makes me think there's fire behind that smoke."

"What?"

"You know, that whole 'where there's smoke, there's fire' thing. That's this."

I take the bill from Taylor, wishing she'd stay and chat. Much to my dismay, she slips the paper into my hand and keeps moving.

Lark sits back. "Did she have a bad personality? Bad breath? Was she mean?"

I fight a smile from forming on my lips.

I've known Lark since I moved to town. The first day I came to Betty Lou's, he sat in the chair he currently occupies. When he commented he'd never seen me before, I said I was new to Alden. The next thing I knew, he was helping me move boxes and invited me to his house to watch a football game.

Our friendship is the easiest relationship I've ever shared. We both love sports, trucks, and the outdoors. Neither of us likes to text or use social media too much. We can go days without talking, meet for Fish Friday, and fall back to where we left off.

Despite his being my closest and only friend, I know Lark is puzzled. He wonders why I might see a woman for a week or two and then break it off, and he's curious about my disinterest in relationships. Lark would love to understand why I change the subject when he starts discussing getting married and having a family.

But he never asks. And I respect him for that.

"Great personality," I say honestly, because I can't let my frustration with Lark's questions unfairly paint Gabrielle in a bad light. "Breath was a little like pizza, but I'm not mad about that."

Lark laughs.

"Good boy. Go back to your truck. I'll be fine."

I chuckle softly. "You know what? She *was* a little mean, now that I think about it."

"That's my kryptonite. I love a woman that can be a little mean. *A little feisty.*" He growls. "Sex with them is so damn hot."

Taylor leans between us. "This is a family joint, boys. Keep the sex talk down." She looks at me and lifts a brow. "Unless you wanna go out with my—"

"Bye, Taylor," I say, laughing.

She groans and walks away.

Lark settles in across from me, waiting for me to finish my thought. Our conversation will return to Gabrielle, and Lark will keep digging until he finds the information he wants. My best bet is to take control of the chat and find a way to end it. *But how do I do that? What would distract him enough . . .*

Bingo.

"How did you find out about Gabrielle?" I ask, already knowing the answer.

"Della."

"Oh," I say like I'm surprised. "You talked to Della?"

Lark's face reddens, making his blond hair appear even lighter. His eyes glass over like a cartoon character's. If he sighs blissfully, I won't be surprised.

By all accounts, the woman across the street is a knockout. Della is in her mid to late twenties, has a tight little body, and always looks perfect—there's never a hair out of place. She jogs down the street, and every man outside raking leaves stops and stares.

I like her just fine. She's simply not my type.

But she's Lark's.

"She got back to town today," he says. "She called to see if I wanted to hang out this weekend."

"Nice."

"I haven't seen her in a month. I'm probably gonna get off in my pants like a teenager."

I laugh. "Where has she been? I haven't seen her car around in a while."

"She had a couple of contracts out of town," he says.

"What does she do for work again?"

He shrugs. "I really don't know. There's not a lot of talking between us, and the talking we do is more about times and places."

"But you had enough conversation for her to tell you about Gabrielle."

"It's not every day that a woman falls off her porch in nothing but a towel and you have to pluck her out of the bushes. Then she goes back inside with your shirt wrapped around her waist."

"Della saw all of that?"

He nods. "She said you two seemed pretty chatty."

Instead of answering him, I slide my wallet out of my pocket. I find my credit card and hand it to Taylor as she passes.

Lark raises both hands. "Okay, that's fine. You don't want to talk about it."

"There's nothing to talk about, Lark."

He takes a wad of cash out of his pocket and slaps some on the table for a tip. "What are you doing this weekend?"

"I'm going to change the oil in my truck and put some shit up in my garage. The Weatherspoon job kept me running around for the last month. My garage became a drop-off zone for tools and materials. It's driving me nuts."

I take my card back from Taylor. "Thanks."

"No problem," she says. "See you, guys."

"See ya later," Lark says, handing her the cash.

We get up and head outside. The sun has slipped below the horizon. Stars twinkle in the clear sky.

"If you and Della get done early, come over," I say as we reach our trucks.

"I'm going to do my best to make it take as much of the weekend as possible."

Laughing, I open the driver's door. "Understood. Have fun."

"Will do. Try not to organize too much. It's not good for the soul."

I shake my head and climb inside the cab, turning on the engine. Now that the sun has set, the air has a bite to it, and I left my sweatshirt at home. *Gabrielle has my flannel.*

Her waist molded in my hands. Her breath warmed my cheek. The memory of my shirt hanging off her body makes me hard.

I'm sure it was the eventful way we met that makes her impossible to forget. After all, not many exciting things happen in Alden, and seeing a naked woman fall off her porch isn't a daily occurrence.

Especially when they look like Gabrielle.

My heart begins to pound, and my blood runs hot. I grip the steering wheel and imagine the softness of her skin. I think about how her tits hung off her frame in perfect teardrops. The curve of her hip. Her eyes taunted mine like they held the keys to my inner workings.

I didn't know I was capable of responding to a woman like that.

Not after what happened with Izzy.

My fingers release the wheel, and I blow out a breath.

And that's why I have to keep myself in check.

It was a moment with Gabrielle. And it will never be anything but that.

CHAPTER FOUR

Gabrielle

I gather our plates and the empty pizza box off the table, making a mental note to tell Cricket that the boys ate every single crumb.

The news that Alden still doesn't offer recycling to the community blows my mind. The waste management company dropped off our refuse containers earlier in the day, and the poor man appeared mind-boggled when I asked about the bin for recyclables. I'm pretty certain no one has ever requested one before.

Carter's footsteps tap against the floor above the kitchen. He wanted the smaller of the two rooms upstairs. He's convinced the proximity to the router will give him better ping for his video games. *Whatever that means.* Occasionally, a laugh will trickle through the thin walls and make its way to my ears. I stop in my tracks and appreciate the sound every time I even think I hear him.

I turn toward the sink as Dylan enters the room. He barely acknowledges me with a grunt. Already in his pajama pants and no shirt, he pads his way across the room.

"Hey, buddy," I say, dropping the plates into the sink. I try not to look at him like he's a wounded badger, even though that's exactly his vibe. "What are you up to?"

"Getting food."

I drop the pizza box in the trash. "Did you not get enough at dinner?"

"I did. But I'm hungry again."

He doesn't look at me as he speaks. He simply opens the refrigerator and peers inside. I'm not sure he'd acknowledge my existence if I hadn't spoken to him first.

"We don't have much to eat," I say. "I haven't had a chance to go to the store."

The door shuts with more force than necessary. I start to say something—to remind him not to be so hard on our things—but think better of it. This isn't a battle I really want to fight tonight.

"Do we have anything in the pantry?" He spins around and faces me for the first time. "Do we even have a pantry?"

"Yes. We have a pantry." I point at the tall cabinet beside him. "Again, there's not much in there."

"Enough to even look?"

"I don't know, Dylan. But it would probably be faster for you to take five seconds and have a gander rather than stand here and grill me over it."

He narrows his eyes, letting them rake over me as he turns away.

"Did you have fun with Kyle?" I ask as he rummages through the few boxes of crackers and cookies we brought from Boston. "You didn't really say much when you got home."

"It was fine."

"Carter seemed to enjoy himself."

"Well, Carter is seven. Of course he enjoyed himself. He got to hang out with older kids at the rec center." The pantry door smacks shut. "Must be nice to have that kind of freedom at seven. I barely have it at fourteen."

I set my jaw in place and remind myself he's doing this on purpose. He's poking and prodding, trying to rile me up to prove a point. Reacting won't help.

"You don't have anything to say to that?" he asks, lifting a brow.

"I have a lot of things to say to that, Dylan. But I don't have the energy to rehash a topic we've gone over a million times."

"You mean that you don't trust me."

"Dylan . . ."

I look at my son and silently plead with him to stop.

He's not this kid—this argumentative, sometimes hateful, rule-bending person I've lived with over the last year. If he were, I would know. I've known him since before he walked this planet.

I know the sound of his breath while he sleeps, the ticklish spot just behind his right knee, and that beneath his hair are two crowns at the top of his head. There are twenty-seven freckles across his nose and a birthmark resembling chocolate milk on his left inner thigh. He likes to build things and take things apart. He hates needles and apples. And somewhere, buried under a lot of anger and frustration, is a little boy who misses his father.

"Trust is earned," I say carefully. "And you helped your case today by going out with Kyle and coming home on time, not giving him any trouble, and being a good sport about Carter tagging along."

"You didn't give me a lot of choice."

I sigh. "I wanted you to meet people. You'll be going to school with those kids on Monday. Won't it be easier if you recognize some of the faces?"

"It would've been easier to stay in school in Boston. So if that's what you're worried about, you've already screwed me over."

"Dylan . . ." I call after him, but he's on the stairs before I can get his name out.

"Damn you, Christopher," I say, letting the licks of anger stemming from my ex-husband's death burn for a moment.

Chris and I divorced three years ago, when Carter was four and Dylan eleven. Our mutual friends said we had the most amicable divorce they'd ever seen. We tried to explain that we didn't fall out of love—our love just changed. Instead of being spouses, we were more like friends.

"We'll still do life together. We'll just do it from different houses." Christopher smiles at me with the same goofy grin Dylan used to wear. "You deserve a lover, someone to appreciate all the wild goodness you have to offer. This doesn't mean I don't love you, Gabs. It just means that there's someone else out there who can love you better. And I love you enough to want that for you."

Tears fill my eyes as I fight back a surge of emotion. *I miss him so much too.*

"You were supposed to be here," I whisper to the empty room. "You were supposed to help me with this."

I look at the ceiling through the fluid clouding my vision and fight to regain composure.

"Mom! My ping is, like, two thousand, and I'm getting killed before I can even render in!" Carter shouts from upstairs. "My ping was two at home! This isn't fair!"

His little voice makes me smile, even though my heart pulls that he still calls Boston "home." *Of course he does. Give him some time.* I wipe my eyes with my hands and clear my throat.

"Speak English, please!" I shout back.

"Our internet sucks!"

I smile. "I can't help it."

"I can't live like this."

"It's a travesty, I know."

His door closes. His steps are a bit heavier on the floor than they were earlier.

I take a breath and spot the old pancake advertisement my mother hung in her kitchen for decades, tacked to the wall above the baker's rack. My apron, the one Christopher purchased for me the Christmas before he passed, hangs off a hook by the broom closet. The refrigerator holds magnets the boys made when they were younger. School pictures, handprints dipped in paint and laminated for eternity, and one sequined blob I've never entirely understood from Dylan's first-grade year.

Part of me thought I should declutter as we packed up the Boston house. I took each magnet off the fridge, intending to throw them away. But those silly little trinkets help make our house a home. They're a reminder of the continuity of our life together. And in a way, a reminder that there's so much life left to live.

The house is suddenly too small. I'm too antsy.

A chilly blast of air smacks me in the face as I step gingerly onto the back deck. I sit on the porch swing and pull my knees to my chest, balancing my bare feet off the edge. I can hear Carter playing his game—and his frustrations with the ping—as I move gently back and forth.

My attention shifts across the lawn and lands on the lit window at Jay's house. A shadow crosses the pane—a shadow big enough to be him.

Jay.

Goose bumps dot my skin at the memory of his calloused hands against my body. The decadence of his smirk drifts through my mind like a warm, lazy river. The way his gaze penetrated me makes me shiver. *Too bad that was all that got penetrated.*

"Hey." Cricket steps onto the porch, tugging her cardigan closer to her body. "Sorry if I startled you. Dylan let me in."

"He wasn't sneaking out, was he?"

She laughs, sitting next to me. "No. He wasn't sneaking out. He had a box of crackers in his hand."

"He's very irritated that we don't have snacks yet."

"I can't blame him. I'd be irritable, too, if I couldn't snack."

I bump her shoulder with mine.

She laughs. "Kyle said they had a good time at the rec center. He said Carter was the life of the party and that Dylan got off to a slow start but wound up making a few friends. That's good news."

"Kyle is my new favorite person in the world."

"He's a good boy. Now, what are you doing out here all by yourself? It's so chilly," she says, burrowing into her cardigan again. "Aren't you cold?"

"A little bit. I just needed some fresh air."

"Are you okay?"

"Yeah, I'm fine." I sigh, gazing at the stars.

There's something different about sitting on the deck at night and conversing with someone instead of doing it over the phone. Taking up space next to her and being honest and vulnerable is such a blessing. It's validating and freeing, and for once, I'm not alone.

"I've spent the last year at a standstill," I say, the words flowing easily. "Christopher's car accident threw all of us for a loop, and I'd like to say that I've spent the months since making sure the boys are okay. But if I'm being honest, I've had to grieve too."

Cricket touches my leg. "Of course you have, honey. I'd know you were lying if you said otherwise."

I look at my cousin and smile softly. "I told Della today I wanted to have fun again. But it's more than that. I want to feel *alive* again. You can have a fun night or weekend—and I want those too. But I also want to walk through my everyday life and feel like . . . *me*."

"This makes me happy to hear."

"It does?"

"Yeah. It does." She pushes off and starts us swinging again. "I hoped coming home would give you some room to breathe again. You've had a lot on your plate."

You're telling me.

For the last thirteen months, I've spent every waking hour keeping a careful eye on the boys. I had to sort out Christopher's estate since he left everything to me for safekeeping for the kids. And that, on top of watching out for the boys' emotional well-being, has consumed me. Drowned me. It's all depleted me in so many ways.

"Yeah, you're not wrong," I say. "I've spent much of my energy and spirit on other people, not that I'd have it any other way." I drop my gaze to my feet. "But I'm ready to climb out of the trenches and live my life again. *But* . . ."

Cricket rubs her hands together and then blows into them.

"It's not that cold," I say, shaking my head.

"Maybe not for you." She repeats the action and then drops her palms onto her lap. "Do you want me to give you permission?"

"Permission? For what?"

"You've spent this whole conversation trying to convince one of us, if not both, that you deserve to get back out there again."

Oof.

"Gabby, it's *your life*. You don't need anyone's confirmation or approval to live it however you want. And if Christopher were here, he'd say the very same thing."

Even though she's wrong—I wasn't seeking her approval for anything—her words touch my heart.

"Thank you," I say, fighting a lump in my throat.

Her eyes sparkle. "You're very welcome. Now, can we go inside? Because I'm turning into a sheet of ice out here."

"Wear a coat next time," I say as we get to our feet.

But just before she steps into the kitchen, she pauses by the railing.

"What happened here?" she asks, her brows pulled taut.

My gaze flips to Jay's house just as the light goes off.

The story is on the tip of my tongue, but I bite back the words before they can pass my lips.

Maybe it's a story for another time. Maybe it's a story I keep to myself. Either way, I don't want to share it. Not yet.

I gesture for her to go inside. "Oh, nothing. It just broke this afternoon. I'm going to fix it tomorrow."

"I'll get the first aid kit ready."

"Hey!"

We laugh as the door shuts behind us.

"I'm going to head home," she says, continuing through the kitchen to the front door. "I just wanted to check on you. And I didn't want to hear another thing about golf. Peter is on this golf kick, and it's driving me batty."

"Well, thanks for coming by. I'm sure I'll see you tomorrow."

She stops on the threshold. "Tomorrow is the first Saturday of the month."

"Okay . . ."

"Della, our friend Scottie, and I all get together on the first Saturday of the month. We have cocktails at one of our houses at seven. This month, we're at Della's. So if I don't see you before then, I'll see you there."

"What if I can't come?"

She laughs and makes her way down the sidewalk. "You can come, or I'll come get you. You only have to go across the street. No excuses."

It's very matter-of-fact—a simple explanation to a question she deems a joke. Even though people demanding my time usually make me want to push back, this time, it feels nice.

"I'll see you there," I say just before she's too far down the street to hear me.

Before I close the door, I glance to my left. I hope the darkness conceals my wide eyes at Jay's shirtless figure across the way.

My gaze follows the lines of muscle down his back. The security light overhead illuminates him. He grabs something from the cab of his vehicle and then heads back to the house. But just as he reaches the garage, he looks my way.

His steps stutter. My heart skips a beat.

I wait for him to say hello or smile. Instead, I only get a half wave, half salute before he disappears into the garage.

"Men," I mutter, shutting the door behind me.

CHAPTER FIVE

Gabrielle

"What in the world . . ."

I groan, shielding my eyes from the bright morning light. The sound coming from beneath my bedroom window begins again.

My body aches as I roll onto my side. Muscles I didn't know I had throb. Scratches litter my arms and legs, thanks to my fall from grace yesterday.

I want to curl up on the soft mattress and go back to sleep. But I'm jostled awake not only by the thumping outside but also at the time shown on the clock—nine thirty.

"Crap," I grumble.

The hardwood is cool against my feet. I reach into my small closet and grab my robe, tying it haphazardly as I head for the stairs. Both boys' bedroom doors are open, and the rooms are empty.

"Boys!" I call down the staircase as I try not to trip over the edge of the robe. I poke my head into the living room. "Dylan? Carter? Where are you guys?"

I take the corner to the kitchen and almost run into my oldest son.

"You scared the shit out of me," I say, jumping back.

"Better go wipe your ass, then."

"Dylan James." I glare at him. "Watch your mouth."

"Sorry."

He's not sorry.

I pour myself a cup of coffee, thankful for automatic machines. *First things first.* "Where's Carter?"

"Your golden child rode his bike to the park with a kid we met yesterday."

"Does this kid have a name?"

Dylan shrugs.

"So you just let your little brother go off with an unknown person in a new town?"

"Look, Kyle knew the kid. Carter played with him for two hours yesterday, and his mom was walking with them. And considering this is the cheesiest town in America, I'd say he's fine. Chill out."

I hold my steaming cup between both hands. "Dylan, after I drink this and can think clearly, you and I are going to have a conversation about your attitude."

"Wasn't it you who said last night that you didn't want to rehash conversations that we've had a million times?" He shrugs and starts up the stairs. "But whatever. All I got is time."

I think he mumbles something like *"Until I'm eighteen,"* but I'm not sure.

The mug is at my lips when the pounding starts again. I jump, dousing my front with hot liquid.

I want to cry. I want to yell at whatever is making that damn noise. I want to pour the coffee down the drain and go back to bed until Dylan grows out of the stage that makes me understand why some animals eat their children.

"Ugh."

I set the mug down and grab a hand towel. My jaw is set, and a growl is on my lips. I throw open the door ready to brawl.

"What the hell is going . . . *on out here.*"

My voice softens until the last of my words are barely audible.

Holy. Crap.

Jay kneels on the deck, looking like a freaking snack. A tight white T-shirt that's thin enough to snuggle his back and arms lies over the ridges and valleys of his body. Jeans hug his thick thighs. A tool belt wraps around his narrow waist. He looks up at me, does a quick scan from head to toe, then lifts a brow and goes back to work.

I vaguely remember putting on a pair of shorts with jelly beans on them that barely cover my ass and a white tank top, no bra, before I went to bed last night. *Better keep this robe pulled tight.*

"Your little boy is riding his bike with Hayes Collins," Jay says without looking at me. "His mom, Freya, works at the city building, and his father is the principal at the elementary school. They're both good people. He'll be okay."

What? I groan. *They're going to think I'm a terrible mom.*

He stops drilling for a moment. "I heard you inside, talking to your other boy. The one with the mouth."

"He has a mouth, all right," I say, blowing out a breath. The attempt at slowing my heartbeat down to a regular speed isn't successful. "Those people are going to think I'm awful. Maybe *I am* awful."

"Relax." He drills another screw into the post and then checks it for sturdiness. "Your older boy told her it was fine. No one is judging you."

I hope that's true. "How long have you been here?"

"Twenty minutes or so. Saw your kid out here and figured you were up." He glances at me over his shoulder. "I see I was wrong."

I'm not strong enough to deal with two males with attitudes without coffee.

I start to answer him, to justify myself by saying that I never sleep this late. I can't remember ever sleeping past eight o'clock. But I don't owe it to him, or to anyone, to justify anything . . . even if he has nice muscles and is fixing my railing.

"What are you doing out here, anyway?" I ask.

He groans, standing up. He sets his drill on the railing, which is secured to the posts once again.

"I told you this was on my list," I say.

"Yeah, well, I'm a carpenter by trade, and I happened to have a box of decking screws handy." He nods to the other side of the deck. "I fixed a piece over there too."

"I'm probably going to have to shore up this whole thing."

The corner of his lip twitches. "Or at least wear clothes out here."

I roll my eyes as my cheeks flush. "And I thought you were a gentleman. *My hero.*"

"You thought wrong." Even as he says it with pursed lips like he means it, his eyes shine with a kindness that makes my stomach flutter. "Do you want me to check the front porch too?"

"I didn't know I was getting a new house and my own personal carpenter. I would've paid more."

He doesn't flinch.

"I'm kidding," I say, slipping off my robe.

Jay's eyes drop to my chest, and I'm quickly reminded of my state of undress. *And* that my white tank is wet from the spilled coffee and that my nipples are undoubtedly putting on a show.

Not that he probably hasn't seen them already.

I clear my throat and put my robe back on. "Thank you for coming by this morning and fixing this. It is very kind of you, and I appreciate it."

"It's no big deal."

"It *is* a big deal." I smile. "I might be a mess, but we aren't a charity case. I can take care of us. I promise."

His head tilts as he takes me in, as if he's choosing his next words carefully. The longer we stand face-to-face, the squirmier I get.

"Do you want a drink?" I ask, needing to fill the silence. "I just made a pot of coffee."

I think he's going to decline. He seems surprised, maybe even taken aback, at my offer. But so am I.

What am I doing, asking a man I just met to come inside my house for a cup of coffee? I don't know him enough to be letting him into my house. Many men who wind up being serial killers start off hot and charming.

Although he's not exactly charming . . .

"Coffee seems like the least I can do," I say, nibbling my bottom lip. "Are you feeling okay this morning?"

"What do you mean?"

"You know, from your fall yesterday. Are you feeling all right?"

"Oh. *That.*" I glance down and grimace. "Just some scrapes, and I'm sore as heck. I convince myself I'm still twenty-one, but something happens like this, and I'm quickly reminded that I'm thirty-eight."

He grins. "Wait until you hit forty. Getting out of bed runs the risk of pulling a muscle."

I laugh and motion to the house. "So, coffee?"

"Sure."

I reach for the door, but he extends his arm before me and grabs the handle. He pulls it open and waits for me to go first.

"You're so certain you're not a gentleman, and then you do things like this," I say, going in first. His cologne envelops me as I pass him. *Goodness, he smells yummy.* "I'm not sure what to make of you."

He slips his tool belt off and sets it on the deck before following me inside.

I take out a mug and fill it for him. Then I top off mine.

"Do you take your coffee with cream or sugar?" I ask.

"Nope. Black is great." He takes the proffered mug. "Are you a cream-and-sugar drinker?"

"I used to be. I didn't want it if it wasn't the color of caramel and tasted like candy. But I overdid it one year with a cookie-flavored creamer, and now the smell of creamer makes my stomach churn."

He leans against the counter and scopes out the kitchen.

"I haven't had time to decorate," I say. "Much to Dylan's dismay, I haven't even gone to the grocery store yet."

"Who is Dylan?"

"The one with the mouth."

He nods, sipping his drink.

The room feels smaller, warmer . . . cozier with him in it. I'm surprised it doesn't feel odd having him in my space. I haven't had a man in my home since Christopher died.

"So it's just you and the two boys here?" he asks before taking another drink.

"Yeah. I grew up in Alden, actually, and moved away for college. I met their father there. We got married and moved to Boston. I've lived there ever since."

He watches me over the rim of his mug, his eyes sparkling in the sunlight from the window. "Where's their dad?"

I take a deep breath and blow it out slowly. I imagine Christopher whispering to me, telling me to relax. To trust myself. To enjoy this interaction. But that doesn't make it easier to speak about his death.

"Their dad, his name was Christopher—he passed away."

Jay's eyes widen. "Shit. I'm sorry."

"Thank you." I sigh. "We had been divorced for a few years, but he was still one of my best friends. Chris was a great dad, and I hate the boys won't—"

"Where is my backpack?" Dylan's voice and footsteps on the stairs interrupt me. "I knew it would get lost when you told Carter he could use it. Now I can't find it, and I know you . . ."

My blond-headed child skids to a stop when his gaze settles on Jay.

"What were you saying?" I ask, lifting a brow.

"Who is that?" Dylan asks, motioning toward Jay with his head. His features make it clear he's not happy to see a man in the house.

"I'm Jay. I live next door."

Dylan turns his attention to him. "Why are you here?"

"I was fixing your deck, and your mother invited me in for a cup of coffee."

"You don't have coffee at your house?" Dylan asks.

"Dylan!" I hiss.

He glares at Jay. Jay looks unbothered. He lifts his mug and slowly sips, never taking his eyes off my son.

"Have you unpacked your drill?" Jay asks, setting his drink on the counter.

My heart pounds as I watch them go back and forth.

"What?" Dylan asks, his facade cracking.

"Every post out back needs a couple of screws put in them," Jay says. "I didn't look at the front, but I'd imagine it's about the same. You're gonna want to get on that before someone gets hurt."

Dylan pulls his brows together. "I don't understand."

"What's there to understand? You came in here and talked to me like a grown man, so I'm reciprocating. There are a lot of grown-man things that need to be done around here. Let me know if you need to borrow any of my tools." Jay places his cup in the sink. "Thanks for the coffee, Gabrielle."

"Yeah, of course," I say, scrambling to understand what just happened. "Thanks, Jay."

He winks at me before slipping out the back door.

As soon as it shuts, Dylan sparks into motion. "Why the heck was he in here?" he asks, pointing at where Jay stood.

"Dylan, I know you're going through a lot right now, but—"

"You can't just have men in here. You don't even know him."

I blink slowly. "Young man, I'll have whoever I want in my house."

His chest rises and falls as if he's struggling to keep himself in check.

I take a deep breath and remind myself that I'm the adult, the parent, and it's my responsibility to stay calm and help my child handle himself.

Lord, help me.

"Do you want to talk about anything?" I ask.

He shakes his head like he's disgusted by the question.

"Do you want to talk to someone else—"

"Don't start with the whole therapist thing again," he says.

"I'm just giving you the option."

"I don't want it."

"That's okay. But you need to figure out how to handle your emotions, because you're being a jerk to me, and now to our neighbor, and that's *not* okay, Dylan."

He narrows his eyes.

"I love you, buddy. I'm here. I'll always be here—*on your team*," I say gently. "But please remember that I'm a person and I have feelings too. And the way you've been talking to me hurts. I don't want to punish you and make your life harder, but I can't let you think that your behavior is okay."

I brace myself for the incoming onslaught of words, *of defiance*, that's been the norm lately. Instead, he looks away and swallows heavily.

My head begins to pound. I pinch my temples as fatigue begins to settle in my bones. I am so tired of this, but I don't know what to do.

"Look, maybe I've let you get away with too much lately," I say. "Maybe some of this is my fault. Maybe—"

He throws himself at me, pulling me in for the tightest hug. He buries his face in my shoulder and squeezes me.

I hold the back of his head with one hand and hug him with the other. All the while, my heart breaks.

Oh, my sweet boy.

Tears spring to my eyes as he clutches me for dear life—like maybe he needs this as much as I do. I don't dare speak. I don't tell him how his pain is mine and I feel it in the depth of my soul. I only hold him, swaying gently back and forth, and comfort my child. Loving on him in the only way he'll accept right now.

Holding him like this reminds me that he's still a baby, no matter what's coming out of his mouth. *My baby.* And he may be down a father, but I'm still here.

"I love you," he says into my robe. Then he pulls back.

His eyes are glassy as he wipes his hands down his face.

"I love you," I say. "More than you'll ever know."

Shades of fear and hope mix in his light-brown eyes. *Hold on to hope, baby boy. We'll get there.*

Dylan turns on his heels and moves quickly up the staircase. I wait until I hear his door close.

I exhale harshly, the weight of the world sinking onto my shoulders.

My coffee doesn't sound appetizing anymore, and I turn toward the sink to dump it out. Before I can take a step, my gaze is drawn out the window and across the lawn.

Jay stands in front of his garage, watching me.

I give him a little smile.

He gives me one back before disappearing inside.

CHAPTER SIX

Jay

"How in the hell do I collect all this junk?" I ask the empty garage.

I survey my day's work. Three filled garbage bags, many empty boxes, and a Christmas tree that stopped lighting up two Christmases ago sit beside the open garage door. It took me most of the day to comb through the shelves lining the back wall. I could've been quicker, but cleaning always helps me feel more in control.

It also proved to be a good distraction.

Every time I stood still without particular focus, my mind would drift to the house next door.

I grin as I remember Gabrielle's fieriness this morning. The way she stomped onto the deck with wild hair and sleep in her eyes. The coffee that stained her tank top. Her nipples pressed against the fabric.

My muscles tighten in my core. *That woman is something else.*

I dig into the final drawer in my toolbox, sorting nails and screws. With each bolt dropped into the proper bin, I'm reminded of another part of Gabrielle that I like. *That I can't stop thinking about.*

The brightness of her smile when she's teasing me.

Her full lips form a perfect pout when she's thinking.

The richness of her personality, the sound of her laugh, and the look on her face when her son stormed into the room.

My stomach tightens at the memory.

"Their dad, his name was Christopher—he passed away."

A screw pings against the container as it's placed inside.

"So that's what's going on with the kid," I say, heaving a breath.

It must be a total nightmare for the kids and Gabrielle not to have a male figure in the boys' lives. They have no one to turn to for help when testosterone rages and questions arise about shit they don't want to talk to their mother about. And Gabrielle has to deal with that on her own. I can only imagine how hard it is to navigate the emotions and situations—that is, I could imagine it if I wanted to.

I don't.

I glance at the calendar hanging above my workbench. Next to the month's inspirational saying is her picture. Big brown eyes. No front teeth. A smile as big as Texas. And like it always does, the image punches another hole in my heart.

"Hey, mister." Gabrielle's little boy stands in the driveway, holding a basketball. "I'm Carter, and I live by you. Do you have a pumper for my ball?"

Freckles lie across his nose and cheeks. His dark-blond hair is messy and curls at the ends. There's a hole in the knee of his jeans, and his blue-and-white-striped hoodie is dirty.

"A pumper?" I ask.

"Yeah. Watch." He drops the ball to the ground. It lands with a thud. "See? It doesn't have enough air in it to bounce."

"So you're looking for an air compressor."

He peels his hoodie off and tosses it on the ground. "Is that a pumper?"

"Yes. That's a pumper."

"Okay. Do you have one? Because my new friend Hayes is really good at basketball, and so are his friends. But I stink. I need to practice bouncing it."

"Dribbling it."

He tilts his head to the side like I speak a foreign language.

"When you bounce it, it's called dribbling," I say.

"Oh. So, can I use your pumper?"

I want to tell him no, to go home and forget I live here. The last thing I want, the last thing I need, is to be marked as the guy next door who can help with shit. Even though I've already done that. Twice.

Ugh. These people are going to drive me nuts.

I start to speak, but his toothless smile gets the best of me.

"Fine," I say, shaking my head. I walk over to my air compressor and flip the switch. It kicks on. "We have to let it get to pressure first."

"Okay." Carter picks up his ball and comes into the garage. He gazes around with wide eyes. "*Wow.* You have a lot of stuff."

"Yeah."

He points at a table saw in the back. "What's that?"

"It's a saw."

"For what?"

I sigh. "Cutting wood."

"Do you cut a lot of wood?"

"I'm a carpenter, so yeah. It's my job."

"Cool." He nods, moseying around like he owns the place. "That's a good job."

"I'm glad you think so."

"Do you think it's a good job?"

What is this? An inquisition? "Yeah. I guess."

"When I get older, I'm going to be a fireman." He giggles, looking at me over his shoulder. His green eyes, the same color as his mother's, twinkle. "Can I tell you a secret?"

No, you cannot tell me a secret.

"I really only wanna wear the costume and shoot water out of the big hose," he says.

I can't help myself. I laugh, motioning for him to come to me. "I understand how that's appealing, but you should really want to do a job because you like the actual job."

"What does *appealing* mean?"

This kid. "Give me your basketball."

"It means *give me your basketball?* That's cool."

"*No. Appealing* means it sounds nice. Now give me your basketball."

He shuffles the rest of the way across the floor and hands me his ball.

I place the needle into the rubber. It inflates in seconds. Carter watches with rapt attention.

"That's magic," he says, bouncing around on one foot. "I'd use that thing for all kinds of stuff."

I hand him the basketball and then turn off the compressor. "Like what?"

"I bet I could use it to blow the food off the dishes when Mom makes me help her clean up after dinner."

"Probably wouldn't work."

"Why not?"

"It'd break the dishes, and it wouldn't sanitize them."

He looks up at me through thick lashes. "What's that mean?"

"What's what mean?"

"Sanitize."

His endless questions are annoying, so I try to hold on to that feeling. But the longer he stands in front of me with his curiosity and boundless energy, the harder it is to stay that way.

I fold my arms over my chest. "If you sanitize something, it means to kill all the things that might make you sick."

He nods appreciatively. "That's great."

Carter drops the ball and begins to dribble it around the garage. I watch him, trying to figure out how to kick the kid out of here without being a dick. Because it isn't his fault I don't want him in my space. He didn't do anything wrong.

Neither did I.

I watch as he tries to dribble between his legs but fails miserably. I want to give him pointers, to tell him to keep the ball bouncing steadily and closer to his body. But I don't.

It's not my problem.

Still, he is so cute with his tongue hanging out while focusing on his coordination. His curls bounce right along with the ball. He gets the hang of it just before it hits his foot and rolls across the floor.

"Oops," he says, chasing it.

I sort the last of the screws and nails and then close the lid to the toolbox.

"Hey, who is that?" Carter asks.

"Who?"

"That." He points at the picture beside the calendar. "That girl. Is she your daughter?"

My heart pulls so tight in my chest that it knocks the wind out of me. Aside from Lark, I haven't talked about her to anyone in four years. She's resided in my heart and in my mind—a block of sweet memories that no one can take away from me. Not even Melody.

"Is she?" he asks again, his ball tucked under his arm.

I nod, staring at her picture. "Yeah. That's my little girl."

Hearing the words aloud sets a sharp pain in motion. It ricochets in my rib cage, puncturing me in as many places as it can.

"What's her name?" he asks, unaware that his questions are slowly killing me.

He watches me closely, genuinely curious. I don't know how to answer him. I don't even know how I got this deep in a conversation with the kid from across the way, but I need to figure out how the fuck to get out of it.

And stay out of it.

"Does your mom know you're here?" I ask, hoping he'll take the bait.

"Um, no. She doesn't know that. But she's busy getting ready to go with Cricket and some other ladies for . . . I don't know what they're doing. But they're going to Della's. Whoever that is."

I glance at Della's. "Are you supposed to be home with Dylan?"

"How do you know Dylan?"

"I met him today."

"Was he a jerk face to you?"

I struggle not to laugh. "That's not a nice thing to say about someone."

"It's the truth," he says with more moxie than I've ever had. "If he doesn't want to be called a jerk face, he shouldn't be one."

I have no idea what to say. Dylan *is* a jerk face, from what I can tell. So do I agree with him or try to dissuade him from calling his brother names?

Wait. This has nothing to do with me. *Carter needs to go home.*

"You know what? I have a bunch of stuff to do. Why don't you head back home?" I ask.

Instead of leaving, he remains rooted in place. He furrows his little brows and studies me like I'm a puzzle he has to finish before going.

I sigh, hoping the sound encourages him to hurry.

It doesn't.

"You give . . . lonely vibes," he says, satisfied.

It's my turn to be puzzled. "Excuse me?"

"You're lonely, huh?"

What? "Carter, it's been good chatting with ya, kid, but it's time for you to leave."

He bounces his ball again. "You can come to dinner at our house. Mom always says we can fix an extra plate if someone needs it."

"I have food, but thank you."

"But you're lonely."

"I'm not lonely."

He looks up and gives me a cheesy grin. "Yeah, you are. And you're getting cranky."

I snatch his ball midbounce and carry it to the grass by the driveway. There I set it gently on the ground.

"Your face doesn't look happy, and you don't want to talk about stuff," he says, frowning. "You're sad."

This fucking kid. "I'm fine. And I'm closing this door."

"Cran-ky." He laughs wildly. "Thanks for pumping up my ball, Mr. Crankypants."

My head hurts. "Goodbye."

I press the button by the door leading into the house before Carter can come back in. The garage door begins to descend.

Carter crouches down from the other side and waves, bending until he's on all fours. Finally, the door seals us apart.

"Your face doesn't look happy, and you don't want to talk about stuff. You're sad."

"Damn kid," I say, marching into the house.

"You give . . . lonely vibes."

Who does that kid think he is? *Lonely vibes?* Lonely vibes, my ass. And what kind of elementary school kid says things like that?

We're gonna have to have some boundaries around here.

I grab a beer from the fridge and carry it into the living room. Instead of figuring out what I'm having for dinner, I plop on the recliner and flip on the television. I don't bother finding a program to watch. That's not the point.

The show makes noise in the house so it doesn't feel so empty. It doesn't seem as inviting for my thoughts to stray to things I don't want to think about.

How will I survive, living by these people? One interaction with Carter and I'm afraid I'm going to crack. One interaction with Dylan and I want to whip him into shape. Every interaction with Gabrielle makes me want to have another.

Take a breath, Jay.

All that is superficial. I don't *really* want any of it.

I don't want to talk about my little girl. I don't give a shit what Dylan does or does not do. And Gabrielle—I only *think* I want to see her again. Down deep, I don't. Because I know what will happen if I do, and at the end of the day, being involved with anyone, let alone a woman with two kids, is the last thing in the world I'm interested in.

And that's a fact.

I take a long pull of my beer.

My phone buzzes in my pocket, so I set my drink down and pull it out. The number shows the name of the owner of the farmhouse we're supposed to start work on Monday.

"This is Jay," I say into the line.

"Hey, Jay. This is Larry Harris."

"Hi, Larry. What's going on?"

"I have bad news. The permits for the remodel weren't approved."

My brows rise. "Really?"

"Yeah. I just found out. My wife went to pick them up this morning and was told there was a holdup. They said they'd call us on Monday to go over it." He groans. "I'm sorry, Jay."

I press my head against the chair and close my eyes. "Yeah. Me too. Keep me posted, I guess."

"Absolutely."

"This will throw off our schedule, but I'm sure you know that."

"I do. Actually, is there any way we can set to start next Monday? To give me a week to get this fixed?"

"That'll work. It's not ideal, but I can make it happen."

He sighs. "Thanks, Jay. Again, I'm sorry. I'll be in touch."

"Talk soon."

I end the call.

A whole week with nothing to do and new neighbors already getting under my skin.

I better find something to keep me busy.

CHAPTER SEVEN

GABRIELLE

"Come on in, Gabby," Della calls from the other side of the screen door.

Laughter and soft music greet me as I step inside the small bungalow.

Della's home is absolutely adorable and more feminine than I would've predicted. The white walls and ceilings are extra bright compared with the warm wooden floors. Instead of one giant chandelier overhead, there are five smaller lights. None of them match, yet somehow, they do.

The living area on the right is comfortably decorated with accents of pink and turquoise. A large art piece resembling paint thrown onto a canvas and smeared hangs above a slim fireplace. Ahead is the kitchen, where Della, Cricket, and a dark-headed woman I've never seen before are gathered around an island.

"Hey," Della says, waving me in.

"There you are. I thought I would have to come and get you," Cricket says, grinning.

"I argued with myself for ten minutes over whether I should bring something. Otherwise, I would've been on time."

"Like I told you, the hostess takes care of everything," Cricket says, her emerald-green blouse complementing her red hair perfectly.

Della smiles, looking up from a chopping board. "Besides, we don't get fancy. Especially me. I keep it as simple as possible."

"Gabby, this is our friend Scottie," Cricket says, motioning to the dark-headed woman sitting beside her. "Scottie, this is my cousin Gabby."

"It's so nice to finally meet you, Gabby," Scottie says, grinning.

"It's nice to meet you too."

"Scottie lives catty-corner to me," Cricket says. "Her house has flower beds that look like a magazine cover."

"That's your house?" I ask, lifting a brow. "Oh, my gosh. It's beautiful."

She waves a hand through the air. "Thank you. But it's pathetic, really. I gave up on men and decided that I was going to channel all my passion into gardening." She laughs. "Let's just say I didn't imagine I'd have this much time to perfect the art."

"Scottie is on a self-inflicted hiatus from men," Della says, squeezing a lime into a glass.

"Not true." Scottie points at her friend. "I did take a hiatus from men. But I called it off a year ago and haven't found a suitable candidate to ease me back in."

"I don't want to be eased back in," I say, coming around the island to stand beside Della. "It's been so long since I had a man that I don't want there to be anything *easy* about it. Just give it to me, baby."

Della bumps me with her hip, making me laugh. Then she hands out palomas with a salt rim and fresh lime wedge.

"If you don't like tequila, I can make you something else," she says. "I ordered enchiladas and rice from Gran Ranchero and thought palomas would go perfectly with it."

"Della refuses to cook for us," Cricket says, taking her drink.

"Wait, Alden has a Gran Ranchero?" I ask. "When did that happen?"

"Because I want you all alive and well, not knelt over your toilets fighting for your life," Della says to Cricket. Then she turns to me. "No, Alden still just has Betty Lou's. I was in Logan today and picked it up."

"That makes sense. I was wondering how I missed a new restaurant in town." I laugh. "Tequila is great. Thank you."

The three friends argue over a pot roast Della recently made—or tried to make, depending on who's talking. I sit on a barstool and sip my drink.

I didn't realize how badly I needed this evening until now. How much I missed having girlfriends.

The tequila is potent as it hits my stomach. Instantly, liquid fire flows through my veins. I close my eyes and enjoy the sensation of giving up a bit of control and stress.

I enjoy being a woman with a life outside of her kids.

"Are you guys ready to eat?" Della asks, pulling two silver containers from the oven. "Damn, this smells good."

"I'm starving," Scottie says.

Cricket wipes lime juice off the counter and then lines the limes, salt, and tequila up in a tidy little row. Scottie plucks paper plates and plastic forks from a cabinet. Della uncovers the trays and finds serving utensils.

They work together like a well-oiled machine. There are no directions given, no questions asked. They move alongside one another with an ease and trust that prickles something in my soul.

What would it be like to be a part of a group like this? To have friends with whom you can simply exist without making excuses or worrying whether they'll show up—friends who just get into your cabinets and help clean up after you?

Scottie looks at me and smiles. *I hope there will continue to be space for me here.*

"I'm just sitting here," I say. "What can I do to help?"

"Come make your plate," Della says, offering me one.

"Don't worry. By next month, Cricket will be ordering you around." Scottie laughs. "Enjoy it while you can."

Cricket huffs. "That's not true. I don't order people around."

Della looks at my cousin over her shoulder. "You literally texted me this morning and told me to make sure my laundry wasn't in the living room tonight."

"Excuse me for not wanting to dine next to your G-string again," Cricket says, placing an enchilada on her plate.

"You can't come by unannounced and complain about the state of my life," Della says. "If I had known you were coming, I would've put my stuff away."

"She has a point, Cricket," Scottie says.

Cricket groans. "You all are incorrigible."

Della looks at me and winks. "Come on. Let's eat in the living room. It's more comfortable in there."

We take our food and drinks and follow her through the house.

"Tell us about you," Scottie says as we sit on the white furniture. *It's clear Della doesn't have kids.* "What do you do for fun?"

I set my plate on the coffee table. I start to speak—to answer her question. But nothing comes out. *How do I not know how to answer that?*

"No one has asked me that in a very long time," I say.

"I didn't mean to put you on the spot," Scottie says.

"Oh, you didn't. It's just wild that I haven't thought about what I want to do for fun. I want to have more fun, sure, but I don't even know what that means." I frown. "How sad is that?"

Cricket scoops up a forkful of rice. A smirk plays on her lips. "Isn't that a website you frequent, Della? Adult Fun Finder?"

"Close. But not quite." Della smiles smugly. "But you should try the websites I frequent, Cricket. Those ironed curtains will pale in comparison."

I laugh at them. "Speaking of ironing curtains—which is Cricket's idea of fun, not mine—I do enjoy a good do-it-yourself project."

Cricket groans.

"Stop it." I point my stare at her. "I'm good at them. You only see them through video chat. You've never actually seen one of my completed masterpieces in person."

"Because every time Peter and I would come to Boston, you'd insist on meeting us in the city."

"Because the city is fun. I loved having an excuse to do all the things with you instead of you sitting around my house fixing everything."

"Oh, I would not . . ." She stops, tucking a strand of hair behind her ears. "*Okay.* Maybe I would've done that."

I take a bite of my enchilada.

"Do you work, Gabby?" Della asks.

"She has the wildest job ever," Cricket says, eyes glittering. "Go on. Tell them."

"I used to work at a bank," I say, resting my fork on my plate. "But when my ex-husband, Christopher, died, I was his beneficiary."

Della flinches. "Your ex-husband made *you* his beneficiary?"

"He knew I'd make sure the kids were taken care of," I say with a simple shrug. "And he built a very successful veterinary business while we were married. He said that I deserved to reap the benefits if something would ever happen to him, because I sacrificed alongside him for years."

"And you divorced this guy?" Della asks. "He sounds like a dream."

My heart softens. "He was a really good man. He just wasn't the man for me anymore." I shrug again. "Anyway, his estate has allowed me not to work this past year. I'll go back to work as soon as the kids are settled. But it's been a huge privilege to be able to sit with them in their grief."

Cricket smiles, perching on the edge of her chair as if she can't wait a moment longer for me to get to the point. "Gabby gets paid to name babies."

"What?" Scottie asks, laughing.

"You do not," Della says, surprised.

"I didn't mean for it to be a thing—and I don't get paid enough for it to be a real job," I say. "I just offered names on a social media post. The next time I opened the app, my comments had gone viral. People were messaging me, asking me for suggestions. Now I have a page for it and charge a small fee." I look at Cricket. "It's more of a hobby than a job."

"So that's what you do for fun," Scottie says. "You're a baby-naming DIYer."

"Do you want more kids?" Della asks.

"No."

My quick response gets a laugh from the women around me.

"I can't have babies anymore," I say. "I had a partial hysterectomy a few years ago. But even if I could, it would be a no. What about you? Do you have kids? Want them?"

Della nearly turns green. "If I have kids, that would be a sign that I'm not in control of my decisions and y'all need to get me help."

"And yet she has tons of sex and doesn't want kids," Scottie says, falling back into the cushions. "I want kids and haven't had sex in what feels like forever."

"You're too picky," Della tells her. "Lower your standards a little."

"Della!" Cricket protests.

Della rolls her eyes. "Calm down. Sometimes the best sex is with the guys that aren't husband material." She leans toward Cricket. "*And that's fine.* Not all sex has to be with a goal of procreation."

"I agree," Cricket says, sitting taller. "But I still think you can have fun sex without lowering your standards."

I've known Della for only a few hours, but I already know one of her quirks. The corner of her lips twitches when she's about to say something she knows will set Cricket off.

"Fun sex is called *fucking*, Cricket," Della says, watching her friend closely so as not to miss a moment of her reaction. "When was the last time Peter fucked you?"

"We have fun sex a few times a week," Cricket says, meeting Della's stare head-on.

Della doesn't respond with anything more than a hum.

Cricket makes a face at her and then turns back to me. "Remember what I said last night about ensuring your definition of *good time* matches hers?"

I look at Della and grin. "I think we're on the same page."

"Oh, good lord," Cricket says, getting to her feet. "I'm getting a bottle of water. Does anyone else want one?"

"I need another paloma." Della stands. "You haven't touched yours, Scottie."

She picks up her glass. "Sorry. The entertainment has been entertaining."

Della peers into mine. "Want another?"

I should say no. My tolerance for tequila is low. But I'm really enjoying myself . . .

"I'll take one more," I say, handing her my glass.

She follows Cricket into the kitchen.

I take my phone out of my pocket and check for missed calls or messages from Dylan, even though I would've felt it vibrate against my leg. Since our hug, he's been a little less abrasive. I expected more of a pushback when I asked him to watch Carter this evening. Surprisingly, he agreed with little more than an eye roll.

A part of me wonders if he doesn't secretly enjoy spending time with his brother. I never asked him to watch Carter in Boston. They spent little time alone together. But in the few days we've been in Alden, they've been together a ton.

Maybe it's because there aren't a ton of alternatives. Or maybe the slower, small-town life is as good for him as I hoped it would be.

There are no messages, so I type out a quick text to check in.

Me: Are you and Carter doing okay?

I expect it to take a long time for him to reply. Instead, he surprises me and sends a selfie of himself with his brother in the living room. A drama about a boy doctor is on the television in the distance.

My heart warms.

Me: I love you guys.

There's no reply.

I sigh, putting the phone back in my pocket. "Sorry. I just wanted to check on the boys."

Scottie smiles. "No worries." She shifts in her chair. "You know, when I was eight, I lost my father to cancer."

"I'm so sorry."

"It's okay. Clearly, that was a long time ago."

I give her a small smile.

"But what I want to say is that my mother cried and had her moment. Then she picked herself right back up and lived her life. I don't know how she did it, looking back. But I remember thinking that if she could smile again, so could I. We didn't realize it then, but she helped us heal by healing herself. She went out with her friends and took us to the movies, and we took vacations. And eventually, she started dating again. Mom wound up married to the best human in the world."

"That's great, Scottie."

"So while I don't know what you're going through and hope you don't think I'm putting my nose where it doesn't belong, I just wanted to share that with you. I have experience on the child side of that coin. Thought it may help."

Her words touch me—not just because of what she said. It's that she said it. That she cared enough to share something so private with a woman she doesn't really know.

"Thank you," I say. "It means a lot that you told me that."

"Of course."

Voices grow louder as Della and Cricket return.

"Just try it," Della says, taunting her. "He'll blow more than his mind."

"You are filthy." Cricket hands me my glass and then takes her seat. "You don't have to do . . . *all of that* to keep a man happy."

Scottie and I exchange a grin.

"So, Gabby . . ." The way Della says my name tightens my stomach. "What did you think of Mr. Stetson?"

"Who?"

"Your neighbor. *Jay Stetson.*"

Oh, crap.

The look on her face makes it abundantly clear that she either heard about what happened or . . .

I gulp.

Jay wouldn't have told her . . . would he? *I* haven't said a word to anyone about falling off the damn porch. But if he didn't tell her, that leaves the other option.

Della licks her lips. "I saw."

"You saw what?" Cricket asks, looking between us.

I take a long—too long—drink of my paloma. The tequila burns down my throat, splashing into the pool of liquid that's been churning for a while. Heat shoots through my veins as my mind settles on Jay.

"Oh, it's no big deal," I say, practically breathing fire from the drink. "One of the rails on my back deck broke, and I fell off it into the bushes."

Della does that thing with the corner of her mouth.

"I was in a towel," I say quickly before she can out me. "And Jay had to come over and help me out of it."

"Out of the towel or out of the bushes?" Scottie asks.

Della bursts out laughing.

I give Scottie a look.

"Hey, I'm just saying . . ." Scottie whistles through her teeth. "I'd shed my towel for that man. Have you seen him shirtless? Hot damn."

"He was nice but a little distant." My brows pull together. "I wouldn't say he was unfriendly. Just . . ."

"He's just Jay." Della shrugs. "I can be over here in a string bikini, bent over my lawn mower, and the man doesn't look at me twice."

What? With those curves? How is that even possible?

Cricket sighs. "He's always polite. And he sometimes stops and talks to Peter if he's working on the front lawn. But I don't think I've ever seen him with a woman."

They chat about Jay before the conversation moves to what color Scottie should paint her kitchen. As they discuss paint colors and tile patterns, my mind drifts elsewhere.

"I can be over here in a string bikini, bent over my lawn mower, and the man doesn't look at me twice."

Della is stunning and sexy—all the things I'm not. I'm disheveled most of the time, rocking my mom bod and a messy bun. If Jay isn't looking at her when she's barely dressed and practically begging for his attention, the odds that I'll get it are slim.

But do I even want it?

My body tingles as I think about him watching us through the window. The surprise I felt, finding him fixing the deck without being asked. The ease with which he handled Dylan's attitude.

All that felt good in so many ways.

Supported. Cared for. Seen. It strikes a chord deep inside me, reminding me what it's like not to be alone.

I'm so tired of being alone.

I watch Della tell a story, her manicured fingers flying through the air.

By the sound of it, my interactions with Jay were a momentary thing—not a foundation of friendship or anything else. *That's fine.* I don't have the bandwidth to build something real with someone else right now anyway.

But those arms. That chest. The smirk that toys on his lips . . .

I take a long drink of my paloma.

I need to get laid. Stat.

CHAPTER EIGHT

Gabrielle

"Carter! Stop bouncing the ball in the house," I say, angling my voice toward the kitchen.

The incessant rubber meeting hardwood stops. I tilt my head back in relief. Dylan sighs from the sofa across the room.

Despite my making them a meal before I went to Della's, the boys were starving when I returned. I whipped up sausage patties and pancakes after a quick trip to the grocery store, which they scarfed down like wild dogs. I was surprised when neither ran to his room after we cleaned up their second dinner. Instead, Carter took his ball to the deck to practice dribbling. Dylan sat in the living room with me and turned on a murder mystery. I'm sure he did it to torment me, but it's a sacrifice I'm willing to make to spend time with him.

"Want to give me your opinion?" I ask, scrolling to the top of my computer screen.

"Sure."

"I have a pregnant customer with triplets who wants names with a theme. Any theme. Doesn't matter. Two girls and a boy."

Dylan turns the volume down.

"I have Luna, Stella, and Orion. Clover, Daisy, and Clay. Opal, Ruby, and Jasper. Brooke, Cordelia, and Adrian."

He furrows his brows. "People really pay you for this?"

"Look, it shocks me too. But at one hundred dollars a pop, what can I say?"

"You say Ruth, Jackie, and Derek."

"What?" I ask, laughing.

"You wanted themes." He shrugs. "Those are all baseball greats."

Oh. "Repeat those."

"Ruth. Jackie. Derek."

"I'm writing that down. When I looked at their social media, I noticed her husband was into baseball. Those could work."

Dylan grins. "I want half the money if they use my idea."

His face lights up, forgoing the narrowed eyes and pressed lips I'm so used to seeing from him. He's happy—almost carefree. I'd give everything to understand why he flips back and forth so fast. And I'd give even more to keep him like this.

"So what combination was your favorite?" I ask.

"Mine. Then probably the one with Clover. You never hear that as a name. It's kinda cool."

Whoa. A compliment too? What was in those pancakes?

Carter's footsteps echo through the house. They grow louder as he approaches.

"What are you guys doing?" he asks, swatting a lock of hair out of his face.

"I'm finishing up a project. What are you doing?" I ask him.

"Well, I was practicing my dribbling. But I think I'm dribbled out."

Thank God.

Dylan climbs off the sofa. "Hey, wanna hop on and play duos?"

"Let's go!" Carter races up the stairs, followed closely by his brother.

Their chatter hits my heart so hard it takes my breath away. *Why can't it always be like this?*

I close my computer, too distracted to concentrate on my work. Middle names are always the hardest, and there's no way I can think about that now. Instead, I turn to the basket of clean clothes on the coffee table. My mind wanders, flitting from one topic to the next.

I grab the shirt lying on top of the pile and fold it.

"He's just Jay."

Della's words come back to me as I pick up his flannel. *He's just Jay.* What does that mean?

At the end of the day, what it means doesn't really matter. He's my kind, albeit gorgeous, neighbor. That's all.

I carry Jay's flannel through the house and into the kitchen, stopping at the sink. The lights in his house are on. I mull over the idea of returning his shirt or keeping it until tomorrow. While tomorrow would be fine, there's no time like the present.

My stomach tightens. I shoot Dylan a text and then exit the back door.

The night is cool, sending a wave of chills over me as I step onto the lawn. Brilliant stars twinkle overhead in the clear night sky—something I missed in Boston. We didn't live downtown, but even in the suburbs there was enough light to prevent a clear view of the stars.

My anxiety grows as I get closer to Jay's door.

Why did I think this was a good idea again?

Knock! Knock!

Jay opens the door. His eyes widen when he sees it's me.

My jaw drops when I see him.

Even tequila couldn't have prepared me for this.

He's shirtless with a towel thrown over his shoulder. The lines of his shoulders, chest, and abs are covered in a sheen. Sweatpants sit low on his hips.

"Hey," he says, wiping his forehead with the edge of the towel.

Words, Gabby. Use words.

"Hey." I flash him a wobbly smile. "I brought your shirt back."

"Oh. Thanks."

Our fingers brush against each other's as he takes the flannel from me. The contact ignites the alcohol that's left in my system. My knees wobble as I struggle not to melt.

"I saw your little boy tonight," he says.

"You did? When?"

"A few hours ago." He chuckles softly. "That kid is a bundle of energy."

I cringe. "Carter must have come over while I was at Della's. I'm sorry if he bothered you."

"Nah, he just wanted his basketball aired up."

"So you're responsible for him bouncing that thing in the house all night? I ought to make him come over here and practice. He's driving Dylan and me nuts."

Jay steps to the side. "He left his hoodie. If you want to come in, I'll grab it."

"Sure. Thanks."

I inhale a lungful of masculinity as I pass him. It's sweat and cologne—a deep, rich scent that's, in a word, *delicious*. The door closing snaps me back to reality.

"You can have a seat," he says. "I need to remember where I put it."

"That sounds like something I'd do. I put things in a safe place all the time. The problem is that the only thing it's safe from is me ever finding it again."

"It might be on my workbench in the garage. Hang tight."

I sit on his brown leather sofa. "I'm hanging."

His back, in all its glory, is on full display as he leaves the room.

"Just settle down and be normal," I whisper to myself.

The living area is comfortable, with leather furniture and a large brick fireplace. A small desk is tucked into one corner and flanked by bookcases. And instead of trinkets adorning the shelves, it's actual books.

So hot.

"Here you go," he says, returning with Carter's hoodie in his hand. "He left it lying on the garage floor."

"Color me not surprised." I take it from him. "When he was a baby, he used to take his diaper off and leave it wherever he was standing. Then it graduated to socks and then shoes. Now we're at the hoodie stage."

Jay sits in a chair next to the couch. "Be happy. In a few years, he'll be leaving his pants—"

"No, no, no. Don't say that about my baby."

He chuckles.

"I'm not ready for that," I say, wadding the hoodie on my lap. "In other news, it turns out that Della saw the Towel Incident."

"I know."

What? "How do you know?"

"She told my buddy Lark."

"People are talking about it?"

"Didn't you say you grew up here?" He shrugs. "It's a small town. People talk. Although I doubt Lark said anything to anyone but me. He doesn't get in other people's business much."

"Well, thank God for small favors."

He picks up a water bottle from the coffee table and unscrews the lid. "Do you want a drink?"

"I had three palomas at Della's tonight, and that's probably two too many. I'm trying to lay off the fluids because my stomach's still a bit squirrely. My fear of puking is real."

His Adam's apple bobs as he downs the water. I don't know how watching someone drink is sexy, but it is. *It really freaking is.*

The energy in the room is easy. He's almost relaxed. I wonder if it's because we're on his turf, not mine. Every interaction we've had until now has been at my house.

He settles back in his chair. "So did you know Della before you moved here?"

"Della? No. It's such a weird thing. Everyone says that small towns always stay the same. On the surface, that's true. But if you've been gone for a while and come back, you see that some things did change. Buildings are torn down; new homes are put up. The people come and go. I didn't know Della or Scottie when I lived here. But that *was* almost two decades ago." I pause. "When did you move to Alden?"

"About four years ago."

"Why here?"

A shadow filters across his face. Lines bunch around his eyes, and his shoulders are taut. He makes a point of swallowing before he speaks.

"Just needed a change of scenery," he says.

"Where did you move here from?"

"Indiana."

I wait for him to expand on his answer and elaborate a bit. But he remains unflinching.

Okay . . . He's not giving me much to work with, but he's not clamming up. Maybe if I push a tiny bit, he'll give me a nugget of information about himself.

"I had dinner tonight with Cricket, Della, and Scottie," I say. "They said you were a good neighbor."

"They all seem nice."

"Do you know any of them well?"

He shakes his head.

"Why not?" I ask.

"Because I don't care enough to know them well."

His answer is straightforward, but it doesn't satisfy my curiosity. *Why?*

"If you'd like to get to know them, maybe we could have a neighborhood potluck or something and—"

"You're missing the point."

"Which is . . ."

He side-eyes me and sighs. "Look, I appreciate your misplaced sense of . . . whatever this is, but I'm not a people person. I don't need to get to know everyone on the street. I don't want to, as a matter of fact."

I blow out a breath and sink deeper into the cushions. "Aren't you lonely? Don't you miss having connections with people?"

"No." He rolls his head around his neck. "I take it you do."

"Yes, I do. Don't you fear growing old alone?"

"I'd rather grow old alone than with the wrong person, Gabrielle."

My instinct is to argue with him. But that actually makes sense.

Christopher thought the exact same way, so much so that he divorced me. *"I love you too much to let you grow old with the wrong person, Gabs."*

Leave it to me to be attracted to two men who think I'm the wrong person.

"I don't know that I even want to grow old with someone, per se," I say. "I want companionship more than anything. Don't get me wrong. I love *love*. It's beautiful and wonderful when it's right. But I'm not even after that at this point."

Jay leans forward, resting his elbows on his knees. His eyes are clear as he listens. His attentiveness encourages me to continue.

"I just want to feel like a woman again," I say. "Love isn't necessary. I just want a reason to get dolled up on Friday nights. I want someone to laugh with, cuddle up to—someone to have fun sex with."

You're not talking to the girls, Gabby. Shut up.

His brows shoot to the ceiling. He quickly catches himself and smoothens his features.

I scramble, trying desperately to figure out how to sweep this under the rug. *Do I say I was kidding?*

Jay bites his lip and watches me.

Oh, what's it matter? He's just Jay, after all—the guy who won't look twice at Della. He's obviously not interested in me.

"So do you have any friends looking for a hookup?" I ask, smiling sweetly. I might as well lean all the way in at this point.

"No."

The word is rough and raw, uttered with an unshakable confidence. It toys with my hormones. It ruffles my feathers. The single syllable, mixed with the severity in his tone, nearly has me panting.

Why do I always go for the unavailable ones?

He gets to his feet and takes the towel off his shoulders. He wipes his face again before tossing it on the arm of the chair.

I stand, too, and try not to stare at him. He's a beautiful, handsome puzzle I can't quite snap together.

"Thanks for letting me borrow your flannel," I say. "And thanks for helping Carter tonight with his ball."

"It's no problem."

I smile at him and then head for the door.

"I'll tell the boys not to bother you," I say. "And like I said, we are self-sufficient . . . despite the events of the last two days. Don't worry about us being needy and wanting to connect or anything."

It's a joke—mostly. At least, I mean it as one. But when he reaches in front of me to open the door and I look up into his eyes, I'm not sure he took it that way.

He peers down at me with his hand on the knob. A storm wages in those hazel orbs. The intensity of the golds and browns holds my attention, not letting me look away.

Each breath has his chest brushing against my arm. I'm frozen in place, held hostage by nothing but his silent demand not to move.

It's a request I'm too happy to oblige.

"Gabrielle . . ."

"Yes?"

The storm picks up. So does his breathing. My heartbeat races in anticipation of what he's going to say.

Or do.

He licks his lips. His tongue leaves a trail of wetness behind, making him that much more kissable. His gaze drops to my mouth.

My mind races, sorting through a million thoughts powering through my brain at warp speed. *Is he going to kiss me?*

He lowers his face toward mine. I lift my chin to meet him, my breath trembling. This doesn't make a whole lot of sense since he's not into connecting with people—and kissing me would definitely be a connection. *But who am I to turn down a kiss from a sexy man?*

My heart thunders in my ears. I'm barely able to stand. The pressure between my thighs is so heavy, so great, that I squeeze them together, or else I'll moan.

"Thanks again for the shirt," he says, pulling the door open and stepping away.

What the actual hell?

My stomach drops. My jaw goes right along with it.

He makes no move except to blink.

This asshole.

I look at him, narrowing my eyes and smiling facetiously. I don't know what game he's playing, but I'm out.

"You're very welcome," I say.

With that, I pivot and quickly exit his home.

CHAPTER NINE

JAY

"This is a nightmare." I sip my coffee in the same way I would if I were watching a train wreck. Because, really, it's about the same thing. "Don't do that. *Don't do that.*"

Gabrielle climbs a ladder leaned against the house. The legs aren't on even ground, and there's no way it'll stay vertical once she's up more than a few rungs. My stomach churns and I hold my breath.

One step. Two.

"Shit," I hiss as she starts to wobble.

She looks over her shoulder. Then she slowly descends back to the ground. Once her feet are planted on the soil, I breathe a sigh of relief.

My attention slides to the back of the house, where Dylan sits on the edge of the deck. He's looking at a drill like he's never seen one before. *Maybe he hasn't.*

"Stop looking," I mutter aloud, turning away from the window. "It's not your problem."

I force myself into the living room—a space that has no view of the house next door. I've found myself watching them most of the morning like an obsessed lunatic.

It doesn't matter that I have nothing to do today and could so easily have their tasks done in a few hours. It doesn't matter at all. *Why?* Because I'm not getting involved.

Because I almost fucking kissed Gabrielle last night.

Despite that moment being twelve hours ago, I haven't managed to settle down. I'm still buzzed on adrenaline.

I don't know what happened or what came over me. I don't lose control like that. But my lips were inches from hers when reality pummeled me and I realized what I was doing.

Maybe I got sucked into the moment. Maybe her realness, her vulnerability, softened me. It's been a long time since anyone was that open, that honest.

"I just want to feel like a woman again. Love isn't necessary. I just want a reason to get dolled up on Friday nights. I want someone to laugh with, cuddle up to—someone to have fun sex with."

My jaw tenses. So does my cock.

My self-restraint was the only thing soft.

"I might have to move," I say, shaking my head. "If I can't figure out how to handle this, I'll pack up and head elsewhere. Alaska is nice this time of year."

But even Alaska probably isn't far enough away to erase her from my mind.

The problem is that Gabrielle would be an amazing woman to spend time with if I were ready to do that. *But I'm not.* When I imagine holding her in my arms, having her in my bed, losing myself inside her . . . it's immediately followed by a sickness that's all too familiar.

It's one I don't want to have again. I don't think I'd survive it.

"You have to hold the screw in place a second, Dylan," I say, realizing I'm back at the kitchen window. The screw drops to the ground again. "Come on, kid. YouTube it or something."

I glance back to the front of her house and nearly choke.

Gabrielle is standing on the front lawn, facing her house, with a sledgehammer.

"Oh, fuck it." I slam my mug on the counter and charge out the door. "You can't leave well enough be, Jay. You're going to have no one to complain about except yourself."

Gabrielle looks up, propping a hand on her hip, and all but scowls. *She's not happy to see me.*

"What in the world are you doing?" I ask, marching across the lawn.

"What's it to you?"

"I don't know. Call me a concerned citizen."

She makes a face that tells me to fuck off. "It's demo day. So if you'll excuse me, I have work to do."

"Look," I say, frustration growing. "I know demo day is cute on all the home renovation shows. But in the real world, all that smashing something with a sledgehammer is going to do is make a bigger mess to clean up."

"And?"

I roll my eyes. "What are you trying to do?"

"Right now, I'm trying to get a very nosy *and unwelcome* neighbor to leave me alone."

Her little jaw is set in place like a wannabe badass. Her tits are about ready to spill out of her skewed tank top. She has a pair of safety goggles dangling around her neck and boots on—with her shorts. It's hard to keep a straight face.

"Let me help you," I say, struggling not to smile.

"You've already thanked me for the shirt." She turns toward the porch. "You've done enough."

Oh. That's what this is about.

She pulls the sledgehammer back, ready to attack a defenseless spindle. I snatch it from her hand as she brings it forward.

"Hey," she yelps, spinning around. Her hand is still cupped where the handle was. "What are you doing?"

"Will you stop being so dramatic and talk to me?"

She snorts. "You are hilarious. *Hilarious.* I'm dramatic and you want to talk. I'm in stitches over here."

"Then you should see me when I'm trying to be funny."

"I had a front-row ticket to it last night, bucko."

I smirk. "Bucko?"

She waves a hand in the air. "I don't know. My grandma used to say it. But that's not the point." She steps my way. "The point is that—"

"The point is that I didn't kiss you last night."

Gabrielle sucks in a breath and, for once, doesn't speak. I'm completely aware that Dylan could walk around the side of the house at any moment, so I speak quickly and quietly.

"I think that was more effective at getting you to stop talking than kissing you would've been," I say.

That brings her back to life.

"Do you want to know what I'm mad about? Fine. I'll tell you," she says. "It's not because you didn't kiss me. Believe it or not, I'll survive without kissing you. What pissed me off was that you made me feel like a complete fool. *You* initiated the situation. *You* acted like you wanted it. And then when I opened myself up to it, *you* laughed in my face."

"I *did not* laugh in your face."

She glares at me.

The hurt in her eyes swims to the surface. Her lips tip toward the ground. Her voice is filled with frustration and edged in hurt. *And I kick myself for it.*

I didn't anticipate her thinking I was fucking with her. *Doesn't she realize that she's the prize?* Any man in their right mind would kiss the hell out of her.

Clearly, the problem is me. *Doesn't she see that?*

"Gabrielle, I'm sorry," I say, looking her in the eye. "I was going to kiss you but thought better of it at the last second."

She flinches but recovers quickly.

Fuck. "Look, kissing you would've been giving in to the moment. Did I want to kiss you? Of course. You're gorgeous."

You're the first woman that's made my heart race in a long time. That's why you're so dangerous.

Her cheeks flush a rosy shade of pink.

"But it would've been wrong of me to do that because it wouldn't have gone anywhere," I say. "I was trying not to lead you on."

"What's so terrible about me that it can't go anywhere? Hypothetically, of course."

"Not a damn thing."

We face one another, both of us refusing to give in. I'm not looking away first. I want her to see I'm telling her the truth.

I want her to know it's not her who's the problem.

Finally, her shoulders slump. "Whatever. Give me my sledgehammer back."

"If you want to take the spindles out, all you need is a hammer." I point at one of them. "But look at how they're attached. They're nailed on the outside. So if you go whacking it from this side, you're not going to pop it out. Not easily, anyway."

"Oh." She leans forward to investigate. "So I need to be on the porch and hitting it out toward where we are now."

"It would be much easier and much cleaner."

She huffs. "Fine. Good point. Thanks."

"Get yourself a hammer, Miss Fix-It." I swing the sledgehammer as I walk away. "I'm going to show your kid how to use a drill."

"I can show him."

I look at her over my shoulder. "This is painful to watch. Don't make me suffer longer than necessary."

She holds my gaze for a few seconds. As each second ticks by, the look on her face shifts from annoyance to a playful arrogance that has my cock hard as hell.

"If you want to stick around, do it," she says, smirking. She glances down my body to the bulge in my pants and then lifts her eyes back to mine. "I'm going to make you suffer as long as I can."

I narrow my gaze. *Walk home. Turn around and get the hell out of here before you fuck everything up. Now, Jay.*

But even as I think it, I find myself at the back deck with Dylan.

"What are you doing here?" he asks, getting to his feet once I'm around the side of the house. The drill hangs at his side.

I wish I knew. "Need some help?"

"No."

I lean the sledgehammer against the deck. "All right. No worries."

He clenches his jaw and doesn't speak.

"Look, man, I'm not your enemy," I say.

"I'll be the judge of that."

Ah, there's the mouthy little shit I remember.

Dylan will play hardball, and a part of me respects the hell out of that. Sure, he's being a little fuckhead. But he's trying to be a man in the best way he knows how. He's trying to protect his mother and his home from me, the guy who instincts tell him might be preying on them.

He's not wrong, and I don't want to negate his innate sense to listen to his gut.

I need to figure out how to convince him to let me help while still letting him have dominion over his space.

"Hey, I don't blame you," I say. "Always trust your gut."

His brows pull together in confusion.

I peer over one of the loose rails I saw him fiddling with from my window.

"Oh, I bet you'll have a hell of a time with this one." I point at the edge of the rail he was trying to fix. "Is that giving you shit?"

He nods warily.

"You probably don't have any screws long enough to attach it, do you?" I ask.

"No. But I'll get some."

I run a hand down my jaw. "I'm a carpenter and have seen this many times. You can try the screws, but you'd be better off just replacing the whole board." I shrug. "That's just my professional opinion. Take it or leave it."

He swallows hard, watching me carefully. "Why are you being so nice to us?"

His question puts me on the spot. It throws me off for a moment. *Why am I being so nice to you?*

"I mean, I know why you're being so nice to Mom," he says. "You probably want to do her."

"Well, Dylan, that's not a conversation I'm going to have with you."

"But why are you being nice to me?"

My heart tugs in my chest, and I decide to be honest with him. "Because I hope someone is being nice to my daughter right now . . . just for the sake of being kind. No ulterior motives."

"All right." He pauses. "Where does she live?"

I blow out a shaky breath and yank the board in question off the deck. *That's enough honesty for one day.* "I have a whole bunch of these in my garage, taking up space. Want them? I'll help you carry them over."

His eyes search mine.

"You'll be doing me a favor," I say, hoping he'll follow my redirection. "I was going to donate them somewhere anyway. You might as well take them. I gotta get them out of my way."

I'm not sure he's going to go with it. Finally, he sighs. "Sure, I guess."

We set off for the garage, Dylan a couple of steps behind me. I give him a few minutes to get his head together and to come up with a plan on how he's going to handle this. If I don't, he'll act like a child out of habit, and no one wants that.

I can also use a few minutes to get my head together. This morning has gone sideways in ways I didn't predict.

We enter the garage and I sort the boards, gathering a stack that will work for him. The noise keeps us from having to speak for a while. *Thank God.*

"If these are too long, just mark where they need to be cut, and we can cut them over here," I say, motioning toward my saws.

"Yeah. Okay." He holds his arms out while I put the boards across them. "You're really just giving these to us?"

"They've sat here for months."

He nods. "Okay." He looks around. "You have a lot of tools."

"I've liked building things since I was your little brother's age."

"You know Carter?"

"He came by last night wanting me to help him with his basketball. The kid never stops moving."

Dylan grins. "That's Carter." His affection for his little brother is clear. That's interesting, considering I've seen how he talks to everyone else. "So how did you learn how to build things?"

"Practice, mostly. I went to a trade school while I was in high school and learned the basics. It's a lot harder than people think."

"So do you build houses or what?"

"I don't build them from the ground up. That involves a lot of shit that I don't want to deal with. I do a lot of renovations, and sometimes that means adding a room or taking one down. That kind of thing."

"That's pretty cool."

"There are worse ways to make a living."

He nods, seemingly satisfied by his investigation of me. "Does that offer to help still stand? Not because I can't do it. But because, you know, it might go faster with two guys on the job."

"No problem. I have some time on my hands."

He smiles, relief written all over his face. "Thanks. What did you say your name is?"

"I'm Jay."

"I'm Dylan."

"All right, Dylan. Let's get over there and get to work."

We start back across the lawn. Gabrielle watches us from the front porch. Her grin says, *Thank you.* My wave says, *Don't worry about it.*

But *I* worry about it. I worry about it a whole damn lot. Because helping a single mother I'm wildly attracted to is the last place I need to be. It's a place I swore to myself I'd never be again.

I know that.

So why didn't I simply just stay away?

CHAPTER TEN

Gabrielle

I collect the broken spindles littering the ground and make a pile near the driveway. The front of the house looks a little bare without them, but no spindle is better than missing every third and every sixth one being broken.

My muscles groan as I stare back at the house and take in my handiwork. *Not bad.*

Aside from the spindles, the steps leading to the porch are gone. I tore out all the weeds popping up in the landscaping and yanked a few plants that were overgrown. The porch light that hasn't been changed since at least the eighties is now in the trash can.

I still need to clean the baby trees out of the gutters.

The ladder leans against the house right where I left it. I shake it, summoning the courage to give scaling the rungs another shot. The gutters were going to be my first plan of attack, but I chickened out when a not-so-strong breeze nearly yeeted me across the lawn.

It felt like that, at least.

"Woman up, Gabby," I say, sliding gloves out of my pocket and onto my hands. Then I grip the rails. "Get your butt up there and do the damn thing."

Voices drift around the house, replacing the hammering and drilling from the last couple of hours. I place one foot on the lowest rung. Dylan and Jay will be here any second, and they'll try to talk me out of going up there. *Heck, they both have already tried today.* Besides, if I'm ten feet up in the air, it'll be harder for Jay to bring up our earlier conversation.

"Look, kissing you would've been giving in to the moment. Did I want to kiss you? Of course. You're gorgeous. But it would've been wrong of me to do that because it wouldn't have gone anywhere."

Hmm. *Right.*

The gutters, Gabs. Get to the gutters.

The ladder is steadier than it was earlier. Still, I keep my weight leaning forward so I don't tip backward. There's no need to play with unnecessary risks any more than I already am.

Jay's voice is warm, and the deep notes find me before I find him. The sound drags across my body, caressing it in a way that isn't safe for a woman this far off the ground. Come to think of it, it wouldn't be safe if I had both feet planted firmly on the soil either.

"Thanks again for the shirt."

"Thanks again for the shirt," I say, mocking Jay's words that echo through my head. I scoop my hand in the gutter and fish out a heavy, water-laden pile of yuck. *I ought to throw this on you, Jay.*

Why has he convoluted my brain with all his mixed signals? He doesn't want to connect with people. He accepted my coffee. He almost kisses me, calls me gorgeous. He went out of his way to help my sons. He doesn't want anything, obviously, between us, but how am I supposed to understand his behavior?

Why come over here? Why show up for us two days in a row? Why air up Carter's ball and help Dylan fix the porch?

My insides clench as I recall the bulge in his pants.

I don't think he's screwing with me to be a dick. But he's screwing with me, nonetheless. *And I plan on screwing with him right back.*

I drop the pile of yuck into the bucket I hung off the ladder earlier.

"Mom on a ladder never ends well," Dylan says.

I look down at him. "Very funny."

"I'm going inside and taking a shower. I don't want to see how this ends."

"Did you get the deck all done?" I ask, ignoring Jay standing next to him.

Dylan nods. "Yeah. Jay helped me." He peers at him out of the corner of his eye. "He let us have some boards."

I can't quite work out Dylan's tone. It's steady and void of overt sarcasm, but the edges of his words are a little too raw to be conversational. *I hope he wasn't a complete brat to Jay all afternoon.*

I move my attention to Jay. The sight of his sweaty T-shirt clinging to his body makes my mouth water. *Play it cool, Gabby.*

"Thanks again for the boards," I say, mimicking his words about the flannel.

He nods knowingly, shoving his tongue into his cheek. I smile with a cockiness I might regret later. *Oh well. Gotta roll with it now.*

"Can I go in?" Dylan sighs.

"Yes. You can go in," I say. "Make sure you thank Jay for his help."

He hops over the missing stairs and lands on the porch. "I did."

"Dylan . . ."

The door closing is his response.

I look at the sky. "I love him. I love him. I love him."

Jay chuckles.

"I hope he wasn't so moody with you—*whoa*!" I lean forward and grip the rails so tight that my knuckles burn.

Jay's gaze is hot on the side of my face. I don't dare look at him.

"Why don't you come down from there?" he asks carefully.

I take a deep breath and twist to the gutter again. "Because I'm cleaning the gutters."

"I'm sure it can wait a few minutes."

"Nah, I'm already up here." I drag my hand through the sludge and dump another handful into my bucket. My stomach turns at the smell. "Gosh, that reeks."

"If you come down, I'll finish the job for you."

"Thanks, but I got it."

"Gabrielle . . ."

It's the way he says my name that does it. *Gabrielle.* Like he's exasperated that I won't listen to his direction.

Well, Mr. Stetson, screw that.

"Look," I say, turning until I can see him. But either I move too fast, lean too far away from the house, or the ladder is lopsided . . . Or maybe it's a combination of the three. For whatever reason, the ladder begins to tilt backward. I slam my chest against the rungs and force the top rungs to lie snugly against the roofline. *"Ho-ly crap."*

My heart thunders. Sweat dots my back. I calculate how many broken bones I might wake up with tomorrow if I don't start remembering I'm ten feet off the ground.

When I glance down, Jay's hands are on the ladder. Judging by that heavy scowl on his face, he's displeased.

This shouldn't be that hot.

I don't tell him that this isn't helping. Maybe he's keeping the ladder from rocking, but that won't stop me from falling if my knees turn to gelatin from the heat in his eyes. His grip on the rails isn't going to stop me from sliding straight down the metal as I melt into a puddle of orgasmic need.

He smirks.

I didn't say that out loud, did I?

"Look, I'm sure you can do this on your own," he says. "But taking a little help when it's offered isn't a sign of weakness. It's a sign of strength."

I roll my eyes.

"Come on, Gabrielle."

"Come on . . . what?"

I return his smirk as the innuendo hits him in the face. His eyes darken.

Yeah, Jay. Imagine me just like that.

"Don't worry," I say. I slide my gloves off and drape them over the side of the bucket. "I don't expect an answer. I already have it."

"Answer it, then."

I watch him over my shoulder. His features are severe, his jawline so sharp it could cut granite. It would be so easy to let him win this battle of wits . . . if I were willing to lose.

"I can come on whatever I want as long as it has nothing to do with you." I grin, lifting a brow. "Right?"

His eyes narrow.

"Oh, stop it," I say, sighing dramatically as I move down the rungs. "Calm down. I know you don't want me." *Or so you say.*

He barely steps back enough to make room for me to get down.

My butt, then my back, brushes against him as my feet drop to the ground. A blast of heat burns through me and pools in my belly. Turning around is going to be akin to fireworks—I know this. But I also know I can't refuse to face him either.

I brush my hands off and sidestep away from Jay. "So was Dylan a pain in the butt, or did he remember some of the manners I've worked hard to instill in him?"

"He was fine." Jay's words are strangled. *Tight.* "He learned a few things."

"It's always a good day when you learn something new."

He clears his throat. "Looks like you got the spindles out. But what in the hell happened to the stairs?"

"Oh. *Those.*" I focus on the spot where steps once stood. "They weren't level, and I about fell through the right side yesterday afternoon while carrying groceries. I figured I'd rebuild them tomorrow when I put in the new spindles."

I wait for him to respond. Once it's clear he's not going to, I finally look at him.

A grin graces his lips. His arms are folded across his barrel chest. Amusement plays across his features in the most relaxed, carefree way I've seen him.

It's a sight to behold.

"Let me get this straight," he says, shifting his weight. "You're going to fix the railing. Build new stairs. Clean the gutters. What else?"

"Well . . ." I turn to the house. "I think there used to be a ceiling fan on the front porch. So I'm going to see if I can figure that out. I'm going to install security cameras. Those are on their way from an online store. I want to do a little painting and fix a toilet that won't stop running. Oh! And some of the outlets in the house need to be replaced. They're on a dimmer switch, and it's going bad. So the lights just kind of pulse in some rooms, giving us a headache." I point at Jay. "But you can't tell Cricket that."

"Why not?"

"She thinks I can't do electrical work."

He hums. "I've not seen you in electrical action, but I'd wager that Cricket is right."

I gasp. *"Rude."*

He chuckles and moseys around the front lawn, stopping at various places to check out the house from different vantage points. I have no idea what he's doing, but I could watch him move around all day. *Even if I am mildly irritated at him for second-guessing my skills.*

Finally, he stops traveling and makes his way back to me.

"The project I'm meant to work on this week got called off," he says, slipping a hand into the front pocket of his jeans.

"Okay . . ."

"Let me come over and help you."

"Absolutely not."

He rubs his forehead.

"I told you that we're self-sufficient over here," I say, then wince. "I mean, your help *has* been appreciated. But we aren't a charity case."

"No one said you were."

You implied it, though. I grab a rake off the porch and gather the weeds I pulled earlier.

"You're sweet to offer," I say. "But this stuff is fun for me. It's the only fun I have left, and I don't want to contaminate my happy place with someone helping me out of pity."

"It's not out of pity."

I stop raking. "Then what is it?"

He holds my gaze as he walks to me. Every step he takes cranks up the temperature between us. He's controlled and intentional.

He stops inches before me, towering over me by nearly a foot. His cologne fills the space between us with a scent I sniffed out of his flannel before I tossed it in the washer last night. It's comforting and exudes strength, giving me a spark of excitement.

"Why can't it be as easy as I have time on my hands and you have work to do?" he asks.

"Because no one wants to work if they don't have to."

"What do you want me to do? Do you want me to stand in front of my window and watch you climb the ladder and nearly fall to your death?"

I gasp. "First, I didn't almost fall to my death. Second, I don't care what you do. And third, what is it with you standing at your window? It's a little creepy."

He rolls his eyes.

He's more agitated than I expected. And although I don't understand why he's hell-bent on helping me, I can't say I don't like it or that I don't want him to. But winding him up—watching the self-contained Jay Stetson start to lose his precious control—is fun.

Besides, *he* almost kissed *me*. He has it coming.

"Hey," I say, swinging my hips more than necessary to pick up my water bottle. "Did you ever think of any of your friends that might be looking for a hookup? They could come over and help me. It'd be a two-for-one. He could work with me and then *work me.*"

And . . . *he delivers.*

Jay cuts the distance between us in half. His eyes flare with irritation. His fists clench at his sides. He peers down at me like he wants to rip me in half—and I consider offering an invitation. But he's already made it clear that's not happening.

I'm not one to beg.

Although, I think he's one to lie.

"Does that question bother you?" I ask, fluttering my lashes. "Because it seems like it does."

Instead of answering me, he starts across the lawn. "What time are we starting tomorrow?"

"What?"

"What time do you want me here in the morning?"

I laugh. "I said I didn't need your help."

"I'll be here at nine," he says over his shoulder.

His insistence on helping me makes me smile. Sure, I can do all this on my own—or I can try, anyway. But having Jay around is exciting. And if I get to watch him work and get all sweaty for a couple of days, that's just the cherry on top.

"Fine," I say. "But you're my assistant. Remember that."

He shakes his head and disappears into his house. Even though I don't quite understand what he's up to, I smile all the way into mine.

CHAPTER ELEVEN

Gabrielle

"You cook just like Grandma," I say, putting away the last plate. "Dinner was delicious, Cricket."

Cricket's kitchen is the opposite of mine. The stove itself probably costs more than every appliance in my kitchen. It's emerald green with gold knobs that complement the bespoke refrigerator across the room. She has a mixer, chopper, and slicer for every meal-prep step. It's quite a change from my cupboard's single can opener and cutting board.

"Oh, that's so sweet of you to say." She smiles over her shoulder. "One of my regrets is that I never had the chance to cook with her. I mean, sure, we mixed and stirred. But I never got to stand in the kitchen and create a meal with her."

"She would be impressed by you."

My cousin beams.

"What's for dessert?" Peter comes into the kitchen and hands Cricket his tea glass. "Did you make a sheet cake?"

"No," she says, setting the glass in the sink. "I made a pineapple upside-down cake instead."

"Oh. I thought we talked about a sheet cake?"

"We did. But I changed the menu, and a sheet cake didn't go with our entrée, dear." She gives him a forced smile and turns to me. "Would you like a piece of cake?"

"I would!" Carter races into the room, sliding the last few feet in his socks. "I love cake."

I tousle his hair. "Don't run in the house, Carter."

He leans his head back and smiles wide.

"So, what's it like to be back in Alden, Gabby?" Peter asks.

"We love it," Carter says. "Don't we, Mom?"

He takes a slice of cake from Cricket.

"Sit at the table in the dining room with that," I say.

Peter grins as Carter holds the cake like a prize while walking to the dining room. "He's a cute kid. I remember when Kyle was that little. Feels like yesterday." He stands tall. "Speaking of the devil . . ."

Kyle walks in, looking like the spitting image of his father. He wraps an arm around my neck in a faux headlock. "Some of my friends are going to play ball at the rec center. Can I go?"

"Be back before it gets too late," Cricket says. "You have school tomorrow."

"For goodness' sake, Cricket. The boy's sixteen. Let him live a little."

She whips around with the cake server in her hand. "I know how old he is, Peter. I was there when he was born."

"I'll be back by eight." Kyle lets me go. Then he steps between them, kissing his mother on the cheek. "Dinner was great."

"Thank you."

"Bye, Gabby," Kyle says.

"Goodbye."

He knuckle-bumps his father, and Peter follows him out of the room.

Cricket's cheeks are flushed the same color of red as her apron.

"Hey, are you okay?" I ask, moving closer to her.

She drops the server on the plate with a bit more force than necessary. "Yes. I'm fine. Just aggravated."

"Mom, can I go with Kyle?" Dylan stands in the doorway. Uncertainty is clear on his face. "He asked me to."

"Sure. Have fun."

He nods warily and disappears around the corner.

Cricket removes her apron and tosses it on the counter.

"It's none of my business, and I don't want to pry," I say carefully. "But I'm here to listen if you need to talk about anything."

"I'm fine, Gabby. But thank you for the sweet offer."

The fire in her eyes tells me she's not fine. But it also warns me not to poke.

A loud crack rumbles through the air, garnering an eye roll from Cricket.

"What is that?" I ask.

"Kyle's truck."

"Oh. That *is* a little . . ."

"Obnoxious?" she offers. "I loathe it. It's so tacky. But Peter took him to get the . . . whatever parts to make it sound like that. So what can I say?"

The look on her face tells me she's probably said a lot about it. And was completely ignored.

"That's one good thing about being a single parent," I say. "There's no one to argue with or to trump me. I am the final say."

"So what did you think of Della and Scottie?" Cricket asks, her voice an octave higher than usual. "Della can be a little forward, and Scottie a touch dramatic. But they're very sweet."

"I thought they were great. They both seem like they could be a lot of fun."

"They can be fun, all right." She glances toward the sound of Peter's voice in the living room. "Would you like to sit outside on the patio? It's a beautiful evening."

"I'd love to."

The sun is warm as we sit on the wicker chairs facing Bittersweet Court. A butterfly flutters around the flower bed between the patio and the road. It moves happily from plant to plant, as if it has no care in the world. *Wouldn't that be nice?*

I spent most of Reverend Smith's sermon early this morning pondering my life and elbowing Dylan to keep him awake. Seeing so many friendly, familiar faces when we walked in gave me energy. Sitting in the pew where our grandmother and my mother once sat was inspiring.

I come from a long line of women who are strong. Fierce. Who made it through the Great Depression, divorce, miscarriages, house fires, and more. They suffered, yet their resilience, grit, and determination drove them forward. They kept moving. And somewhere between the sermon and "Amazing Grace," I realized I'm in that group too. I made it. *I just need to keep moving forward.*

But just because you've made it to the other side of the fire doesn't mean life returns to the way it was before. Once you've been through the flames, you're burned. Those scars never totally heal.

What will my life look like now that I'm on the other side? It's been so long since I was in life mode, not survival mode, that I'm not even sure.

"What are you thinking about?" Cricket asks.

"If I told you, you'd laugh."

"Try me."

I settle back in my chair. "Okay. I was wondering what living a normal life looks like."

"What?" She smiles but doesn't laugh. "Are you serious?"

"Yeah. I've tiptoed around for months, waiting for the sky to fall at any minute. I'm just now feeling like it might be okay to breathe. If I put roots down and take a step forward, maybe the world won't slam my hopes in my face."

"Oh, honey." She grabs my hand and gives it a gentle squeeze. "This last year must've been just awful for you."

"You know, I've had that thought every day for months. *'This is awful.'* Over and over. But maybe thinking that kept me there, if that makes sense. When Reverend Smith started the sermon, he began with a passage about forgetting former things and not dwelling on the past. And my mind just took off."

She smiles.

"Scottie said something to me yesterday, too, that's been gnawing on me. I've been waiting for Dylan to change his behavior. But maybe I'm keeping him from doing that because I'm not changing mine." I turn to face her. "Maybe I need to start going forward for him to know it's safe."

"I love that."

Me too.

We sit quietly, watching the butterflies. Carter comes out and dribbles his basketball up and down the sidewalk. His tongue sticking out the side of his mouth makes Cricket and me laugh.

"I'm going to go inside for a minute," Cricket says. "Do you need me to bring you a drink when I return?"

"No, I'm good. Thanks, though."

She stands and goes back into the house.

I take out my phone and scroll through social media. I'm midcomment on a friend from Boston's post when a text buzzes.

Hey, it's Della. I got your number from Cricket.

My fingers shuffle over the keys.

Me: Hey.

Della: Do you have plans for Friday night?

Me: No.

Della: Great. Let's go out and have some drinks.

I read her text again. *"Let's go out and have some drinks."* When was the last time I went out on a Friday night?

"What's wrong?" Cricket asks, taking her seat.

"Della just asked if I wanted to go for drinks on Friday night."

"Well, it would be memorable. I'll promise you that."

I smile at her. "Should I go?"

"You've been saying you want to put a step forward. Here's your chance." She flicks a piece of dust off her armrest. "I'll keep an eye on the boys. Peter will be gone golfing for the weekend, so it'll give me something to do."

"Would you want to come with us?"

She laughs loudly. "With Della? No, ma'am. I'm a happily married woman and want to keep it that way."

I laugh, too, and text Della back.

Me: Let's do it!

Della: 🎉 I'll confirm the time with you later.

Me: Sounds great.

"Is she really as wild as you say she is?" I ask, setting my phone on the edge of a plant stand.

She considers this. "Yes and no. She did have two very burly-looking gentlemen leaving her house within five minutes of each other. And I have heard tales of her, another couple, caramel sauce, and a blow dryer."

"Really?"

She shrugs.

"Mom!" Carter's little voice echoes down the street. "Mom!"

I look up to find my son running down the sidewalk with his ball tucked under his arm. Another little boy runs alongside him.

"Mom! Can I go to the park with Hayes?" he asks, dragging in a breath. *"Please?"*

"My mom is going too," Hayes says, pointing to a lady coming up the sidewalk, pushing a stroller. "See? That's her."

Carter bounces up and down. *"Please?"*

"Let me talk to Hayes's mom first," I say.

The boys accompany me, one kid attached to either side, to the woman, as if I might lose my way.

"I'm Freya," she says, grinning.

"Hi. I'm Gabby. I wanted to say thank you for keeping an eye on Carter the other day. My son Dylan said he met you and gave Carter permission to go with you."

"I hope that's okay."

I smile. "Of course. I just didn't want you to think I was a bad mom. We'd never met before, and my little boy just traipses off with you to the park."

She laughs. "I make it a habit never to judge moms. I know how hard it is. Besides, Dylan was very polite and got my name."

He did? He didn't share it with me.

"And I saw Jay Stetson working on your deck," she says. "I thought if you had a problem with me taking Carter, Jay could assure you I'm not a childnapper."

"Yes, he did mention that he knew you and your husband."

Freya gives the baby in the stroller a pacifier. "We need to get moving, or my little lovebug in here will start screaming like she has for the last five hours." She laughs. "The joys of motherhood."

"Good luck."

"I'll just drop Carter off as we walk by in an hour or so," she says.

"That's perfect. I'll be home by then."

She nods, gathers the kids, and heads for the park.

Just as I'm about to return to Cricket's, a black truck comes down the road. It slows as it approaches and rolls to a stop next to me.

Jay slides sunglasses off his face. He looks over my head and gives Cricket a little wave. Then he turns his sights on me.

"Are you any more agreeable this afternoon than earlier this morning?" he asks, grinning.

That grin could melt an iceberg.

I return his grin. "I'm always agreeable, Jay. I don't know what you mean."

He chuckles, the sound electrifying the air between us.

"Where are you off to?" I ask.

"I'm headed to the grocery store. Since I'll be home all week, I gotta grab breakfast and lunch stuff." He licks his lips. "What are you up to?"

"Cricket made dinner. We're just sitting out here and enjoying the day. I'm probably going to head home soon and try to get a bit of work done."

"Oh. What kind of work do you do?"

"I name babies."

His eyes go wide. "You've got to be shitting me."

"No." I laugh. "I name babies as a side hustle."

"People pay you for that?"

My laughter gets louder, and I don't bother to reply.

"All right," he says, shifting in his seat. "I better go. Enjoy your Sunday."

I tap his truck and take a step back. He pulls away slowly. Once he's down the road, he picks up his speed. The rumble of the engine growls through the air.

"What was that all about?" Cricket asks.

I jump to find her standing on the sidewalk behind me. Her arms are crossed over her chest, and a knowing grin is painted on her red lips.

"That was nothing. He just said hello," I say.

"Gabrielle, Jay Stetson says hello to no one on this street. Not willingly, anyway."

I lift my chin and step off the road and next to her. "He speaks to me."

"Interesting."

"Well, we are neighbors, so it makes sense. Right?"

"Yes," she says curiously. "But it is surprising. He's quite reserved. It makes me wonder . . . Have you already wooed the mysterious Jay Stetson with your womanly wiles?"

We both laugh.

I think again of the "almost" moments.

"But it would've been wrong of me to do that because it wouldn't have gone anywhere."

"No," I say, sighing. "He said that there could never be anything between us. But that doesn't mean I don't like flirting with him."

"You and every other woman in the world. But he doesn't flirt back with the others."

I gaze down the street. He's long gone.

"He doesn't exactly flirt with me either," I say. "And if he does, he makes sure to temper it with something that reminds me that he will never act on it."

She hums. "Well, then, I guess you just see what happens."

"Nothing will happen, Cricket. He's made that loud and clear. And I'm just overly needy because I haven't had sex in a long damn time." I wink at her. "But I will sharpen my skills on him this week to use Friday night with Della."

"Oh dear."

I laugh at the expression on her face. "On that note, I'm heading home. Thank you for a wonderful Sunday dinner."

She gives me a quick hug. "I love that you're here."

"Me too." I pull away. "Thank you for helping me and the boys get settled in. Alden is feeling like home again."

Life is feeling so much less . . . lonely now.

"Well, we are glad to have you back."

Cricket heads into the house, and I walk toward home.

CHAPTER TWELVE

JAY

"Jay, I'm really worried about you," I say to my reflection in the bathroom mirror. "What is wrong? Why are you doing this? You can go get a piece of ass if that's what you're after."

My stomach twists because that's not what I'm after. Not specifically, anyway.

I shove away from the vanity and head back into my bedroom. I whisper a prayer that it somehow started storming in the last twenty minutes, making outside housing projects out of the question. But as expected, it's the brightest day Ohio has seen since I moved here.

Damn it.

Feelings that I'd forgotten existed surge inside me. It's that need to be around someone, that almost unbearable urge to say their name. It exceeds wanting to fuck or to fuck around. It's bigger than that. It encompasses all the senses—seeing her smile, breathing in her perfume, touching her soft skin, listening to her laugh. The only thing I don't know is how she tastes.

"Fuck," I say, growling into the air. *I'll never find out how she tastes either.*

I could say no. I could just not show up or tell her that I got busy. Nothing would be worse for the wear. Even though I shouldn't, *I want to see her.*

As preoccupied with Gabrielle as I am, I'm that angry with Melody. I haven't been angry with her—not like this—for a long time. The sentiment was more bitter. Loathing. So disgusted that I couldn't even think about her. But now that Gabrielle is next door and I can't manage my damn self, I'm pissed as hell at Melody for doing this to me.

She didn't just take my beautiful daughter. She took away my future.

I shove my feet into my boots and head for the door.

Birds welcome me outside with a song. I pause on the porch and take a moment to focus, to center myself for the day ahead.

"I can be around her," I say to myself. "Have fun with her. I just can't cross a line."

My stomach tightens and I know I'm right. I know I'll stop before I cross a line. I don't think I could cross it if I wanted to.

"Good thing I'm not paying you!"

I turn toward the sound of Gabrielle's voice. She's standing on the back deck, coffee in hand, with a pink bow wrapped around her ponytail.

This woman is going to be the death of me. "Why is that?"

"Because you're late."

I start across the lawn. "Traffic was a mess."

She grins. "That's what they all say. Want some coffee? The kids are at school today, so it's not as hostile an environment as it was on Saturday."

I hop onto the deck and jump to hold the door for her. She smiles, nodding appreciatively as she enters first.

"I'm not going to say Dylan and I are friends," I say. "But I think we made headway."

Gabrielle pours me a cup of coffee. "He didn't say anything bad about you last night." She hands me the mug. "I mean, he didn't say anything good either. So take that for what it's worth."

I chuckle.

"Let me send this email, and then we can get started," she says, sitting in front of her computer. "If this woman doesn't name her twins Elodie and Ophelia, I'm going to die."

"So people really pay you to name their kids."

Her fingers fly across the keyboard. "They pay me to give them suggestions. It's really hard naming kids." She pauses to watch me over her shoulder. "Do you have any kids?"

I clear my throat and sit across from her. "No kids I've ever named."

It's a curious answer to an unwanted question. *Why do these people keep harping on me having kids?* First Carter, then Dylan, and now Gabrielle.

She pulls her brows together but goes back to typing. "Then you don't know how hard it can be. And sometimes it becomes too emotional, and the parents argue. Getting a third party involved helps." She hits "Enter" with a flourish. "There. Sent."

Silence descends upon us. In any other time and place, I'd welcome it. There's something great about being able to sit in the stillness with another person. But with this woman and her questions and innuendos, I'm better off filling the void.

"So what's on the agenda today, Boss?" I ask.

"Ooh. I could get used to that."

I look at her over my mug. "Don't."

She laughs. "I really don't know where to start. There's so much to do that I kind of just want to not do any of it today."

"You tore the steps off your front porch."

"So?"

"So? You can't just leave it that way."

She shrugs. "I mean, *I could*." A grin slips across her face as she reads my annoyance.

This woman.

"I fixed the drain in the sink last night," she says, closing her computer. "Do you know how to stop toilets from running?"

"Generally, you just adjust the float in the back. That is, unless the guts in the tank need replacing."

She grimaces. "Toilets give me the ick. Could I fix it? I'm sure I could. But if you could fix it . . ." Her nose wrinkles like she's bracing for me to say no.

I can't tell her no. Case in point: I'm here. If I were able to resist her, I wouldn't be standing in her house and on my way to fix her damn toilet.

Try harder, Stetson.

"Where's it at?" I ask.

"Up the stairs. Second door on the right. It's the boys' bathroom, so be warned."

We get up from the table and I start toward the steps. She doesn't follow.

"Are you coming up with me?" I ask.

"I have something to finish down here. Then we can work outside."

I shrug. "Fair enough."

The stairs creak as I climb them, and the landing squeaks as I step onto it. There are two doors on my right, one at the end, and two on my left. As instructed, I enter the second one on my right.

The bathroom is small. Light-blue paint, the color of a baby bird egg, is on the walls. The shower is the color of mustard. *I wonder how old that thing is.* And the toilet, as promised, is running.

It takes all of a minute to make it stop. As I'm placing the lid back on, I hear Gabrielle shriek and a loud *pop* from downstairs. The power goes off at the same time.

Shit.

"Gabrielle?"

"Do not tell Cricket about this."

I chuckle, shaking my head as I go back downstairs. "Don't tell Cricket about what?"

"In here," she says from the living room.

She's standing next to an outlet dangling from the wall. She gives me a sheepish grin.

"That's electrical," I say.

"I know it's electrical." She rolls her eyes. "I can change an outlet."

"Well, by the sound of it, you just shocked the shit out of yourself."

She fake cries, making me laugh.

"It hurt," she says, shaking her arms. "It went all through my body and, like, sizzled me or something."

"This is why Cricket told you no electrical."

"Cricket needs to mind her own business."

"Where's your breaker box?"

She shrugs. "I have no clue."

"Does this house have a basement?"

"Yes. The stairwell is in the hallway off the kitchen."

"Do you have a flashlight?"

"Yup." She holds up her phone. A light shines from the top. "See? I'm prepared."

I sigh. "Okay. Show me the stairwell, please."

She leads me through the kitchen to a short hallway. At the end, there's a laundry room. She points to a closed door on the left.

"That's it," she says, thrusting her phone my way.

"What are you doing?"

"Giving you the flashlight."

"Oh no, Miss Fix-It. You're coming too."

She gasps. "I'm not."

"Yes, you are."

Her jaw clenches. "Jay, there was a snake outside a couple of days ago. Basements are snake havens. And spiders. And bugs. And . . . just do it for me, please?"

It would be so easy to do it for her. But this isn't like the railings or the stairs. If those break, she could wait days, even weeks, for someone to help her if she couldn't manage. But a thrown breaker? She needs to know where her breaker box is located.

"Come on," I say, coaxing her to me.

"No."

"Gabrielle."

"Jay," she whines.

"Where's that *can-do spirit* now? Huh? Where's that *'We don't need your help*?"

"It's with the electricity. It's gone. Now please go flip the breaker and bring back my spirit."

I open the door and let my eyes adjust to the darkness. The stairs look pretty sturdy—probably twenty of them or so.

"You need to know where your breaker box is, Gabrielle. Come on."

She glares at me and steps behind me. "You're going first." Her wrist rests on my shoulder with the phone dangling from her fingers. "Here."

I take it. "You know, when I offered to help you, I didn't realize it would be this involved."

"That's your fault. I fell off a deck, and you had to rescue me. I have a hard time believing you didn't realize this would be so involved."

We step into the darkness. Gabrielle keeps a hand on my back at all times. She's giving me the lightest touch, but it feels like it's burning into my skin. The heat bolts through me and coalesces in my cock.

Good thing it's dark.

I wish it didn't feel so good to be with her. I wish she had something annoying about her that made it easy to sit at home with a beer on my day off like I usually do. But that's not the case. And it's problematic.

"Jay . . ." She stays up against me from behind. "Do you see the box?"

I swing the flashlight around the basement. It's bigger than I anticipated. "No. Not yet."

Something scurries in the dark. Gabrielle yelps and dives under my arm.

With her breasts pressed against me, her arm slung around my back, and her head buried into my side, it's like fireworks going off in every corner of my body.

"Relax," I say, guiding her through the darkness. "I got you."

"I like when you say that to me," she says softly.

"When I say what?"

"I got you."

My heart starts to pound.

"I know it's a figure of speech," she says. "And I know you're not saying it in any kind of way. You're not leading me on. But it's nice to have someone like this, you know?"

Yeah. I know.

I didn't know. I hadn't known that I'd missed this at all.

Careful, Jay.

"There it is," I say, shining the light onto a silver box on the wall. I sigh in relief. "Let's get this thing open."

She releases me, and I miss her touch.

"Look," I say, prying the door open and flipping the main breaker. The power flickers on. "Did you see how I got that open?"

"Yeah."

I peer down at her. She didn't see shit.

I grin at the way she investigates her basement, studying each corner like a clown might jump out from behind a wall at any moment. Slowly, she gets farther away from me and starts to mosey around.

"It's nice and dry down here," I say. "But you would've known that, had you had an inspection."

She laughs. "Don't start on me about that."

Gabrielle stands away from a half wall separating two spaces but bends over to see on the other side. Her ass is up in the air, the ends of her shorts riding up to the sweet spot where her ass meets her thighs.

I could slide up behind her, pull those shorts to the side, and sink my cock deep inside her. She would push backward, grinding against me, then look over her shoulder at me and beg for it harder.

Stop it, Jay.

"I don't see any snakes, so that's good," she says. "Hey, did you ever catch that one that tried to eat me?"

"It didn't try to eat you." *But I might.*

She faces me. "Did you catch it?"

"Yes, I caught it. You're safe."

"Good." She looks around. "Are you ready to go back upstairs?"

"No more electrical for you."

She huffs as I hand her the phone back. "You are no fun."

Oh, but I could be.

Her eyes darken. "What did you just think?"

"About what?"

"What just went through your head?"

"Why?" I ask.

"Because you had this look in your eye, and I want to know what caused it."

I consider lying to her. It would be the mature thing to do. But something tells me she'll call me out for it and this conversation will take ten times as long—and I'll wind up telling her anyway.

"You want to know what I was thinking?" My head screams at me to stop. To not put this into the world. To not go this far. "I was thinking how you'd sound bent over that wall while I nailed you from behind."

Her breaths come out in quick gasps.

"Would you scream for me, even though you said you don't?" I ask, holding her gaze. "Would you moan? What little sounds would come out of your mouth when you're coming all over my cock?"

I watch as her chest rises and falls.

"That is what I was thinking," I say before turning to the steps.

"Wait."

I keep moving. I can't stop. I shouldn't have said that—I shouldn't have taken it there.

Gabrielle squeezes between me and the stairs. She hops on the bottom one and faces me so there's little more than our clothes between us. Her eyes are wild, and she's panting as if she's out of breath.

My blood burns with the need to have her on me and over me. An unbridled demand screams at me not to let this moment pass.

This is what I've needed to break the darkness I've lived in for so long. Her laugh. Her smile. Her playful demeanor.

But if I do that, how does it end? How do I guarantee it doesn't end with one or both of us getting destroyed?

She lays a finger against my lips.

"I would scream for you," she whispers. "I would moan your name. I would tell you how good you feel inside me, and I'd beg you to give me more."

My God.

She pulls her finger away and searches my eyes. Finally, she smiles. Sadly, maybe.

"I don't know what you're doing, Jay, but you don't have to be scared of me."

Before I can reply, she walks up the stairs and leaves me behind. I'm grateful for it. Because I don't know what in the hell just happened.

"I would tell you how good you feel inside me, and I'd beg you to give me more."

No, I do know what happened. I played with fire, and now I'm about to be burned.

CHAPTER THIRTEEN

Jay

How ya doing, Jay?" Mr. Thomas asks from the other side of the counter.

The door chimes as it swings closed. The Thomas Hardware Store sign vibrates against the glass, creating its own alert.

The hardware store can't have changed much since it was built in the early 1900s. A layer of dust sits on just about everything, which would lead one to believe they aren't busy. *They are.* Aside from Betty Lou's, this is the busiest place in Alden.

"I'm good, Mr. Thomas. How are you?" I ask.

"Fine, fine. This rain could stop, though." He whistles through his teeth. "Three days of it in a row is about enough for me and my arthritis."

"Every sports injury I've ever had has been aching this week."

He lifts a brow. "You played sports? Where at?"

"Back home in Indiana. A little town in the middle of a cornfield."

He looks me up and down. "You look like a baseball player."

"Thanks." *I think.*

I chuckle, glancing around the store. I'm the only customer at the moment.

"How's work goin' these days?" he asks, busying himself with a stack of papers. "I know you've been in here a lot, so I reckon that means it's good."

"Yeah, it's good. I've got one on hold until Monday and another . . . rained out."

Mr. Thomas glances out the window at the overcast day. "Okay. Sure. I hear ya."

I frown. *It's not rained out. I'm just a fool, and I'm sure he knows that now.*

Whatever. I have bigger fish to fry.

Gabrielle has been out of sight since I left Monday after the whole breaker box incident. I caught a glimpse of her a couple of times, getting in and out of her car, but unlike every other day she's lived on the street, she's not been outside. *And I hate it.*

The rain hasn't helped the situation at all. It started Monday evening, and there has been at least a mist since. I love a few days off work, but this time, I'm going stir-crazy.

"Do you have my bill handy?" I ask, pulling out my wallet.

"I bet we do. Gimme a minute to sort through this stack."

"You know, if you'd get online, this would be a lot easier."

He snorts. "Not happening. We've made it fifty years without going online. I reckon we can go a few more." He licks his finger and then pulls out a sheet. "Here you go. This one is yours."

I take a look at it. If it were anywhere else, I'd go line by line. But if there's one thing I'm sure of, Mr. Thomas is exactly right—to the penny.

"Looks good to me," I say, signing the bottom. Then I hand him my credit card. "Here you go."

"Thank you, Jay."

He shoves my card into the machine, and I sit on one of the stools at the counter. If there's another thing I'm sure of, it's that Mr. Thomas will take forever to actually take my money. It's the only bad thing about finding him at the desk and not his helper, Frank.

"Where's Frank?" I ask.

"Ah, his wife's gout is back. I told him to take the day off. I can handle it in here."

I nod, watching him punch buttons, and then grow frustrated. *You'll get it. Keep trying.*

My lips twitch as I remember the last time I said that—to Carter not more than twelve hours ago, when he came over to use my pumper.

"I can't dribble, Jay. I'm not a good dribbler. Maybe I need more air," he says, defeated.

"You'll get it. Keep trying."

It took everything I had not to ask him about his mother. I led him in that direction, hoping he'd offer up a nugget of information about what she was doing, but he didn't. Instead, he told me all about his day at school, why Hayes is his new best friend, and how he really wants a dog but his mom said absolutely not.

I get up, too antsy to sit still. Mr. Thomas starts all over, so I wander around the store.

I should have talked myself out of this headspace by now. Three days without seeing Gabrielle should be long enough to remember that I'm better off alone. It should be enough time to convince myself that it was lust talking and not actual attraction.

She's a single mom. How could I possibly be attracted to that again?

The chimes ring out, followed by the smacking of the sign. I look over my shoulder at the door and see Scottie. She finds me immediately and waves. After a quick chat with Mr. Thomas, she makes her way back to me.

"Looking for a new hose?" she asks.

"What?"

She points at the shelf behind me. "Hoses. Are you looking for a new hose?"

"Oh. No. I'm just killing time while he figures out how to take my payment. I keep a tab open here and pay him every Thursday."

"I see. Where's Frank?" she asks.

"Brenda has gout."

"Ah." She nods. "Got it." She shuffles around, pretending to be interested in birdseed. "So what have you been up to lately? Anything fun happening on your end of the street?"

"No. What's happening on yours?"

She rolls her eyes. "It doesn't matter what's happening on mine. Your side is the interesting one."

"How do you figure?"

"That's what a little birdie told me."

I smile. "Is that why you're looking for birdseed?"

"What?"

I point at the shelf behind her. "Birdseed. Are you making friends with birds?"

She bursts out laughing, her cheeks turning pink. "Good one."

"I try." *But I really don't.* I avoid interaction with Scottie and Della—with all the women I routinely encounter. Keeping them at arm's length prevents them from poking around, from showing up on my doorstep with a casserole like Cricket did the day I moved in.

It saves me from winding up at their house, fixing their electricity, and fucking myself up.

"So the girls and I had dinner at Della's last weekend, and I heard you and my new friend Gabby got acquainted." Her eyes sparkle with mischief. "What do you think about your new neighbor?"

Internally, I groan.

This is the most I've ever talked to Scottie in the four years I've lived on Bittersweet Court. *Why am I talking to her now?*

"I'm gonna head back up and get my receipt," I say warily.

"Oh, come on, Jay. Gabby is beautiful. She's single. You should totally make a move on that before someone else does." She shrugs with a nonchalance that goes right through me. "She's the new girl. As soon as word gets out that there's an unattached hottie in town, she'll have a line of men at her door."

I'll fight them all.

My teeth grind together as I stop myself from saying anything. This is none of my business.

So why does it feel a whole lot like my business? Why do I want to do wild things when I think about her with someone else?

It's a question without an answer. A problem with no solution—none that are satisfying, anyway.

I've thought about fucking her. I've thought about just giving in and hoping I can make a one-night stand out of it. Maybe it would remove the intensity and let me think clearly.

But I haven't because I know none of that is possible.

There would be no going back with Gabrielle Solomon. If I touched her, that would be it for me. I don't know how I know that, but I do. It's a fact. And with that comes a lot of heavy shit—opening a huge vulnerability that I'm determined to keep closed.

Alaska, here I come, I guess.

"That's okay with you?" Scottie asks. "You won't mind seeing her with someone else?"

I step back from her. "Why are you doing this? I haven't said more than twenty words since we met. Why are you being so chatty now?"

"Because she's my friend. And friends help each other out when they have an opportunity."

"And you think this is helping her out?"

She smiles. "You're a good guy, Jay Stetson. I've only met Gabby once, but she really impressed me. What's wrong with hoping two good people get together?"

I lift a brow and head for the front of the store. "Leave Cupid's work to Cupid, Scottie."

"You're no fun, Jay."

That's been said before.

Mr. Thomas hands me my card and receipt. I thank him and get out of the store and into my truck before I'm cornered by someone else.

The encounter with Scottie has left me sweating. Thinking about seeing another man walk out of Gabrielle's house in the morning, like I see at Della's, raises my blood pressure.

No one deserves Gabby. I've thought about that—endlessly. It's kept me up at night, preoccupied my thoughts at breakfast, and followed me around the afternoons. It's not even that I'm just attracted to her. It's more than that. That *more than that* is what has kept me inside my own house. In my lane. Out of trouble.

There's nobody good enough for her. Who is trustworthy enough to handle her sweet, trusting personality and feisty, hardheaded nature?

Who can be trusted to get Dylan through his rough years and to keep Carter from having a deflated basketball?

Not me. And not anyone I know.

Probably not anyone in the world.

But that won't stop them from trying. And it probably won't stop her from falling for one of them either.

I turn on the truck and pull onto the street. I consider stopping at Betty Lou's for a piece of pie but think better of it. My mood is trash, and I don't want to be a dick to anyone.

My phone rings, and I press a button on the steering wheel to answer it. "Hello?"

"What are you doing?" Lark asks.

"Driving home from the hardware store. What about you?"

"Driving from one farm to another. I hate it when it's all wet like this. There's mud up to my neck whenever I get out of my truck."

"Change careers."

"But I'm so good at what I do."

"That's what you keep telling me."

He laughs. "I'm calling because I promised one of my customers that I'd visit his son's new bar in Logan this weekend."

I groan because I know where this is going, and I don't feel like going to a bar right now.

"Listen, it's a new place—Murray's on State. He talked it up for half an hour. Then he bought a bunch of shit from me and kept telling me to go. So I said I would. And you're going with me."

"Yeah, about that. I don't think I can."

"You are."

I blink. "What did you say?"

"I said you're going with me. There's no reason for you to sit all by yourself at home this weekend, thinking about Towel Girl and why you can't have her."

Fucker. "That's not what I'll be doing."

"No, you won't because you'll be with me. I promised him I'd go, Jay. And you're my only friend who isn't married and not a total downer."

"Gee, thanks."

"Besides, what else do you have to do?"

I flip on my turn signal and go down Bittersweet Court. "Oh, I can think of a million things I have to do."

"Move them down the list."

"I—"

"Don't care, Jay. I don't give a shit what you're going to say. You're coming with me to Murray's tomorrow. I'll text you with a time later."

Sighing, I slow my speed as I near Gabrielle's.

My heart picks up as I see her car in the driveway. The curtains are open, and Carter is on the porch, dribbling his basketball. He waves and gives me a big, lopsided smile.

I pull into my garage and turn off the engine, switching my phone to speaker. Instead of getting out, I sit in silence.

There's not even a small part of me that feels like going out tomorrow night with Lark. But if I don't, I'll just sit here and ruminate.

Maybe if I go, it'll break Gabrielle's spell on me.

"Fine," I say, climbing out of my truck. "I'll go."

"Attaboy. I'll text you tomorrow. But I'm pulling into this farm, so I gotta go."

"See you tomorrow."

"Bye."

I lock the truck and turn around and— "*Shit!* Carter, my man, warn a guy before you sneak up on him like that."

He giggles. "Whatcha doing, Jay?"

"Just got home."

"Where from?"

"The hardware store."

"Why?"

I groan. "Because I had a bill to pay. Want to know anything else before I go inside?"

He tilts his head to the side. "Still cranky, I see."

"I'm not cranky, Carter. I have adult problems, and sometimes those require being serious." *And not answering a million questions from the kid next door.*

"Do what Mom does when she has adult problems."

Keep talking, kid. "What does your mom do?"

"Well, sometimes she drinks wine. Do you like wine?"

"It's okay. What else does she do?"

"Sometimes she paints the house. One time, she painted the kitchen three different colors in a week!"

I smile. "That's a good strategy."

"And sometimes she cries." His smile wobbles. "She says it's not because she's sad. It's because she's working through her problems and crying helps." He shrugs. "I don't understand, but I guess it makes sense. What do I know? I'm a kid."

A fissure cracks the center of my heart.

I squat so we're eye to eye. "Has she been crying lately?"

"Um . . ." His face scrunches up in thought. "Yeah. Last night, I think. But Dylan was a jerk face to her, and then she lost a middle name or something. I don't know. Apparently, that's bad. And then she said she just wanted a hug. So I gave her the biggest one I could and planted a sticky kiss on her cheek. I'd been eating sticky candy. She hates that. But better a sticky kiss than none. That's what I told her."

He giggles, and the split in my chest deepens.

"It's nice to have someone like this, you know?"

Gabrielle's words from the basement swing through my mind.

She deserves to have someone hold her and to have her back. I know she wants it. And a line of men will wait to give it to her.

Will it be any easier, watching someone else give her their attention? Will it be easier to swallow than not giving her mine?

Damn you, Melody, for doing this to me. And damn you, Scottie, for reminding me.

"You better get home, kiddo," I say, standing up again.

"Okay."

"Do me a favor, all right?"

He nods, his little curls bouncing.

"If your mom looks sad, make sure you give her a big hug. Will you do that?" I ask.

"Okay."

He smiles wide before launching himself at me. His arms wrap around my legs, and he squeezes them with all his might, almost knocking me over.

"What's this?" I ask, chuckling.

He looks up at me. "You seem sad too. So I'm hugging you. Do you feel better?"

"Yes." I pry him off me. He clings to me like a monkey. "But you better get home now."

He sits down, breaking contact. Then he scoots back and stands up.

"Have a good night, Jay," he says.

"You too, Carter."

He picks up his ball in the driveway and dribbles it to the sidewalk.

I shut out him, the ball, and as many thoughts about his mother as I can manage and go into the house.

"But Dylan was a jerk face to her, and then she lost a middle name or something. I don't know. Apparently, that's bad. And then she said she just wanted a hug."

I need to remind myself—continuously—that Gabrielle is not alone. She has her children. Friends. And eventually she'll have some guy wrapping his arms around her, giving her hugs, and helping her not do life alone.

And I'll be . . . here.

As much as that pisses me off, it's the way it should be.

The way it has to be.

CHAPTER FOURTEEN

Gabrielle

"Can you not put everything you see into the cart, please?" I ask my two children.

"But, Mom," Carter says, making my name into a sentence. *"I need these."*

I snatch the box out of his hand. "You do not need liquefied sugar with red food coloring and a sour sprinkle." I put it back on the shelf. "There are so many reasons why that's not happening."

The grocery store in Logan is comfortably busy. There are enough people inside to keep the doors open, but there aren't so many people that I want to start ramming carts with my own. Most people shop at the big-box store across town. I prefer the mom-and-pop establishment that has homemade soaps and trail mix.

"How was school?" I ask Dylan. He hasn't really spoken to me since I picked him up an hour ago. Most of his communication has been via grunts and head nods. It's so fun for me. "Did you have a good day?"

He grunts.

"How about this," I say, picking up a box of instant oatmeal. "One grunt for yes and two for no."

He glares at me.

"Or use English," I say. "It's up to you."

"Sometimes I really don't like you," he says.

"Yeah, well, at least you said it in English."

He rolls his eyes and refuses to look at me.

Carter grabs my arm and rests his head against my bicep. "I had a good day, Mom. I made a free throw during gym class. Everybody clapped."

"That's great, Carter."

"And I made the prettiest flower during art. I know Mrs. Templesman thought so. I could see it on her face." He tugs on me until I look down at him. "You know that face you make when you tell someone their baby is cute, but you really don't mean it?"

I struggle not to laugh.

"The teacher made that face when she looked at everyone's flower but mine." He beams. "I'll bring it home to you once she takes it off the wall in the hallway."

"I can't wait."

"Can I get some beef jerky?" Dylan asks, holding up a box.

"Sure."

He drops it into the cart unceremoniously.

The week has been a bust. The rain kept me from doing any of my outside projects, and my frustration with Jay Stetson kept me from doing many on the inside. Every time I grabbed a hammer, I had to hold myself back from throwing it across the yard and into his window while screaming, *"Get your shit together, asshole."* By Wednesday, I was more frustrated than angry. And yesterday I was more perplexed than frustrated. It's a journey, I've learned, when dealing with my neighbor.

He's handsome. He's fun, when he lets his guard down. He's surprisingly good with the boys.

He has a voice that makes me wobble and a touch that melts me.

And that's why I won't deal with him again.

I stop the cart and pull a bag of popcorn off a shelf. "This might be fun for Cricket's tonight. It's the parmesan kind."

"Can I please stay home alone?" Dylan asks.

"No."

"Mom." His nostrils flare. "I'm fourteen. I'm not a little kid."

"I know, Dylan. And I know I have to let loose of you a little bit. But we just got to town and—"

"And you refuse to let me stay home with Cricket living down the street. You realize you're making me go to a babysitter with my seven-year-old brother, right?"

I sigh. "Kyle will be there."

"He lives there, Mother."

I ignore the stare of an older woman as she passes and stay focused on my child.

"Can we not do this here?" I ask.

"Sure. Let's not ever do it. That's what you want, anyway."

I turn my back to Carter and glare at my oldest son. As I'm about to speak, Scottie's words come back to me.

"I remember thinking that if she could smile again, so could I. We didn't realize it then, but she helped us heal by healing herself."

"The reason you can't stay home tonight is because I'll worry about you," I say calmly. "I don't feel comfortable yet, being out of town while you're alone after dark. But," I say before he can cut me off, "I will start giving you a bit more freedom if you keep going to school and being good with Carter and being nice to me. It's about respect, Dylan. Trust is earned. Show me some respect and I can trust you with a little more."

He sobers a little. "Or you could just stay home."

Is that what this is about? Is he pushing me away because he wants me home? Or is he just upset to see me make plans for the first time since Christopher's passing?

"Look, I need to do this, Dylan. This is hard for me too. But it's time we stop being scared and sad and move on with our lives. We don't have to do it all at once, but we need to take steps in that direction."

"Do you think that's what Dad would've wanted?"

My sweet boy. I grab his hand. "I know it's what Dad would've wanted."

He pulls his hand back and looks away. I sniffle as he joins Carter at the front of the cart.

"Is that you, Gabrielle?" An older man in a golfer's hat stops beside me. "By golly, it is you. How are you, sweetheart?"

It's the way he says *sweetheart* that clues me in. I laugh. "Billy Madrid, how are you?"

"Still kicking," he says, pulling me into a quick hug. "I heard you were back in town. The Alden Social Club was talking about it last night."

"About what, exactly?"

I hold my breath while he explains, hoping there's no mention of a towel.

"Just that Juanita Miller saw you dropping your kids off at school the other day," he says. "We were going to send you a card and invite you to a meeting. But since I'm here, I'll just invite you personally."

"The old Alden Social Club. What are you all up to nowadays?"

"We're still doing charity work, of course." He shakes his head. "Your mother was the best fundraiser I ever knew. She could convince anyone to donate to anything."

My heart swells at the mention of her.

"Hey, Mom," Carter says with Dylan on his heels.

I wait for them to reach us, giving them a look to remember their manners.

"Kids, I'd like you to meet Billy Madrid," I say. "He was the high school principal when I was in school, and he was in a club with your grandma."

"Your grandma was an amazing lady," Billy says, shaking both their hands. "And this mama of yours is pretty special."

"We love her," Carter says, smiling up at me.

"I bet you do," Billy says. "I tell you what, Gabby, finish your shopping. The club meets every Friday at Betty Lou's for fish and Tuesdays for our weekly meeting at the community building at the park. We'd love for you to come by."

"I'll try."

He grins. "It was nice meeting you, boys."

"You too," Dylan says, watching him walk away.

Carter wastes no time in bringing me back to the activity at hand. "So hear us out. We get one cereal that's healthy and one cereal full of sugar. Then we go one bowl healthy stuff, one bowl good stuff."

"Fine," I say, giving in entirely too easily. It doesn't bode well for the rest of the shopping excursion. "Hey, guys. I forgot to get orange juice. Will you run back and get a jug of it, please?"

"Pulp or no pulp?" Dylan asks.

"Some pulp but not to where it's chunky."

They take off to the back of the store with Dylan lecturing Carter on not interrupting people, something I find ironic.

I pause next to the discounted spice bin to check my email. But as I bring it up, a text comes through.

Della: Are you ready for tonight?

Me: I can't wait.

Della: I'll pick you up around eight?

Me: I'm usually in bed at eight. Ha! If I fall asleep, prop me up and put a drink in my hand.

Della: 😮

"Whoa," I say as the cart rattles. An armful of items is deposited with our other items. "That was more than orange juice."

"But it was healthy," Carter says. "String cheese. Yogurt with strawberries."

"Bagels," Dylan says, wincing. "But the cream cheese was dairy. *Ish.*"

I sigh and push on. "You guys have absolutely no idea how much food costs these days. If you keep eating like this, I'm going to have to get an actual job." I laugh at myself. "Come on, guys. That was funny."

"Total Mom joke," Carter says, making Dylan laugh.

"You laugh at a seven-year-old but not me? Cool."

Carter sprints ahead of us and comes back with a box of doughnuts.

"No," I say, shaking my head. "We have bagels and cream cheese, thanks to Dylan. We don't need this much food. It'll go to waste." *I think. With the way they've been eating, maybe not.*

"These aren't for us," Carter says.

Dylan looks at me, his brows pulled together.

"Then who are they for?" I ask.

"Jay."

I slow my walk. *Did he say Jay? Surely not.* "Excuse me?"

"These are for Jay," he says again.

It takes me a moment to get my bearings.

"Why would we get doughnuts for Jay?" I ask, confused.

"Are we talking about our neighbor?" Dylan asks.

I shrug. "I think so."

"Yes, silly. Our neighbor, Jay. How many other Jays do you know?" Carter asks.

I scratch my forehead. "So why are we getting Jay doughnuts?"

"Because," Carter says, as if we're too slow and need to catch up, "he's been sad. So we need to get him a treat. Because that's being nice, and we should be nice to our neighbors. That's what you always say. Treat your neighbors like you want to be treated. If I was sad, I'd want doughnuts."

That was before our neighbor was an infuriating, confusing, gorgeous man that I'd like to forget exists at this point.

Dylan looks at me. "Ball is in your court."

I start to speak but stop. I have so many questions that I don't know where to start.

"We haven't seen Jay since last weekend," Dylan says. "How do you know he's sad?"

Well, I saw him Monday in the basement, but that's neither here nor there.

"Maybe you haven't seen him, but I have," Carter says, bouncing from one foot to the other. "I saw him yesterday."

"Where?" I ask.

"I went to his house. My ball needed air again, and I was gonna ask to use his pumper. But he was all cranky again, so I didn't ask."

I force a swallow. "Didn't I ask you to leave him alone?"

"Yes, you did. But he's my friend. And he's having adult problems and is sad. So I have to see him. That's what you do. You taught me that."

I never thought I would regret teaching my child manners. But here we are.

"Why do you think he's having adult problems?" I ask as nonchalantly as I can manage while my brain is working overtime.

"He told me." He shrugs, placing the doughnuts carefully into the cart. "I gave him your tricks and told him to try them."

My eyes bulge. "What did you tell him?"

"That you drink wine. Or you paint a room a bunch of times. Or . . . you cry."

I briefly close my eyes and try not to die on the spot.

Dylan makes a face. "Carter, why don't we go see if there are any watermelons?"

"Okay!"

I give Dylan a smile as they scamper off to the produce aisle.

"Let this go," I whisper. "It doesn't matter what Carter told Jay. Jay's nothing to you. And he wants it that way. So who cares?"

I glance down at my phone and see another text of a devil emoji from Della.

"Go have fun tonight and keep going forward," I say softly. "Fuck Jay."

Just not literally.

CHAPTER FIFTEEN

Gabrielle

Murray's on State, a bar that just opened if Della is to be believed, is hopping. It's one of the more upscale bars I've visited—not that I've visited many. But I do appreciate the forest-green walls, bronze accents, and that the music's not blaring so loud that you can't hear yourself think.

Heads turn as we make our way to the bartender. I skim the crowd, wondering whether I'd recognize my high school classmates if I saw them. *Or would they recognize me?*

I pick at the scalloped, plunging neckline of the black, formfitting shirt I found in a box in the back of my closet. It's the sexiest thing I own. With distressed jeans I bought in an emotional shopping binge a few months ago, and a pair of heels so the jeans don't drag the ground, it's very nineties. Della said I look hot. I'm choosing to lean into that opinion and not focus on the way my stomach is rounder than it was twenty years ago.

"Hey, ladies," the bartender says. "What can I get for you tonight?"

"Amaretto sour," Della says. "Gabby? What about you?"

Is this kid even old enough to serve us alcohol? I shake my head. "Lemon drop martini, please."

"Coming right up," he says with a wink.

"So what do you think?" Della asks. Her bright-red lips split her cheeks. "I've never been here before, but I heard it was the place to be these days."

"The only place I know that is *the place to be these days* is drop-off at the school by seven fifty. If not, they're tardy."

Della laughs. "We're expanding your horizons. By the end of the night, you'll forget all about drop-off."

I hope so.

The bartender hands us our drinks, assuring us the first one is on the house, and takes a tip from Della. Then we work our way through the growing crowd to a table along a wall.

"It's been so long since I went out that I almost forget how," I admit, taking a sip of my drink. *Whoa, that's strong.*

"You are in good, capable hands tonight." She leans forward, her cleavage on full display. "If you see anyone you're interested in, let me know."

I laugh. "What are you talking about? It's not that easy."

"What do you mean, *it's not that easy*? Girl, men are the most predictable animals on the planet. I can read them like a book."

"Is there a course to take for that?"

"It's called having a stripper as your mother." She lifts a brow, grinning. "And she was a damn good one, let me tell you. Some of my friends' parents were doctors and lawyers, and my mom raked in double the amount of cash they did."

Is she serious?

"It was a business to her," Della says. "She used her body as a tool, just like a CEO uses his brain."

"Is that something you just grew up knowing?"

"Until I was eighteen, I thought she was a traveling nurse." She laughs. "I found out when a guy I was dating in college happened to go to her club and saw her. Awkward conversation. Dropped the boyfriend. But there was this . . . missing piece between Mom and me that fell into place."

I take a drink and then set my glass on the table. "Is that why you're so confident? Is that why you have such a . . . free, I guess, way about you? Because you really don't seem to care what anyone thinks."

"I don't care." She shrugs. "My confidence comes from being raised with a very body-positive mindset. It was all presented at an age-appropriate level, of course. Just because she was a stripper doesn't mean she was a bad mom or negligent."

"Of course not."

"In a way, she was a better parent. She taught me to be proud of myself. To take care of myself. I remember her telling me from a young age that I was in charge of my body. I grew up not being ashamed of it." She takes a drink. "What about you? What was your life like growing up?"

The alcohol heats my skin, and I welcome the warm, relaxing sensation that eats away my stress—if only for a while.

"I was raised here in Alden, remember?" I swirl the liquid around my glass. "There was an expectation of modesty. We didn't talk about sex or things like that. My friends and I would secretly trade romance novels to try to learn what we could."

"Ah, the perfect romance hero. That's where you went wrong."

"No, they exist. But finding one isn't as easy as breaking down in the middle of a cornfield. They don't pop up out of nowhere."

She grins. "I'm sure they do exist. I'm just too jaded to want the perfect hero."

"Why is that?"

She studies me for a long time, pausing to take a long drink. The hairs on the back of my neck prickle.

"I don't tell people what I do for a living. Not because I'm ashamed," she says. "Just because I don't want to hear the judgment."

"Okay . . ."

"I clean houses topless."

My eyes widen. "What?"

She shrugs. "I have a roster of men—most of them business owners or men who travel to town regularly for golf or business meetings. And I clean their homes or wherever they happen to be . . . topless."

"In Alden?"

"*No.* I go to Cleveland or Cincinnati. I have a security guy who goes with me to make sure nothing goes wrong, and we run background checks. We have nondisclosure agreements. I don't really even take new clients at this point, because my regulars treat me so well."

I glance at her chest. *I bet they do.*

She sighs. "Look, Gabby, we only live once. Why not live life the way you want? Why be scared or tiptoe around it? Grab whatever it is that makes you happy and run while you can." She snickers. "People can judge me while sitting at home in their miserable, boring lives while I take my money and head to Italy for a month in the summer and Germany for December."

"Grab whatever it is that makes you happy and run while you can." Her words ring through my brain on repeat.

"Excuse me for just a moment," she says. "I'm going to go say hello to a friend."

"Sure. Go. I'm fine."

She slides out of the booth and sashays her way across the bar. As soon as she's gone, I let out a long, hasty breath.

"Grab whatever it is that makes you happy and run while you can."

It's been a long time since I had the ability to think that way. And as much as I love the sentiment—and the freedom that comes with it—it's not that easy. I'm a single mother. Yes, I can try and plan and want to integrate things into my life that make me happy. But at the end of the day, those plans are contingent upon how they impact the most important thing in my life: my children.

They are my priority.

I'll have to find a happy medium, a balance between what invigorates me but doesn't detract from the boys. I hope to God I can find it.

I can imagine Christopher saying those words to me too. *"You deserve a lover, someone to appreciate all the wild goodness you have to offer."*

I did have a wild goodness about me then. I lived my life instead of surviving it. I went after what I wanted.

How do I get back to that, get back to her?

"Gabby, I'd like to introduce you to a friend of mine. This is Heath and his friend Bryant," Della says, snapping me out of my reverie. "Guys, this is my new neighbor, Gabby."

Wow.

If someone asked me to select two men from this bar that Della would know, it would be these two. They're young—midtwenties, at best. Fit as hell. Their arms stretch the fabric of their Polo shirts, and their necks are nothing short of tree trunks. And their smiles? To die for.

Della and Heath sit across from me. His bright-blue eyes are the same color as his shirt.

I look up at Bryant. "Do you wanna sit?"

"I hope we're not interrupting anything," he says, sitting next to me.

Charisma pours out of him as he watches me with a cocky grin. He chews gum with a deliberateness that draws attention to his mouth. I can imagine those lips doing many things to a lucky lady.

"So, Gabby," he says, ignoring the others. "Tell me about you."

I take a drink to wet my throat. "What do you want to know?"

"We can cut to the chase, and I can ask if you're single."

His smile is devilish, and I feel it in places that could get me in trouble.

I laugh.

"Why are you laughing, mama?" he asks.

My laugh grows louder. "I get that's a slang term these days, but it's awkward when I could almost be your mother."

"Age is just a number." He smirks. "And you're *fine as hell*."

Oh.

He licks his lips in an overt suggestion—one I have no problem understanding. It's the understanding part that causes my skin to feel too small for my body.

This is what I've been after. A fun, casual night with a guy to get me back in the saddle. And by the looks of Bryant, he'd be a whole lot of fun.

The Gabby from Boston, from before Christopher's death, would've known what to say. Hell, she'd have already said it. I'd be sitting on this guy's lap and working him up. He'd be eating out of the palm of my hand.

But now, I hesitate. A snack is sitting inches from me, and nothing comes out of my mouth. Time is ticking and he's waiting for a response. But the more time passes, the more frantic I get.

I don't know what to say.

Suddenly, the thought of going home with Bryant is overwhelming. It's not what I want. Not at all.

What I want is back on Bittersweet Court, hiding secrets and pushing me away.

I look at Della across the table. *What do you do when the thing that just might make you happy refuses to let you try?*

"Hey, Heath," a voice says, coming our way. An attractive man with dimples approaches our table. "How have you been?"

"Well, if it isn't Lark Johnston." Heath stands and shakes Lark's hand. "It's been a long time, buddy. How have you been?"

"Hanging in there," Lark says.

"Lark, this is my friend Bryant."

Bryant nods at Lark. "Nice to meet ya."

"Same," Lark says, flipping his gaze to mine. There's a twinkle in his eye that tickles my curiosity. "And who are you?"

"Babe, this is my new neighbor, Gabby," Della says. "Gabby, this is Lark."

"Babe"? Interesting.

Lark's grin is cheeky. "It's nice to meet you, Gabby." He and Della exchange a look that I can't quite read.

Lark sits next to Della. He wastes no time pulling her into his side and whispering something in her ear. She gazes up at him and winks, making him laugh.

My stomach tightens, although I'm unsure why. Everything is going well, and my tablemates are chatting away like old friends. *Why do I feel like I'm on the ledge, waiting to fall?*

"So," Bryant says, casually, "are you single?"

"Yes."

"Great."

"But," I say, holding a finger between us, "I'm not here to pick up a guy."

Even though that's exactly why I was here originally.

"That's fine," he says. "You don't have to pick me up. I'll pick *you* up."

"You're cute."

He scoots closer, his body rippling with energy. "I'm a lot more than cute. Give me a chance."

I force a swallow and lean back, trying to get a grip on the chaos inside me. Luckily, I'm saved from responding when Lark speaks loudly.

"There he is," Lark says, looking over his shoulder. "I was afraid you got lost."

"It's Jay Fucking Stetson," Heath says, laughing. "Hell, brother. I haven't seen you in ages."

Say what? The room begins to spin. *Did he just say Jay Stetson?*

My gaze whips to Della's. She grins, shrugging.

I close my eyes.

"Are you all right, mama?" Bryant asks.

This is bad. This is so, so bad.

I open my eyes and am immediately clobbered by a blaze of heat from the side.

"Do you know Bryant Shoals?" Lark asks. "And that is Gabby, a friend of Della's."

Fuck. My. Life.

"Nice to meet you, Jay," Bryant says, still angled my way.

Everyone stares at me, waiting for me to say hello. I slowly bring my eyes to Jay's. Our gazes collide so hard that I flinch.

Jay's jaw flexes. He works it back and forth while gripping his glass so hard his knuckles turn white. Even though he's pissed, he's so damn handsome that none of these men even come close.

But what does it matter how attractive he is? Or how strong the connection is between us? He's made it clear: he may want me, but he'll never give in.

"Good to see you again," I say, my voice even.

"Is it?" Jay asks, the words cold and clipped.

His indignation angers me. He has no right to be mad. My choices are none of his business.

"Yeah," I say, lifting a brow. "It's always nice to run into neighbors when we're out and about. How else would we see each other?"

Bryant scoots closer. "If you were my neighbor, you'd be seeing *a lot* of me."

Jay pins me to my seat with his stare. The intensity makes me shiver.

"Do you want to see a lot of me tonight, mama?" Bryant asks, giving me a cocky grin. "Say the word and we'll get out of here."

I pull my eyes away from Jay and land them on my seatmate. Knowing Jay's watching my every move, I lean toward Bryant.

"You certainly seem like a man who knows what he wants," I say, coyly.

I can almost feel Jay bristle from across the table.

Bryant leans so close he nearly touches me. "I want *you*."

"Tell us, Gabrielle," Jay says, his voice eerily calm. Everyone at the table quiets. "What do you want?"

My heart thunders as I absorb the heat in his eyes.

"Hey, man," Bryant says. "Fuck off."

Lark hops to his feet, positioning himself between Bryant and Jay.

Jay lifts a brow at the man sitting next to me. "Choose your battles carefully, little boy."

"Who the fuck do you think you are?" Bryant asks, getting up. A vein throbs in his temple. "Why don't you go back to wherever you came from and leave my date alone?"

What?

Lark holds one hand on each of their chests. "Let's not do this here."

"Bryant, what are you talking about?" I ask, disbelief at his audacity mixing with frustration. "I met you ten minutes ago."

"That's not the point," he says, squaring his shoulders to Jay.

Jay takes a step back. He looks Bryant up and down, then turns to me. He says something to Lark that I can't hear before disappearing into the throng of bodies that now pack the bar.

A collective sigh rushes around the table moments before chatter breaks out again.

Bryant starts to sit back down, but I shimmy to the end of the booth.

"Excuse me, please." I get to my feet. "I'll be back, Della."

"Gabby . . ." she calls after me, but I'm already two layers deep in the crowd.

My breathing is ragged as I pick my way through the bodies. I don't know why I'm chasing him. It's probably not a good idea, especially if he's as angry as I think he is. But I'm angry, too, damn it. He doesn't get to waltz in here and act like a jealous boyfriend.

I scoot out the door. The chilly wind of the evening hits me in the face. My body is too heated, too worked up, to shiver.

The parking lot is busy. Cars fill the spots and line the street in front of the bar. I scan the area for Jay.

"Where are you?" I mutter.

I'm about to give up when I spot him nearing his truck. Irritation floods me again, growing heavier and thicker as I get closer to him. I nearly jog the last few yards to catch him before he gets in his truck.

My palm smacks the hood, making him jump. He twirls around, one arm poised to throw a punch. But when he sees it's me, he doesn't throw. He only scowls.

"What the hell was that back there?" I ask, throwing my hands on my hips. My breaths billow in the air. "What are you doing?"

"*You* wanna ask *me* what was going on back there?"

"Yeah, I do. I was sitting there with my friend, having a drink and enjoying my night. And you come in and ruin it."

His jaw flexes. "No, I'm pretty sure he'll still take you home."

"I meant with Della. I don't want to go home with that guy sitting beside me, you asshole." My hands fly through the air. "I just want to have one good night where I can have fun. Where I can dress cute and have adult conversations. Where I don't have to figure out what's for dinner and hear about *pings*." I suck in a breath. "I don't want to sit at home another night and wonder why you—"

His mouth crashes against mine. He holds my face in his hands and pivots us so that my back is against his truck. The metal is cool through the thin fabric of my shirt, a stark juxtaposition to the heat radiating off Jay.

My knees go weak.

He controls my mouth like he owns it. Kissing and licking as if I'm the oasis he's been searching for.

His fingertips burn into my face, pinning locks of hair against my cheek. The air is scented with his cologne and peppered with soft moans that escape my throat. Peppermint stings my tongue as his wraps around it in a lazy dance like they've done it before.

I wrap my arms around him, pulling him closer, and give back as good as he gives.

"Jay," I say, struggling for air once he pulls away.

His eyes are wild. His chest heaves as if he just ran a mile. His lips are swollen and red, a reminder of the kiss we just shared.

He searches my eyes as if he's desperate to find an answer to a question I don't know. I just look at him, pulling down all my defenses, giving him access, silently pleading with him to find what he's looking for.

"I gotta go," he says, stepping away.

"Jay, *no*."

He unlocks the door and opens it. "Go back inside, Gabrielle."

"What the hell are you doing?" I ask, moving out of the way. "Jay! Stop it."

He climbs in the truck and starts the engine. Before he closes himself in, sealing himself away from me, he sighs. "I'm sorry."

"Jay . . ."

The truck lurches forward, and he pulls out of the parking lot, leaving a trail of dust and a confused, splintered heart behind.

CHAPTER SIXTEEN

Gabrielle

I hand the driver a cash tip. "Thanks for the ride."

"Anytime. Have a safe night out there, ma'am."

Shivering, I close the door of the rideshare and step onto my driveway. Lights are off in most of the houses down Bittersweet. Most, but not all. The kitchen light is on at Jay's.

"Go back inside, Gabrielle. I'm sorry."

I touch my lips, remembering how his felt against them.

Why? Why is he doing this? I don't believe Jay is a bad guy. *So why is he being a jackass?*

I stare at the sky, hoping the night air will bleed into me and help me calm down. But the longer I absorb the stillness of the dark, the more I recall why I'm here and not out having fun with Della.

Because of Jay.

"Damn you," I say, ignoring my better judgment and marching down the sidewalk toward his house.

There's nothing to say to him. And by going over there, all I'm doing is letting him know he gets to me. That his behavior, *and that kiss*, affected me. I'm not helping my case by pounding on his door.

My knuckles rap hard against the wood anyway.

I'm just going to tell him to stay away from me. Draw some boundaries. Let him know I'm done playing his games.

My blood pressure rises as I knock again. This time, he answers.

The door pulls open with a flourish. He's lost his shirt and his shoes but held tight to the fire I saw firsthand an hour ago. Anger is painted across his face.

I meet him glare for glare.

"Don't you ever—*ever*—do that to me again," I say, halfway shouting. "Don't come at me, in a public place with an audience, no less, and act like you have some kind of say in what I do." I lean closer, fury bubbling in my stomach. "You're the neighbor, Jay. *Just my neighbor.* And if I want to go home with a guy—*oof.*"

His lips cover mine in an instant. The contact is a douse of gasoline on an already raging fire.

He's greedy this time. *Hungry.* He's as desperate for contact as I am.

One hand palms the back of my head, holding me against him. The other is around my back and cupping my ass with a ferocity that almost hurts.

I'm against his bare chest. Heat radiates off his tanned skin. We're a whirlwind of lips, tongues, gasps, and moans. He pulls me closer to him and kicks the door closed.

The slam echoes through the room.

My hands run up his torso, appreciating every ridge and line. Then they roam across his shoulders and to the sides of his face, cupping his cheeks in my palms.

His kisses are urgent—*demanding.* He nips my bottom lip before planting kisses down my throat.

I moan, unable to take the intensity of the buildup in my core. My head spins as he kisses down my throat, then runs his tongue up to my ear. It's too much of everything.

It's not enough at the same time.

Oh, that feels so good.

"I'm still mad at you," I say, barely able to get the words out.

He walks me until my back hits a wall, never breaking his kiss. His mouth takes mine *hard*, his tongue dragging over my bottom lip. My knees buckle. I'm held up by the drywall behind me and Jay Stetson's hot body in front.

"You're driving me nuts," he says, the words peppered in between kisses.

My head digs into the wall as I wind his hair through my fingers. "Who do you think you are—*oh, my fuck*."

His palms slide beneath my shirt, dragging roughly from my hips to my chest. My breasts in his hands—with only a piece of lace separating them—melts me.

I'm a rioting mess of need, want, and desire. *So much fucking desire.*

"Right now, I want to make you forget about that bastard in the bar." He stops kissing me long enough to take the hem of my shirt and lift it over my head. He tosses it unceremoniously across the room. "How do you feel about that?"

"That depends on how you're going to achieve it," I say as his lips find mine again.

I find the waistband of his jeans, dipping my fingers behind it and drawing them to the button in the front. He leans away so I can unfasten them. His eyes are wild, yet cautious as he peers down at me.

"I want to fuck you, Gabrielle."

That's never sounded hotter. My thighs squeeze together, desperate for relief. That one simple sentence is the strongest foreplay of my life.

His button frees and I drag the zipper down slowly, letting my knuckles brush against his hard cock. I hold his gaze and watch his pupils dilate.

"I want you to fuck me too, Jay," I whisper, gripping his sides. "But I need you to stop with the games."

"There are no games."

I chuckle, pushing the jeans down his legs. "I beg to differ." I drop to the floor with them, tossing them away once he steps away from the fabric.

Grabbing the backs of his thighs, I kneel in front of a completely naked Jay.

My God, he's a work of art. He's a mix of smooth skin and rough edges, soft dips, and hard lines. Powerful and capable, yet attentive and maybe even sweet.

His cock is thick and hard as I wrap my hand around it. Precum glistens on the tip. All I can think about is how he'll feel buried inside me—stretching me while I quiver around him.

I stifle a moan at the thought alone.

"There are no games, Gabrielle." His eyes burn with sincerity. "What you think is a game is me trying to protect us both."

"Protect us from what?"

He studies me, searching my face. Then, as if relief washes across him, he grins. "From my stupidity, I guess."

Shivers race through me at his genuineness. This might be the first time I've seen a completely unprotected Jay. And damn it if it's not beautiful.

"You have been a fool," I say, grinning back at him.

I rise up on my knees and stroke him. His eyes widen. His mouth falls agape. I'm so wet that my thighs are sticky, and I can barely move without my clit screaming for attention.

But first, my attention is on him.

I look up at him through my lashes as his eyes darken. His anticipation of my mouth covering the head of his cock feeds how powerful I feel. The always-controlled Jay Stetson is threatening to come apart in my hand.

"You're lucky," I say, swiping the liquid off the tip with my thumb.

"Why is that?"

I smirk. "Because I didn't go home with Bryant tonight." I pop my thumb in my mouth and suck the saltiness off. "Think: I could be at his house, on my knees, ready to put his cock in my mouth."

His Adam's apple bobs. "Now isn't the time for you to get cocky."

I stroke him again, earning a hiss. Knowing how much I turn him on is a heady feeling—one I could get used to.

"I'm not getting cocky," I say, fighting the heat rushing to my pussy. "I'm stating facts."

His eyes blaze. "If you would've gone home with him, I would've—*fuck!*"

He throws his head back and groans, flexing as I pull the head of his cock into my mouth. Watching him struggle to stay in control is the power play I didn't know I wanted. Muscles in his neck and chest strain as I flick my tongue across his tip.

I give his balls a gentle squeeze, stroking him slowly with enough pressure to have him hissing through his teeth.

Watching him is intoxicating. I'm dizzy, almost drunk with adrenaline. It's been too long since I experienced this.

He reaches for me, threading his fingers through my hair and guiding me up and down his length. Saliva drips down his shaft. I take him deep in my throat, then swirl the head around my mouth, using the underside of my tongue to dance in a slow circle around it.

"Stop," he says, the words strangled.

I tap my tongue against the tip and gaze up at him. "You sure?"

He groans. "I said it, didn't I?"

"Now isn't the time for *you* to get cocky."

I rise higher on my knees and take him deep again. I'm soaking wet, sure that the dampness is visible through my pants.

He tugs on my hair, pulling me away.

I release him and rock back on my heels. He stares down at me, the tension between us thick. The air crackles with suspense, but neither of us moves more than the rising and falling of our chests.

"I'm telling you, Gabrielle," he says, nearly panting. "If we do this—if we fuck—things will be different between us."

"Do you mean this is a one-night stand and you'll ignore me after?" I smirk. "Oh, wait. You do that anyway."

"Keep it up."

"And what, Jay? What are you going to do?"

I narrow my eyes, fully aware I'm playing with fire.

He motions for me to stand, never breaking eye contact. I get to my feet and ignore my heart thumping so hard I can almost hear it.

"Turn around," he says, the words a command and not a request.

I pull my hair over one shoulder and face the wall. I feel him step closer to me, and every cell in my body reacts to his proximity. My breath stalls in my chest as his fingers brush against my back.

My bra is unfastened. It falls from my front and onto the floor.

He moves until his front is against my back. My head falls against his chest as his arms wrap around me. My jeans are next as he unfastens them, pressing light kisses to the crook of my neck.

I pant, leaning my head to the side to afford him all the space he wants.

"You're so damn beautiful, Gabrielle," he breathes against my neck. "Fuck, I couldn't stay away."

He says my name as if it's something to be treasured. I gasp a breath, fighting hard not to move, not to turn around and kiss him.

His palm lies on my stomach, and then, one painfully slow inch at a time, it moves down to my groin. His fingertips slide under my panties until they reach the top of my pussy.

I widen my stance, overwhelmed with sensations. The rough pads of his fingers hovering just above my throbbing clit. The soft presses of his lips up and down my shoulder. His hard body providing support since my legs have jellified.

"You're wet," he says before nipping at my earlobe. "I want to bury myself inside you."

"Please."

"Look at you, using manners." He chuckles, sucking the bend of my neck. "I will. Just because you said *please*."

"Now—*ah!*"

He finds my clit and rubs slow circles around the swollen bud. Fireworks shoot from my core, spreading like lava through my veins. I sag against him, only to have him wrap his other arm around my middle, holding me tight to him.

He slides one finger inside me, and then two. The way his fingers bend causes him to graze just the right spot with each movement.

"Let's get one thing clear," he says, his tone suddenly hard. Gruff. Serious.

It sends a chill down my spine, and I wiggle against him. His cock digs into my ass, reminding me of what's to come.

"What?" I ask, the question a beg.

"This isn't a one-night stand."

"What does that mean?" I squirm, helping him remove my jeans and panties. "What do you want, then?"

I barely get the denim kicked to the side when he spins me in his arms. The golden hue blazes as he pins his sights on me. I'm breathless.

I don't know where this is going, or why we're doing this now. We're both amped up. We aren't thinking clearly. But something tells me this isn't the first time he's thought this through.

"If we do this," he says, sober as a judge, "it's not a one-night stand."

"Then what is it?"

He takes a step forward. I take one back.

"I don't know," he says, swallowing. Beads of sweat dot his forehead. "But I know that if I know what it's like to be inside you, it's not something I'm going to be able to forget."

I have a feeling I'm going to feel the same way. "Meaning?"

He moves toward me again. I take another step back.

"That means if we fuck, there are no more assholes in the bar. Not until we figure things out between us."

My back hits the drywall and I'm pinned against it. He stares down at me, waiting for my response.

Doesn't he know he already has me?

I smile at him. "Fuck me, Stetson."

He scoops me up, balancing my thighs on his forearms and digging his fingers in my ass. My back slams against the wall, rattling a shelf so hard a picture falls to the floor. Our kisses are frenzied, feverish—as if there's a timer ticking and we have to get in as much as we can while we can.

He carries me around the sofa and lays me on the carpet in front of the fireplace. The fibers bite into my back, irritating the scrapes from the wall. But I don't care. I need him inside me more than I've ever needed anything.

"I need to get a condom," he says, his nostrils flaring.

"Wait." I pop up on my elbows and try not to be distracted by his body. "I can't have kids. And I haven't had sex in . . ." I try to calculate the months. "Look, math is impossible when you're this turned on."

He smirks.

"But it's been a very long time, and I've had all the tests," I say, trying not to whine.

"I had a physical just before you moved in. I'm good to go."

He doesn't move, giving me a moment to think it through. I respect the hell out of that. But I also need him inside me.

"Then for the love of God . . ." I groan, gritting my teeth as I will myself not to tackle him and ride him until I come.

He stalks my way, dropping to his knees and then hovering over me. He gazes down at me with a rogue look in his eye.

"How do you want this?" he asks.

I lift my legs and lock them around his hips. "Do I get to do this more than once?"

"I sure fucking hope so."

"Then make me come, Jay. I need it. *Now.*"

He chuckles, the sound low and gravelly. It prickles my already sensitive libido. He positions himself at my opening. Then holding my gaze, he enters me in one hard, swift, delicious movement.

I yell, lifting my chin to the ceiling and closing my eyes for fear they'll pop out of my head. I'm filled so completely, so fully, that I only pray I'm breathing.

He pumps in and out of me. "I thought you weren't a screamer?"

"Me too," I say through gritted teeth.

"You feel so good, Gabrielle. Even better than I imagined."

My hips tilt for him. "Right there. Oh, my—*fuck, Jay.*" I wince at the force of the waves rolling through me. "Right there."

"Watching you makes it hard not to lose it."

Tears dot the corners of my eyes. Every muscle tenses. I grip his shoulders as my legs begin to shake.

"Look at me," he says. *"Look at me, Gabrielle."*

I open my eyes. He holds my gaze.

His arms shake and my knees fall to the side. My ankles slip apart and down his sides.

The carpet burns my back. I simply don't care.

He fucks me harder, deeper, watching me with rapt attention.

"You're so damn beautiful, Gabrielle. Fuck, I couldn't stay away."

His cock is phenomenal, *but the way he looks at me? The way he says my name?* That's the true event.

I've never felt more beautiful, more wanted, in my life.

"I'm going to come," I say, bracing for the surge of energy building in my core. "Just a couple more times and I'm . . ."

The words won't come out. They're stuck in my throat.

Sweat drips from his chin and hits my chest.

"Where do you want me to—"

"Ah!" I yell, my body trembling uncontrollably.

"Fucking hell," he says, thrusting faster. "I'm getting too close. I'm going to have to—"

The orgasm hits me like a freight train. I yell again, too enveloped in bliss to be embarrassed.

"Don't stop," I say, my tits bouncing as he drives into me. The force of the orgasm is too much, too hard. I close my eyes and absorb the intensity. "God, Jay. *Don't stop.*"

"Fuck!" He slams into me. The sound of our bodies together fills the room. "Gabrielle . . ."

I force myself to look, to watch him fall apart. And it's a sight worth the effort.

His arms shake. His throat flexes. His jaw clenches so hard I'm afraid it'll break. His hips roll as he empties himself, milking every bit of the orgasm that just destroyed me in the best way.

He's a vision of masculinity—of a beautiful man falling apart . . . over me.

I lean up, taking his face in my hands. He looks down and his arms buckle. I pull him to me, taking his mouth with mine.

He falls onto his shoulder, then brings me against his side.

Finally, I pull away, desperate for air. As soon as we're apart, we look at each other and laugh, collapsing onto the floor.

"That was worth it," I say, catching my breath.

He rolls onto his side and stares at me. "Worth what?"

I know what I'm about to say is going to set him off. But I can't resist.

"This was totally worth not going home with Bryant."

I barely get the words out before he's on top of me, and I'm giggling like crazy.

CHAPTER SEVENTEEN

Jay

The moonlight streams through the windows of my bedroom. Shadows flicker across the wall, the limbs of the giant oak tree outside the window blowing in the breeze. I pull Gabrielle closer to my side and breathe her in.

For the first time in four long, hard years, I feel as though peace—if only a sliver—is attainable. Usually, I lie in bed and overthink—ripping apart every decision, every conversation I've had, that brought me to this place. A place that most nights I loathe.

No one enjoys being bitter—anger is uncomfortable—but both emotions have dominated my life for a long time. I've both hated it and wished it away, and held on to it, because it was better than the alternative of feeling sorry for myself.

"What are you thinking about?" Gabrielle whispers into the quiet.

"Not much. You?"

She hums against my side.

"I thought you were asleep," I say.

"I was, but I'm not used to having someone in bed with me. Every time it registers that there's a body beside mine, I wake up."

Please say no. "Do you want to go home?"

She raises her head high enough to look at me. Her eyes are sleepy, her lids heavy. She's absolutely beautiful.

My chest tightens as if it's putting on armor. I know the feeling well. But this time, I don't want to wall off from the perceived threat. The idea of having anything more than a sheet between us is unfair. It's just not that easy to break old habits.

"Do you want me to go?" she asks.

"Come here."

I pull her down so that her head rests against my chest, and I wrap my arms around her, snuggling her beneath my chin.

"Can I ask you something?" She draws designs with her fingertips on my stomach. "I don't want to pressure you. I'm just curious."

"Okay."

The designs on my abs slow. "I want you to know you're right. What you said earlier—that if we have sex, it'll be hard to forget." The circles stop and her palm lies flat against me. "It's already hard to forget."

I watch the ceiling fan spin in methodical circles.

Those words were a warning—to me, as they were to her. Verbalizing what I knew to be true, that if I slept with her, I was giving in to the feelings I've had for her since I saw her lying in that bush.

That I wanted her.

But I feared it would be more than that. *Knowing* what she felt like would shift the *want* to a *need.* Seeing her with that asshole at the bar set off a jealousy that I didn't expect. Thinking of her with someone else now . . . I can't.

"So . . ." she says, prompting a response.

"You didn't ask me anything."

I feel her smile against me. "All right. Let me rephrase." She pauses. "Where do we go from here?"

Shit. I blow out a breath slowly.

"I'm not pressuring you," she says. "When I left the house tonight, I wasn't sure I was ready for more than a one-night stand. But you don't want this to be that, and I don't think I do either. But I also don't think it's that simple."

"I don't think it is either."

"We live next door to each other. I've not even known you for a month. But here I am, in your bed, after a night that's definitely on my list of best nights ever—"

"Hey," I say, tightening my arms around her.

She laughs. "And I'm wondering what this looks like in the morning."

I take a deep breath. "What do you want it to look like?"

"I don't know."

Her body tightens as the words pass her lips. She rises off me, moving her hair to one shoulder. She twists and faces me, my shirt she slipped on earlier for a kitchen run hanging off her shoulders.

I put my hand on her thigh and give it a gentle squeeze. Her next words are going to determine the course of our future—either together or separately. What I want may not be the right thing, or the best thing. I may also not have a choice.

She frowns. "Just a warning: this is going to go deep fast."

The words are softened with a wink, which somehow dispels my fear.

"So," she says, letting her shoulders fall. "Christopher and I didn't end on bad terms. We were still friends, *good friends*, and had the wherewithal to realize we were better friends than lovers. That was three years ago. It took me a solid six months after our divorce to even consider dating again. But even once I found my footing and started seeing other men, I never, *ever* brought them home with me. The boys have never seen me with a man other than their father."

Oh . . .

"So when Dylan walked in and found you in the kitchen, that was a new experience for him," she says. "Not saying that it excuses his animosity. But maybe it explains it."

I nod because it does, even though I didn't need that explanation.

Dylan might be a *jerk face* to his mother, but his behavior in the kitchen was born out of a desire to protect her. It was based out of love. I respect that.

I nod again, giving her space to sort the thoughts I see swirling in her gorgeous eyes.

"This probably sounds ridiculous to you—"

"No," I say earnestly, "it doesn't. You're a good mom. Of course they're the first thing on your mind. They should be."

"I'm saying all of this, and it sounds ridiculous *to me* because I barely know you, Jay. I would never bring up . . . our future at this point with someone else." She grimaces. "I must sound like a loon."

"You do not sound like a loon. You sound like an adult that wants to have a conversation about our situation, and that's respectable."

She sighs. "So you understand?"

"Yeah, I understand. I share your hesitations. And I think it would make a lot of sense to figure out where we stand before you go home and it's awkward."

She draws her knees up, covering them with my shirt. I wonder if it's an unconscious demonstration of her protecting herself from me. I wish I could tell her not to. But I can't.

Because I don't know how to answer her questions.

"Can I be honest with you?" she asks.

"Please."

Slowly, her arms release her knees, and they fall back to the bed. The shirt hangs freely again. I think her cheeks flush, but it's hard to tell in the darkened room.

"I really like you, Jay. I like having you around, talking to you, and having sex with you." She grins. "And it might be too fast, and I might be too forward—and I don't know how to balance it all—but I don't want to go back to the way we were earlier tonight. It would kill me to have this invisible fence between our yards that apparently only Carter can cross."

I chuckle. "I do have a nice pumper."

"That you do." She puts a hand on my cock and squeezes it through the sheet. "I keep thinking about things my friends have said to me lately. About how you have to move on and show the kids that it's safe to do that. That we only live once and have to make ourselves happy."

"Do you think I could make you happy?"

"Yes."

No hesitation. *How can she be so sure?*

The weight of the last few years sits squarely on my chest. It's a burden I've carried with me, that I'll continue to carry with me. But something makes me think that if I unload a bit of it onto Gabrielle, if I'm honest with her about where I'm coming from, maybe a few blocks of the load will dissolve and I can move forward.

My heart pounds at the thought of it. *What would this mean? What would getting to know Gabrielle and her boys do to me?*

Can I handle that? Do I want to handle that?

"What are you thinking?" she asks, her voice wobbling.

It's now or never.

I sit up, letting the sheet pool at my waist. I fight the anger and resentment bubbling to the surface. *No, Jay. This isn't about Melody. This is about Gabrielle.*

She takes my hand and laces her fingers through mine. It's as if she knows I need the contact. I grin, realizing how things between us are so natural. Yes, they may be quick. But that doesn't mean they're wrong.

I look at the ceiling and let out a short, tight laugh. "Believe it or not, I've avoided this situation, this conversation, for years."

"You don't have to tell me anything you don't want to."

I rise up, holding her chin in my hand. "Yes, I do." I press a soft kiss against her lips before resting against the pillows again.

Anxiety builds, making my palms sweat. *What if she thinks I'm a fool? What if she thinks I'm weak? What if she thinks I'm still hung up on Melody and she wants to call this off?*

"Jay," she says, my name falling from her lips. "You don't have to talk to me. But I wish you would."

Go. "Nine years ago, I met a woman through mutual friends. We had a blind date at a bowling alley, of all places, and hit it off."

Gabrielle doesn't blink. I give her hand a squeeze of reassurance—for us both.

Sweat dots my back as I prepare to talk about the one thing in my life that almost killed me. The only thing that I've ever been scared of. *How do I talk about the most devastating part of my life?*

Why do I suddenly feel the need to?

Because this is Gabrielle. And she just might be worth the vulnerability.

"Melody, that was her name," I say. "She and I spent almost every day together after that. I found out on that first date that she had a baby, a daughter named Isabella. She was eleven months old."

My throat tightens, burning so hot it's hard to speak.

"We dated for a couple of years and then they moved in with me," I say, remembering the day they pulled up in Melody's compact car. "We celebrated Izzy's third birthday in my kitchen."

"That's a cute name for a little girl."

I smile sadly. "She is a cute little girl." *Or she was. I don't know anymore.*

A shadow passes across her face, but it disappears as quickly as it arrived.

"Things were great for a year or so," I say. "And then . . . they weren't."

"What happened?"

I shrug. "What happens when you're in a relationship that you never should've been in to begin with?"

"Oh, Jay . . ."

"She wanted to get married. And the more she asked, the more demanding it got, and the further I got from wanting to marry her. She guilted me over Izzy—that Izzy called me Dad, and how could I refuse to be a legal family? How could I do that to them?"

Gabrielle covers our hands with her other one. "That's unfair."

"She turned into a person I didn't recognize, and if I'm being honest, I probably wasn't my best either. There was so much resentment on both our parts. So much bad behavior." My heart squeezes. "But in the middle of it all was Izzy. A baby girl that I raised from before she could walk."

I blow out a breath, wanting desperately to stop. But knowing I can't.

"That kid was *my kid*, Gabrielle. She was my daughter. Her biological father was never in the picture, and I was all she knew. We went fishing together. Played basketball. Had tea parties and watched princess movies." I fight back a swell of emotion. "Ever seen *Beauty and the Beast*? It's a good one."

Gabrielle lets go of my hand and sits at my side.

"I came home from work one day," I say, grinding my teeth. "And they were gone."

She gasps.

"Everything. Gone."

"Jay."

"She left a note that she was moving to Oregon with her sister since I had no intentions of making her my wife. And she was changing her number and never to contact her again or she'd call the authorities."

I stare at the wall across the room.

"I don't know what to say to that." Gabrielle pauses. "I'm sorry, Jay."

I shrug. "Yeah, well, there's not much to say."

My heart broke into a thousand messy and angry pieces over this . . . and I never thought those pieces could fit together again. I never wanted them to. It was never a consideration. *Until now.*

"Did she ever try to contact you?"

"Once. She called and let me talk to Izzy. I think she was trying to get me to come after her in some fucked-up game with our daughter as bait."

"I'm so sorry."

I sit up. Gabrielle lays an arm over my shoulders and rests her head on my arm.

My throat is dry. My stomach is twisted. My legs itch to move—to get up and pace, to distract myself from thinking about it.

But I don't. I want Gabrielle to hear all of it so she understands.

"I've thought a million times that I should've just married her," I say, my voice hollow. "Would it have been that bad? Who is really getting punished here? *Me and Izzy.*"

"You can't marry someone you don't love, Jay. You can't marry them because they're holding something—your daughter, for goodness' sake—over your head. That's . . . *that's cruel.*"

I look at her, taking comfort in the concern in her eyes.

"But would it have been better for Izzy?" I ask.

That's the million-dollar question. The one that keeps me up at night. *Did my decision ruin that little girl's life?*

"No, Jay. That wouldn't have been better for Izzy. Being raised in a house with two parents that don't love one another, that are always sparring and creating dissension . . . what would that teach her?"

"What did never seeing her dad teach her?" I fight a well of tears from trickling down my cheeks. "Does she think I don't love her? That I haven't thought of her every day for the last four years? Will she grow up and not trust men because I fucked her up?"

Gabrielle crawls into my lap and pulls my head to her shoulder. She holds me close, running her hands up and down my back.

"You didn't fuck her up," she says. "You loved her. You got out of a situation that would've put her in the crosshairs of a lot of unhealthy interactions, even though it's clear it killed you." She kisses my shoulder. "You showed her what love is, Jay."

I lean back and position Gabrielle so she's straddling me. I hold her thighs and gaze up at this woman—this single mom I'm falling for.

"And that's why I'm . . ." I don't know how to finish the sentence. "You know what I mean."

"That's why you're scared of getting involved with me. Because I'm a single mom just like Melody."

"Yeah. Ironic, isn't it?" I sigh. "I'm not saying you'd ever do anything like that."

She smiles. "Of course not. But you'd be inhuman if you didn't have some fear."

I take a long, deep breath and blow it out slowly. "I don't want this over my head anymore."

"Guess we have that in common then, don't we?"

"What do you mean?"

"I don't want to second-guess every move I make anymore either. *I want to live again.* I want to not be scared."

My hands find her hips.

Excitement and anxiety mix together in a cocktail of energy that bubbles in my gut. I can't believe I'm about to say this. But not saying it all is impossible.

Am I doing exactly what I promised myself I wouldn't? It looks that way. Can I see it any other way?

She grins down at me like a fucking angel.

Nope. This is the way it's supposed to be.

"Wanna see what this could be?" I ask. "My track record isn't great, and it might not be worth your time. Come to think of it, I might not be worthy of your—"

"Will you shut up?" She laughs, the sound nothing short of music to my ears. "We can see what this can be if you can stop talking nonsense."

I grin. "Weren't you on me to talk before?"

"Funny how things change, huh?" Her cheeks are split by a wide smile. "I want to be really careful around the boys. I'm not against them knowing we're . . . friendly. I just don't want to shock them, I guess."

Thank God. "Works for me."

"I'm sure it does." She lifts up and pulls the sheet off me. Then she sits her pussy down on my cock. "Do you know what would work for me?"

I groan, guiding her hips down harder. "I hope it includes you riding me."

"Looks like we're on the same page."

She begins to lift but stops. Her hair falls into her face as she lowers her lips to mine, kissing me tenderly.

"Thank you for sharing all of that," she says softly. "It means a lot to me."

"Thank you for listening."

The pain in my soul isn't quite as powerful as it was an hour ago. The load that I carry on my shoulders is a bit lighter. I'm breathing easier.

Gabrielle probably has no idea that I've never told that story in that detail to anyone. She cannot understand the gift she gave me by affording me the room, the safety, to unburden a bit of my pain.

I peer up at her.

There's no judgment in her eyes, no disgust or suspicion. And that brings tears to my eyes.

Gabrielle is the best mother I've ever seen, and it means everything to me to have her understand my perspective and take my side. The guilt that I've carried with me all these years over not marrying Melody is suddenly . . . less. Gabrielle will never know the gift she just gave me.

And I will never forget it.

"Come here," I whisper, ushering her closer to me.

She's so damn beautiful. So sweet, so feisty—so kind. And if I'm careful and play my cards right, she might be mine.

I take her face in my hands and pull her in for a kiss.

CHAPTER EIGHTEEN

Gabrielle

The sun shines brightly overhead as I stroll down Main Street. A light breeze matches my happy-go-lucky energy, which is due, largely, to the vivid memories of the last few days.

Life with Jay since our agreement to see where things could go between us has been nothing short of wonderful. His good-morning and end-of-the-day texts are ridiculously sweet. We've sat on the porch swing after the kids have gone to bed and laughed until we've cried. He comes by for lunch every day, and it ends more often than not with *me* being the main course.

I never knew things could be this good.

I'm not sure what I expected things to be like, mostly because I never expected this to happen with Jay. He was so grumpy and reticent when we first met. He'd certainly mastered the art of keeping people at arm's length, which hurts my heart to think about. *But now?* It's just so . . . easy being with him. It's natural. *It's right.* And every time we're together, whether for a quick minute or a few stolen hours, we just click a little more.

"Hey, beautiful. Where are you headed?"

I slow my speed and grin without looking at the truck crawling beside me. "Actually, I'm prowling around town looking for a hot carpenter. Know where I can find one?"

"It's your lucky day."

I laugh and turn toward Jay's truck. The passenger's side window is down, giving me a clear view of his handsome face.

"What are you doing in town?" I ask. "I didn't think you'd be free for lunch today."

"Well, I had to grab a few things from the hardware store and figured I'd swing by your house to say hello."

His wicked grin tells me it was for more than to say hello.

"Sounds like it's *not* my lucky day at all since I'm not home," I say. "What brings you to town?"

"It's too pretty of a day to sit around." I flash him a mischievous smile. "And I *really* wanted to change the ceiling fan in the living room, but—"

"It's electrical." He shakes his head, amused. "I have a better idea. Want to grab a sandwich at Betty Lou's?"

"With you? I'd love to."

He throws the truck in park and reaches over the console to open the door for me. I climb in, not quite seated before he kisses me.

"So what have you done today?" he asks, pulling away from the curb.

He expects an answer after such a sweet, dizzying kiss?

"Cleaned up breakfast and did laundry. Then I worked on a new name list that's been plaguing me a bit. The woman asked for insect-inspired names because her husband is a . . . whatever-ologist who plays with bugs. I put Cricket on there, obviously. But the rest of them feel so *yuck*."

We pull into Betty Lou's parking lot and get out of the truck.

"What about Beetle?" Jay asks, taking my hand. "Or Mantis."

I lift a brow. "I don't think either name will make the final cut."

"*Come on.* Mantis could work. It's strong." He opens the door. "Masculine."

"Did you know it's well documented that female mantises bite off the heads and consume other body parts of males after mating?"

"And how do you know that?"

I laugh. "I have two sons and they both had an insect era."

We sit at a table in the corner beside a window facing the street. The pampas grass next to the Betty Lou's sign needs a trim, and the whiskey barrels on the front porch have seen better days. Still, the restaurant is quite charming.

"What's the hardest name list you've ever been asked to put together?" Jay asks.

"Ooh, this is tough. Someone asked for a list inspired by national parks. I thought that would've been easy, but I struggled with it for a while. *Oh!* One lady gave me her grandmother's name, which was four names that didn't go together, and asked me to give her ten combinations of names inspired by that. There's only so much you can do with Maude Brandy Sheila Cooke."

Jay smiles.

"What about you?" I ask. "What's the hardest job you've ever done?"

"It has more to do with the customer than it does the actual job. I can build pretty much anything, and I enjoy a challenge. So the harder something is technically, the more likely I am to like it. But sometimes you get a customer that asks for something they think they want. You build it to spec, and then they hate it. *Then* they don't want to pay. That's when things get tense. It's people, man. People are the hard part of everything."

"True, because I wanted to be a hairstylist for about five seconds in high school. That lasted until one day when I was in a salon getting my hair colored and a woman came in and handed a stylist a picture of a celebrity. She was determined that she was going to get that specific cut. The stylist kept trying to gently convince her it wasn't a good idea, but she insisted. So the stylist cut it and the lady *bawled.* She thought she was going to look just like Angelina Jolie and was distraught that she didn't."

Jay starts to respond, but his attention is drawn over my shoulder. His features shift into an amused annoyance. Before I can turn to investigate, a bubbly, college-aged girl appears at our table.

"Hey, Jay," she says, obviously teasing my man. A laugh is on the tip of her tongue as she turns to me. "Hi! I'm Taylor. Welcome to Betty Lou's, and I have to mention how freaking pretty you are."

"Wow." My face heats as I look at a smirking Jay. "Um, thank you, Taylor. That's really unexpected but also very kind."

She smiles. "I'm going to be honest."

"Taylor . . ." Jay says, sighing.

She ignores him. "I've been trying to set Jay up with my boyfriend's mother for months, and he's turned me down every single time. He doesn't even consider it. Lark gives him hell about it, too, but Jay has rudely blown me off without a thought." She stands taller. "Now I see why."

He turned her down?

Jay crosses his arms over his chest and watches me.

"Jay, my guy, I get it and I'm sorry," Taylor says. "Can I get you two anything to drink?"

"Water with lemon, please," I say.

"Make it two—with less commentary next time, please," Jay says.

Taylor laughs all the way to the kitchen.

My curiosity is piqued, and I lean against the table, ready to dig in. But before I can say a word, Jay leans forward too.

We're separated by the napkin dispenser and a small space of laminated tabletop. Lunch patrons buzz around us. But the look in Jay's eyes makes the outside world disappear, and it might just be the greatest feeling of all time.

"So," I say, grinning. "You're getting hooked up on the side, huh?"

"You heard her. She said that I've turned her down for months."

"Why? Have you seen the mom? Is she not your type?"

He reaches for my hand and laces our fingers together. "I don't need to see her to know she's not my type."

"How can you be so sure?"

"Because," he says, staring at our connected palms, "I met this woman recently. And since then, she's all I've been able to think about. Granted, sometimes it's because she's driving me nuts."

I laugh, squeezing his hand in mine.

He smiles. "But she's the only woman that's caught my interest in a long damn time. Hell, I didn't even want to be interested in her but couldn't help myself."

"She must be amazing."

"She is. And every day we spend together, I hope there's another one to follow. She says *she* wants to live again." His smile fades into the shy grin that melts my heart. "But I didn't even realize *I* wasn't living until I met her."

The bridge of my nose pinches like it does just before tears flood my eyes. *How does he do that?* His words touch me in a way he'll never understand. It's not only because I know this is difficult for him to share but also because he's slowly proving to be the kind of man I was too scared to even dream about.

I was content in my marriage to Christopher. He was kind, responsible, and dependable. Loyal. He was an amazing father. We had great conversations and chose vacation spots with ease. I was proud to be his wife.

When he brought up divorce, despite knowing it was for the best, I was still crushed. I realized quickly that it wasn't because I was losing *him*, specifically, that was devastating, though. It was being married to a man who I thought had been the "perfect" husband, who didn't want to fight for our marriage, that hurt. *I wasn't enough.* And that he could let me go so easily.

That was the point of my pain.

I've been scared to dream for something bigger than my marriage. I didn't realize that I was doing it until meeting Jay. My sights have been set on finding someone to occupy space in my life. A man to make me feel less alone. I simply needed a seat filler, and the few men I dated after my divorce were just that.

But Jay? He could build the damn chair. And he'd do it with the very best wood and without missing a screw—no pun intended.

He's slowly opening my eyes, and heart, to the possibility that I might have been shortchanging myself all these years. He's showing me that a man can be my friend and my lover. There can be a roomful of people, and he can see only *me*.

"What are you thinking about?" he asks, stroking his thumb over the top of my hand.

I force a swallow past the lump in my throat. "Nothing, really. I was just thinking that you're pretty damn amazing too."

"I—"

"Gabrielle? Is that you?" A woman I vaguely recognize from my high school home economics class pauses at our table. "I didn't know you were home."

Jay slides his hand from mine and winks at me.

"Yes. I'm home," I say, smiling at Mrs. Weston. "I moved back to Alden with my two boys."

"Carter?" She scrunches her brows. "And Dylan, isn't it? Are those your boys?"

I laugh. "I hope that doesn't mean they've been giving anyone any trouble."

"After my retirement three years ago, I found myself bored out of my mind. So I've been volunteering at the school nearly every day. Last week, I was subbing for Carter's teacher in the elementary." She laughs heartily. "Gabby, let me tell you that your little boy is the sweetest, funniest little thing."

Thank God. My shoulders sag. "I'm so glad to hear that."

"Now, your older boy, he's not quite as . . . chipper," she says, searching for the right word. "I chatted with him for a while the other day in the high school cafeteria. He was very polite and had excellent manners, don't get me wrong. He just seems like less of a people person than Carter."

I force a smile. "I think that's a pretty accurate observation."

"Well, I can't wait to get to know them. I'll tell them I know their mama next time and that might win me some brownie points."

Or not.

Mrs. Weston turns to Jay. "How have you been, Jay? I didn't mean to ignore you. I just haven't seen Gabby in what feels like forever."

"I'm good. I hope you're the same, Mrs. Weston," he says.

"Oh, yes, very well, thank you, Jay," she answers.

She looks back and forth between the two of us. A cheeky grin slips across her face.

"I'll let you two get back to it," she says. "It was great to see you, Gabby. Come visit me sometime. I still live out by the ball fields. You remember where that is, don't you?"

"Of course. It was good to see you, Mrs. Weston."

She smiles at us. "Enjoy your lunch."

Jay nods a goodbye as she walks away.

I settle back in my chair and heave a breath. "You do know that woman is one of the biggest gossips in this town, right?"

"No."

"Well, she is. Half of the town will know she saw the two of us having lunch together by the time I get back home."

Jay studies me. "Does that bother you?"

His gaze is heavy on me as I consider his question. My instant reflex is to panic and say yes, it does bother me. I expect that I *should* want to protect the boys and not have them hear that we're together. I wait for a string of words to form that explains why having lunch in public might not be a great idea just yet.

This is all so new. And Jay doesn't want this in the open . . . *does he?*

"Does it bother you?" I ask instead of answering him.

He's thoughtful before responding. Finally, his eyes lock on mine.

"I want you to be comfortable," he says softly. "If you want to keep this quiet—especially for the boys—then I understand that. That's what we'll do. But if it's my decision to make, then I don't care if anyone in this town knows that I'm interested in you. Because I am." A grin tickles his lips. "I like you, Gabrielle. A lot."

A rush of warmth floods my veins, and I bite my lip to keep from laughing in relief.

"I like you too, Jay. A lot."

"How hungry are you?" he asks.

My stomach clenches.

"Because we can stick around and have a burger," he says. "Or . . ."

I stand up. "Or. I pick *or*."

His laughter is loud as he gets to his feet. He takes a twenty from his wallet and hands it to Taylor as she walks by.

"We gotta get going," Jay tells her. "Keep the change."

Taylor reads between the lines and giggles. "Get out of here before you two set this place on fire."

Jay takes my hand and practically drags me to the door.

CHAPTER NINETEEN

Jay

I rinse my plate and place it in the dishwasher. It's a process that's never made sense to me, but it's a habit I can't break. *Why have a dishwasher if you're going to clean the dishes first anyway?* I don't know. But it's what I do.

Gabrielle's bra hangs off the back of a kitchen chair in the same spot she tossed it a few nights ago during one of our middle-of-the-night rendezvous. Sometimes we don't get beyond the sofa. Other times, we wind up in the kitchen, and I make her a snack so she can relax. My favorite nights include her on my lap in the living room or lying with her in my bed, telling stories and sharing mindless details about our day.

She's become such an effortless part of my routine, such a comfortable and enjoyable addition to my life. *Does she feel the same way?*

My stomach pulls as I consider the potential complications ahead of us—namely, Gabrielle's sons.

I can see a future with her. It's bizarre to consider that I've gone from avoiding any relationship with women—specifically women with children—to wanting to be with Gabrielle daily. But the spark connecting my neighbor and me is different from anything I've experienced in the past. So far, it's extraordinary. And I'm tiptoeing around the hope that maybe it could be long term.

Maybe Gabrielle could be *the one*.

It's too early to determine that for certain, but it's also a strong enough potential that I find myself considering how to handle Dylan.

I scrub my hand down my face and exhale.

"How do I start to gain his trust?" I ask the empty kitchen.

It's such a fine line for all of us. Getting involved in Gabrielle's boys' lives triggers a fear inside me. I can't help thinking of Izzy and how it felt having her ripped from my life. *What if that happens again?* Just as I'm about to spin out of control, I consider the look in Gabrielle's eye when she smiles at me, and I know she'd never do something like Melody did.

Gabrielle is not my ex.

"If Melody had been more like Gabrielle, things could've worked out differently," I say, working my head side to side. Tension rides across the back of my neck.

I've never quite pinpointed the crux of my issue with Melody. It was always a jumbled mess in my head regarding her. But now that I've had time with Gabrielle, it's clear.

Melody was wholeheartedly devoted to her own happiness.

I watch Gabrielle put everyone's needs over her own every single day. She's selfless when it comes to her boys—unconditionally devoted. She talks great about her ex-husband. She was even kind to me when I was a dick to her in the beginning. But that's who she is and a huge part of my attraction to her.

And that element didn't exist in my world with Melody. In fact, her lack of concern for anyone else's happiness is what pushed me away. Now that I think about it, her selfishness also bonded Izzy and me. It was a double-edged sword, making it inconceivable to marry her while simultaneously making it impossible to walk away.

Although I never thought I would think this, I'm so glad she left me. I'm so grateful for the opportunity to know Gabrielle and her family . . . even if it is tricky as hell. Because as much as I know Gabrielle is the opposite of Melody, there are still threads of fear I can't quite shake.

I know I must, though. I want to be open and receptive. Gabrielle, Dylan, and Carter deserve that. I want to be worthy of being a part of their lives and not infect our relationship with the poison that Melody left behind.

At the same time, I don't want to overstep. I don't want to involve myself too deeply in their lives—especially until Gabrielle and I decide it's time to make that move. But it kills me that Dylan is struggling and so full of contempt. I didn't lose my parents as a child, but I did lose a child. Maybe I can relate to him on that level.

My phone buzzes on the table. I swipe it up, buzzing with anticipation that it's Gabrielle.

Gabrielle: Hey. What are you doing?

Me: Pondering life's deepest questions involving dishes. You?

Gabrielle: Wondering why I haven't seen my sexy neighbor all day. ☹

I grin.

Me: Ask and you shall receive. ☺

Gabrielle: It's a beautiful night. Want to come over and porch-swing with me?

Me: I'm on my way.

I pour two glasses of tea and head across the lawn.

The moon is muted as it hangs overhead surrounded by a million silver stars. Frogs croak from the creek behind our homes as I take the steps up and onto the back deck.

Gabrielle waits for me, swaying back and forth in the warm night breeze.

"There you are," she says, smiling from ear to ear.

I press a quick kiss against her lips and take a seat next to her, handing her a glass. "How was your day?"

"You brought me tea?" She faux pouts and it's adorable. "You're so damn sweet."

"Keep your voice down. *Damn.* You're going to ruin my reputation."

She laughs, bumping me with her shoulder. "Thank you."

"It's my pleasure. So, your day?"

"It was good. I worked. Had lunch with Della. Went to the grocery store. What about you?"

I slide my arm across the back of the swing and usher her closer to me. "My day was fine. We got a lot of framing done for the new walls on the addition we're building. Although I had to stay late and talk to the homeowner about a change he wants to make. I need to price all of that out this weekend and get back to him."

"Need help?"

I grin. "You're going to help me with an estimate?"

"If you need help, I will." She blushes. "What? Don't look at me like that."

"Like what?"

"Like . . ." She shrugs, her cheeks rosy. "I don't know. Like I'm goofy or something."

I smile at her. "You are many things, Gabrielle Solomon. But goofy isn't one of them."

Her shoulders soften and she leans against me. My heart swells as I kiss the side of her head.

"Are the boys in bed?" I ask.

"Yes. Why?"

"I just realized I've kissed you twice tonight."

She nods slowly. "Can we talk about that?"

"Sure."

I hold my breath as she sits up and slides away from me. She tucks a strand of hair behind her ear, bringing one knee up and twisting to face me.

Her eyes are wary as she nibbles on her bottom lip. I have no idea what she's going to say—and it could go either way. And the uncertainty turns my stomach into a knot.

"I'm not trying to put anything on a fast-track," she says. "So I don't want you to think I'm trying to put the pedal to the metal, because I'm not."

"Okay."

She sighs, tension written across her pretty face. "I know I said I wanted to keep things away from the kids—and I do. I don't want to start kissing you in front of them or making them feel uncomfortable."

"Neither do I, Gabrielle."

"But I . . ." Her grin becomes shy. "I'm going to be honest with you. I hope this thing between us doesn't stop."

Thank God. I take her hand in mine and squeeze it.

"This is the part where you say you agree," she says, her voice wobbly.

I laugh.

"Jay."

I laugh harder.

"Forget it," she says, trying to take her hand from mine. "I don't even agree with myself right now."

"Stop it."

She huffs with a heavy dose of hesitation in her eyes.

"I didn't think it needed to be said, but no, I hope this thing between us doesn't stop either, Gabrielle."

She grins. "Okay. Good. Then what I was going to say, if you would've just cooperated from the beginning, is that if we're planning on keeping this up, then maybe we start easing the boys into the idea of us. What do you think?"

"I think this is absolutely your call."

"So you would be okay with it? Because I don't know what that looks like, and I don't know how they'll take it—specifically Dylan. It could get ugly."

"Yeah, it could. And you have to be ready for that."

"I am ready for that. I'm happier than I've been in a long time, and I don't want to hide it from everyone. I don't want to go to lunch with you at Betty Lou's and fear that it'll get back to the boys. Sneaking into your house in the middle of the night has been fun . . ."

We exchange a knowing smile.

"But I want to be able to come over in the evening," she says. "And I want you to be able to come over without walking on eggshells during daylight hours too. Like a normal couple."

Gabrielle has no idea what her words mean, and it's a whole lot more than what meets the eye. She's offering a reality I never thought was possible. She's proposing a life I decided long ago wasn't an option.

She's suggesting that I'm the man she wants included in her children's lives. That she believes I'll care for them as much as I'll care for her.

What a fucking concept.

"So what do you think?" she asks.

"I want all of that too."

She starts to speak when the door opens from the house. We both turn our attention to Dylan as he walks onto the deck. He spies the two of us sitting on the swing and scowls.

"Hey, buddy," Gabrielle says. "I thought you were in bed."

"I thought *you* were in bed," he says.

"Jay brought me a glass of tea." She smiles in a futile attempt at disarming Dylan. "What's up?"

He side-eyes me. "I wanted to ask you something, but I can do it later."

"Are you sure?" she asks. "Because I can go inside and we can talk, if you want."

"I'd hate to interrupt your date," he says, his jaw flexing.

This is going nowhere, and it's getting there fast. In a few seconds, Gabrielle will respond, and then Dylan will fire something back to get under my skin. We've done this dance before.

How can I make the boy see we aren't enemies?

"Have you dated before?" I ask him.

"What's it matter?"

"Dylan, please don't be rude," Gabby says, sighing.

I shrug, my gaze pinned on the boy. "I suppose it doesn't."

His brows pull together, clearly pissed. "How did you know?"

"How did I know what?" I ask.

"How did you know that I was going to ask Mom about going on a date with a girl from school?"

Gabrielle's eyes widen.

"I didn't," I say, buying her time to regroup. "How would I have known that?"

"You tell me."

It's purely a coincidence, but one that makes all the sense in the world. *Dylan doesn't know what to do, and he's frustrated about talking to his mother about it.* I remember being that age and the awkwardness of conversing with my mother about such things. Having me here doesn't make it any better.

But it could . . .

"I had no clue," I say, before taking a drink. "But since you're new around here and need tips on where to take your girl, let me know."

He narrows his eyes. "Because you take a lot of women out on dates, huh?"

Gabrielle sighs again.

He's picking a fight in his teenage way. I just need to unpick it somehow.

"Actually, no," I say. "I don't. But I do know where all the restaurants and movie theaters are, and also the hangout spots. So, if you have questions, let me know."

He holds my gaze as if he's processing my offer.

I run my hands down my thighs and then get to my feet. "I have to work early in the morning, so I better get going. It was nice talking to you, Gabrielle."

"Good night, Jay."

"Good seeing you again, Dylan," I say.

"Bye."

I take the steps slowly and then set out across the lawn. Their words are a whisper in the wind as I reach my house. Once I'm inside, I glance through the kitchen window to find they've gone inside themselves.

I won't lie. I wanted more time with Gabrielle, but this is the reality of her life. Her kids come first, and I fucking love that about her.

And Dylan and I might've made the *slightest bit* of headway.

A smile reaches my lips.

Who would've thought that I would be happy about making progress with a woman and her children?

Not fucking me.

But here we are.

CHAPTER TWENTY

Gabrielle

So how are things going?" Cricket asks, meeting me stride for stride on the sidewalk. "Are the boys taking things well?"

"Jay and I haven't been together in front of them as a couple yet."

"Oh." She pumps her arms at her sides as we walk. "That's smart. What's the rush, right?"

I smile at her and hope she doesn't laugh.

I'm practically beaming. My cheeks ache from the smile that's been plastered on my face since last Saturday. It's been a week and I'm still walking on air.

Cricket doesn't laugh. She only acknowledges it with a sly grin of her own.

The sky is gray with black clouds jetting over our heads. A few rumbles of thunder rocked the church this morning, but no rain has fallen. It's the only reason Cricket agreed to walk with me. The sun isn't out.

"You haven't been together in front of the boys, but have you been together without them?" she asks, stepping over a skateboard. "I would imagine you're still in the dating honeymoon phase of things when you can't keep your hands off each other."

I sigh blissfully. "We've been together at some point every day, even if it's for a few minutes. Sometimes it's just at lunchtime when he comes by to eat at my house, if you get my drift."

"Ooh."

"Yeah." I shiver at the reminder of how well that man takes care of *every part of me*. "He's helped me build the new stairs. The boys were home but didn't pay a bit of attention to us. He's helped me with the drains, things like that. I've gone over there after the kids have gone to bed most nights. We've snuck in something every day. We've made it work."

"How long are you going to play it like this?"

"Hey!" Scottie is standing on her porch and waving at us. "What are you guys doing?"

We stop at the white gate across the sidewalk leading to her house.

"We're walking," I say, laughing. "Did you think we were about to break out into a sprint?"

She snorts. "Maybe if it had just been you. The only way Cricket would run would be if Martha Stewart were standing at the end of the road."

"Hey," Cricket says, smiling.

"Della's here if you want to take a break and come in," Scottie says. "But be warned, I'm midcrisis."

Cricket side-eyes me and opens the gate. I pass through without a word.

I still don't know these women, aside from Cricket, well enough to know what a crisis looks like to them. *What are we walking into? Is it a financial situation? A robbery? Did she lose her job?*

"I need to borrow a dog." Scottie waits for us to enter before closing the door behind us. "Or a cat. But cats and I really don't mesh well."

Cricket seems startled by this.

Della pokes her head over the couch and rolls her eyes. Then she holds up a cocktail before sliding back into her seat again.

"I don't understand," Cricket says. "Why on earth would you need to borrow a pet?"

Scottie sits on a wicker chair across from Della. Cricket sits beside Della, and I take up the rocking chair near the window.

The house is quaint and comfy. There are lots of pictures and decorations, most of them in warm reds and golds. If I didn't know it was just Scottie who lives here, I could imagine a family hanging out and sharing meals.

"I met a man." Scottie's eyes sparkle. "His name is Grady Brundage and he's midthirties, so smart, and he likes to garden."

The words almost hold back her entire squeal.

Ice clinks in Della's glass as she takes a long drink.

"I still don't understand where the pet comes in," Cricket says.

"Oh. Right. He's a vet. And I don't have a pet and I really don't want one. But two things," Scottie says, holding up a finger. "One, I can't let him think I don't like animals because obviously he does. He'd take that as a red flag. And two, I don't know how I'll ever see him again if I don't force it."

"Scottie," I say carefully, "I'm not sure if faking a love for animals is a great foundation for a relationship."

"Listen to her," Della says. "She just bagged Jay Stetson."

I stare at her. *How does she know?* I look at Cricket to see if she's guilty, but she just shrugs and chuckles.

"What?" Scottie shouts, her jaw dragging the floor. "Why do you guys never tell me the good stuff?"

"I was only guessing," Della says, winking at me. "I saw Jay go all caveman at Murray's last Friday night, so given Gabby's happy little grin, I figured it was a safe bet."

"Oooh, Gabs. You didn't tell me that part," Cricket says, her hands going to her hips.

I sigh. "I just . . . Of course, there's stuff to tell."

My friends laugh.

"But I wanted to keep it to myself for a little while," I say.

"It's been a while. When do we get the juicy bits?" Scottie asks, rubbing her hands together. "I don't mean this in any disrespectful way, but I've wondered so many times . . ."

A giddiness envelops me, the likes of which I haven't felt in ages. I'd love nothing more than to gab with the girls about my new situation with Jay. But I don't want to take away from Scottie, even though she asked.

"I'll give you all the details later," I say. "But let's solve the vet problem first."

Scottie gives me a soft smile. "You're the sweetest."

"So like I've been saying *for the last hour*," Della says, winding the conversation around. "Find him on social media. Where does he like to hang out? Do you have any mutual friends that could work some magic? Call his office and leave a message. When he calls back, ask him to dinner. Guys love a forward woman."

"Do not ask him out," Cricket says, almost as if she's offended on Scottie's behalf. "You want a gentleman, not a child of a man that has to have a woman lead him. Next thing you know, you'll be paying for the date."

"I'm okay with that," Scottie says.

Cricket's eyes widen. "How?"

"Because he's a veterinarian," Scottie says. "I imagine everyone he takes out expects him to pay. And I want to stand out—show him that I'm a woman in my own right. I can take care of myself."

"And she's *choosing him* to be in her life," Della says, taking the invisible baton. "It makes him feel like the lucky one to be noticed *by her*."

Scottie shrugs in agreement.

"Okay, how did you never meet him before?" I ask. "Everyone knows everyone here."

"He's new. Dr. Kane retired and the animal clinic hired Grady," Scottie says.

"How about this?" Della says, putting her drink on the table. Cricket grabs a coaster and slides it under the glass. "My friend Lark has a dog. I'll borrow it, go see Dr. Hottie, and mention my beautiful friend Scottie recommended him. Then I'll give him your number."

Cricket holds up her hands. "And how is that any different than her pretending to have an animal?"

"Because Scottie's not lying," I say, seeing the beauty in the plan. "Who cares if Della is?"

"I'll say it's my friend's dog. I won't even be lying."

Scottie leans back in her chair and points at Della. "You know what, I like that. I like it a lot."

"Thank God." Della groans. "There's only so many times we can go over this."

"It's perfect, Scottie," I say, giving her an encouraging smile. "You don't want to have to pretend in a relationship. Imagine how hard it would be if we were together and he came by, and you had to try to keep your stories straight."

Cricket stands, her face flushed. "Does anyone need a drink? Scottie, can I make us drinks?"

"You know where the kitchen is," she replies.

Cricket takes Della's glass and leaves.

The room grows eerily quiet once Cricket is gone. Scottie sits on the edge of her chair, her eyes glued to the doorway Cricket just passed through. Della looks at me with raised brows. I run through the last few minutes of conversation and try to figure out what doesn't fit.

"What do you think it is?" Della asks.

"You notice the awkward silence too?" Scottie asks.

I clear my throat. "I can't figure out what happened. We were only talking about Scottie and the vet."

"It's the way Cricket shot to her feet and couldn't wait to get out of the room," Della says before glancing over her shoulder. "Is anything going on with her?"

"Not that I know of," I say.

Scottie shakes her head. "I had lunch with her yesterday and everything seemed fine."

"Here you go," Cricket says, announcing her arrival. "Scottie, you're in desperate need of a restock on your alcohol."

"I know," Scottie says, taking a glass from Cricket. "I keep forgetting."

"How do you forget alcohol?" Della asks.

"I only drink with you guys," Scottie says. "If you're not here or if I don't know you're coming, I never even look in that cabinet."

Cricket hands me a cool glass filled with lemonade and then takes her seat. Her neck is blotchy. I can tell despite her taking her hair down and letting it flow over her shoulders.

"Are you okay, Cricket?" Della asks.

"Me? Yes. I'm fine. Why do you ask?"

Della glances at me. As if we've done this many times before, I jump in.

"You just seem a little off," I say.

Her back is perfectly straight, her chin raised. "It's nothing."

Scottie reaches over and touches her arm. "Are you sure?"

A single, silent tear trickles down Cricket's freckled cheek.

What the hell?

"Cricket . . ." Della sets her glass down. "What's going on?"

My cousin stares at a wall across the room. She sniffles, fighting hard not to break down. Watching her struggle to keep her emotions in check brings my own feelings to the surface.

I reach for her hand, and surprisingly, she places a shaky palm in mine.

"It's what you said, Gabby," Cricket says. "About not pretending in a relationship."

Scottie, Della, and I exchange looks. None of us know what to say. Cricket is the stoic one, the one of the four of us who can put her emotions to the side and think with logic. She's not the one to cry, not even in front of us.

"What's going on?" Scottie asks softly. "Tell us. Let us help."

Cricket laughs, sniffling. "You can't help me with this."

"Are you sick?" I ask.

"Is it Kyle?" Della asks.

Cricket's face darkens. Instead of her growing more frantic or even sadder, as one might expect with an illness or a problem child, an iciness slides over her features. *"It's Peter."*

My brain spins wildly, trying to come up with a possible conflict between the couple that, until I moved onto Bittersweet Court, I thought was perfect. The hotshot CEO and the PTA mom. The sports car–driving husband and the luxury-SUV wife. The charismatic businessman and the trophy wife with their perfect son, on a beautiful street.

What gives? The only thing that I can come up with is the tension at Sunday dinner. *Is it always like that and I just didn't realize it?*

Another tear falls.

"My marriage is falling apart, you guys," she says, the words wobbling. "And I don't know how to fix it."

"Oh, honey," Scottie says, kneeling next to her.

I stand and pull her head into my shoulder. The contact makes her heave a sob. The sound triggers tears for me too.

"What kind of a situation are we dealing with here?" Della asks. "I know a lot of people who can do a lot of things privately, if you catch my drift."

Scottie and I make eye contact and fight a grin.

"No, nothing like that," Cricket says, raising her head from my shoulder. She wipes her face with the back of her hand. Mascara streaks her skin. "Oh, damn it. I'm a mess."

Scottie grabs a tissue and hands it to her.

We take our seats as Cricket straightens herself up.

"Peter is spending lots of time in the office," she says, sniffling. "When he's not, he's golfing or barely being civil to me."

"Is he stressed?" Scottie asks. "Is everything going okay at work?"

"I don't know because we never get that far into a conversation without him being rude and me walking away."

Della sighs. "Fine. I'll ask it. Do you think he's fucking someone else?"

"Della," I say, my mouth hanging open.

"Well, we haven't been intimate in . . . a while," Cricket says, fighting tears again. "I don't think he'd have an affair, but I think that's what most people believe when their spouse starts sleeping with their assistant."

I take a drink of my lemonade and listen to Cricket and our friends banter back and forth. It's easy to forget the trials of marriage when things are going fine or you're out of one . . . and your ex-husband is dead.

All the arguments that Chris and I had come back to me. His long hours at the office. My irritation at being touched after having been handled by a toddler all day. My gas tank being empty when we took my van somewhere as a family.

Despite all that—despite our conflicts and the nights we stayed up late arguing and the long days struggling to make it, praying for him to come home—it was worth it. Every bit of it was worth the energy. Even though it ended in divorce, I'm glad I fought for it every time until it was clear we weren't meant to be.

"What do you want to do?" I ask, cutting back into the conversation.

"I don't want a divorce, if that's what you're thinking," Cricket says.

Della smiles. "Then this is where I come in."

"Oh, God," Cricket says under her breath.

"You can't pay for this level of experience," Della says, undeterred. "Do you want my help or not?"

"Be easy with her," I say, laughing.

"I suppose it wouldn't hurt to hear you out," Cricket says. "I am on the verge of desperation."

"I'm going to ignore that." Della lifts a brow. "Let me break this down into the simplest form. The way I see it, and I'm basically an expert in this arena—Peter needs to have sex to have a connection. You, on the other hand, need to have a connection to have sex."

Wow. That makes sense.

"I feel like I should take notes," Scottie teases.

Cricket watches Della with rapt attention. "Go on."

"I've said it a million times: men are simple creatures," Della says. "But it's not because they're emotionless barbarians. It's because most women don't understand them. You're fighting or there's a communication issue or whatever it is, and you withhold sex because you don't feel connected to him. Or he stops fucking you because he's pissed or hurt, and then he stops feeling connected."

"Peter and I haven't *fucked*, as you so eloquently put it, since before I got Botox and stretch marks," Cricket says, her jaw locked. "That puts us having fun sex at a solid sixteen years ago."

Scottie's wide eyes meet mine over the glasses of lemonade.

I didn't think Peter and Cricket had a wild love life, but I didn't expect it to be nonexistent either. She always paints a picture of a healthy sex life and seems satisfied. She even says they have sex several times a week. So, this? This abject desolation written on Cricket's face? It's as shocking as it is heartbreaking.

My heart aches for the loneliness Cricket must be feeling. I know it well. *But a certain handsome, somewhat irritating man is helping me fix that.*

Della stands. "Where is Peter now?"

"Golfing." She spits out the word. "Why?"

"We're going to your house to pick out the sexiest lingerie you own." Della looks Cricket up and down. "Or we're going to go buy some."

Cricket's face grows red, but she surprisingly doesn't object.

"Then you're going to get hold of his assistant and find out when he has an opening in his schedule," Della says. "You're going to have her pencil in a fake name for a full hour."

Cricket swallows so hard I can hear it.

"You're going to wear that with a trench coat over it," Della says, grinning mischievously. "And surprise him at work."

"I can't do that," Cricket says, squeaking.

"You can. *And you will*," Della says. "Make that connection. Show him what he's missing—what you need."

The room is still for a long second. Then Cricket blows out a quick breath.

"You know what, let's do it. Make me a man-eater like you, Della—with all due respect," Cricket says.

Scottie and I laugh.

We file out the door, Scottie locking up behind us. As we make our way down the sidewalk, my mind begins to wander.

And it wanders to my next-door neighbor.

If things got serious between us, would he fight for me? Would he go to the lengths Cricket is going to keep the passion between us?

I smile to myself.

From what I know, I think he might.

And I think I own a trench coat.

CHAPTER TWENTY-ONE

JAY

"This is officially your longest relationship, right?" Lark asks, his voice filling the cab of my truck through the speakers. "I'm going off Della's terminology here, so God help me."

I chuckle, pausing at an intersection to let a jogger pass safely.

The evening is perfect, with a clear sky and gentle breeze. It made work today so much easier than dealing with the cloudy, off-and-on rain showers of the last couple of days. The sunroom at the farmhouse is starting to take shape. As long as the owner doesn't add on a bunch of work, it'll be a great project.

"Yeah," I say, turning right after the jogger has cleared the road. "This is the longest I've spent with a woman in quite a while."

"And you have no thoughts about getting the hell out of there?"

The question hangs in the air, pregnant with insinuations.

A week or two is usually the maximum amount of time I spend with a woman. That's how long it takes for the superficial layer of our interaction to cease. Beyond that framework comes an actual relationship with actual conversations, digging through childhood stories, and the confluence of our lives that makes me uneasy.

I don't go into situations with a countdown flashing over a woman's head. My extraction from our interactions is organic—a knee-jerk reaction that's rooted in my need to remain unattached. Being single has served me well. Relationships have not.

The engine roars as I turn onto Bittersweet Court.

"I'm taking that as a no," Lark says.

I blow out a breath, wrestling with how to summarize and phrase my thoughts.

"Lark, it's . . ." *Different with Gabrielle. It doesn't feel like a relationship. I've slept like a baby all week and not paced the floor.* "I can't explain it."

He hums.

"Maybe it's because we were sort of friends before things between us changed," I say. "Or, you know, her kids aren't babies. They're older. They had a dad and I'm not filling that role. There's no pressure. I'm an ancillary part of their lives."

I'm an ancillary part of their lives by design . . . and I hate it.

Never in my wildest dreams did I think I would be upset about not being a part of a woman's life with her children. It would be so much easier if I did loathe Carter needing to borrow my pumper and found Dylan's jerk-face attitude annoying. Why do I have to enjoy helping Gabrielle around her house, and why can I see myself sitting at their table for dinner so easily?

"I just want to point out that you're saying one thing but telling me the opposite," Lark says.

Scottie waves from her flower bed. I nod her way in return.

"That doesn't even make sense," I say.

"Yeah, it does. You're saying that you're comfortable with Gabrielle because you don't really matter in their lives. But the tone of your voice tells me that you aren't comfortable being an outsider."

Sometimes, I hate him. "I gotta go. I'm almost home."

"Okay. There's a car show this weekend in Logan if you wanna go. I think they opened the track again, so they'll be racing, I bet."

"I'll let you know," I say, slowing as I pass Gabrielle's house. "I'm pulling in my driveway. Gotta go."

"Later."

"Bye."

Gabrielle's car is in the driveway, and lights are on inside the house. The sun is on the horizon, giving off enough light for Carter to still be bouncing his ball on the sidewalk or back deck. I don't see him.

I park outside and make my way inside as quickly as possible.

Coming home used to feel like walking into a trap. The day was over. All natural distractions were elsewhere, and the silence was deafening. Home was both my refuge and my prison. But lately, it's held more . . . hope.

I toss my keys on the table by the door and slip off my boots and socks.

Instead of lamenting the past as I make myself a glass of tea, my brain skips to the future. It's a relief to have a reason to look forward. But it's also a little nerve-racking too.

How will Dylan and Carter take it when they learn their mom is seeing me? Will they welcome me in? Or will they feel like I'm intruding?

"Hell, how am I going to deal with it?" I ask the empty room.

I take a sip of my tea and ponder the question. It's one I've pondered many times lately. Each time I think about it, though, the idea of being introduced to Gabrielle's children as more than a friend isn't quite so heavy. Maybe it's because what I told Lark is right—they're older. It's much different from Izzy.

Izzy.

Her laughter echoes through my brain, bringing a smile to my face.

She's between Dylan's and Carter's ages now. I wonder whether she remembers me. I'm curious whether she's ever asked for me or quizzed Melody about my absence. She was so little then, and it's been four years. I'm sure any wound has healed by now. Maybe she even has another father figure in her life . . .

The thought is both a gut punch . . . and a wish.

"I hope you have someone loving the shit out of you, Izzy Girl," I whisper. "I hope someone is treating you like a princess."

My gaze is pulled to the window over the sink. Carter is tossing a baseball up in the air between our houses. He can't catch worth a damn, nearly hitting himself in the face every other time.

He's a kid without a father. A little boy whose father probably hopes he has someone loving the shit out of him and his brother.

My heart races.

If it came to that, could I consider stepping into that role? Sweat beads on my forehead. *Could I be the man to those kids that I hope is there for Izzy?*

"Hey! Jay!" Carter yells, pulling me out of my head. The words are muffled as they cross the lawn and travel through my window.

I wave at him.

"Do you have a glove?" He holds his gloved hand in the air and jumps up and down. "Do you have one of these, Jay?"

"Oh, this damn kid," I say, chuckling as I find a pair of slides.

I rummage around the garage, finding my old glove in a tote. I no more than get the garage door button pressed than Carter's face appears inches above the driveway.

"Wanna play catch?" he asks, a smile stretched from ear to ear.

"What happened to basketball?"

He stands as the door fully opens. "Oh, I still like it. But I *really* like baseball."

"You do?"

"Yeah, I played on a team in Boston," he says, talking a mile a minute. "I played on the right side in the grass on the even innings. Step twenty steps behind the first base and then ten steps toward the middle. I stood right there and got every ball that they sent to me." He makes a face. "But the poppers—you know, the ones in the air? Those were hard. One cracked me right in the forehead one time. I had to retire for a while after that."

I try hard not to laugh.

"But I'm back, baby." His fist pumps, leading me into the grass. "And Dylan won't play with me because he's being a jerk face to Mom again and she made him go to his room until dinner. And she's making dinner, so she won't play."

"So, what? I'm your last resort?"

"Don't think of it like that." He runs a half a football field away. "You were my first other pick!"

Fantastic.

"I'm warning ya. I have a good arm on me," he says, heaving the ball my way. It doesn't make it to the halfway mark. He's undeterred, jogging to the ball. "Did ya see that? I told ya I have an arm."

I don't even know where to start with this kid. It's been decades since I played baseball, and I'm not sure if I even remember how to throw it anymore. Furthermore, *how the hell did I get stuck doing this again?*

Carter runs to me and puts the ball in my glove. "Okay. Your turn."

"Hey," I say as he sprints off again. "Not so far."

His hands go to his hips. "Why? Are you not a good thrower?"

"It's been a while and I need to warm up. I need to take it easy at first."

"Fine."

I throw the ball in the air far enough that it almost makes it to him before landing in the grass with a soft thud. Carter, none the wiser, picks it up and presses his lips together.

"That was pretty good," he says. "You'll get there. Keep practicing."

God help me. I look at the sky and try not to laugh. Carter takes this as the perfect opportunity to throw the best, hardest ball he's thrown all day . . . right into my eye.

He gasps as I shout, the mixture of sounds causing the birds in the giant oak tree in Gabrielle's front yard to take flight.

"Jay! Jay! I'm sorry!"

My vision is blurry. I suck in a breath and pat the area around my right eye. It stings with each touch and burns anyway. I can't see Carter in front of me. I know he's there only because he's pulling on my arm.

"Give me a minute, Carter," I say.

I grit my teeth so I don't curse.

"I'm sorry," he says. "You gotta catch with the glove and not your face."

"Excellent advice."

"Yeah, I should've told you that before we started. I learned that on that popper."

Slowly, my vision comes back, but the stinging is still present. Carter is gazing up at me with concern written all over his little face.

I squat down to his level. "Believe it or not, I played baseball when I was little—from the time I was five or six until I graduated high school."

"Really? What happened?"

This little shit. I shake my head and chuckle. "Look, rule number one in baseball is always watch the ball. I didn't do that. And rule number two is to not throw the ball at someone unless they are looking at you. And you didn't do that."

He closes one eye and narrows the other. I'm not sure if he's thinking or mocking me. I don't ask.

"Baseball is a team sport, and we weren't really operating like a team today," I say.

"Okay. So the next time we play, which is probably tomorrow, we need to be a team."

His eyes sparkle and I can't argue with him, or even correct him. He's too damn cute.

"So," I say, "let's not—"

"Mom! We need some ice over here."

I follow his gaze to the back deck of his house. Gabrielle stands on the deck, in about the same spot she was standing the first day I saw her, with a puzzled look on her face.

"Why? What happened?" she asks.

"Jay wasn't watching the ball and it hit him right in the eye. *Pow!*" Carter takes off running toward his mom. "I warned him I have a good arm on me."

I walk across the yard, wishing I had two good eyes to see Gabrielle. Her hair is in a messy knot on top of her head. A T-shirt hangs off one shoulder, highlighting the sweet curve of her neck. Those lips, the same ones I want on me immediately, are curved into a frown.

"Oh, Jay, I'm so sorry," she says, wincing. "I had no idea he was going to get you to play."

"It's fine." I rest my forearms on the railing and look up at her beautiful face. "We're just going to have to issue some ground rules next time. Like no throwing it when someone isn't looking."

She fights a giggle and fails. The sound goes straight to my cock.

"Keep it up," I say quietly.

"And what?"

"And I'll—"

"Hey, can I have a piece of candy?" Carter pokes his head out the door. "Just one. *Pleaseee?*"

Gabrielle grins before turning her attention to her son. "No. Dinner is almost ready."

"Fine." He perks up. "Hey, Jay! Why don't you eat with us?"

His little eyes are trained on me like he's watching for me to slip up.

"Thanks, Carter, but I can't—"

"Why?"

Gabrielle holds up a hand before clearing her throat. She pivots slowly to me with a hefty dose of hesitation in her features. "You know, we do have plenty if you want to come in and eat."

"Yeah. Come on, Jay. You can sit by me. And if you can't see out of your eye, I'll help you eat."

Gabrielle giggles.

"Carter, my man, that's a great offer. But . . ."

I'm ready to turn them down again. Gabrielle and I agreed to take things slow until we knew what we were doing—if anything. But the way she looks at me, like she hopes I say yes, stops me in my tracks.

Is this her way of declaring her intentions? Is she trying to tell me she's ready to be more forward about our relationship than we planned?

My mind races nearly as fast as my heart.

I have two choices. I can retreat, backing out of this and going home. My life will be what it's been for the last four years. Or I can take the invitation, go inside, and share a meal with a woman who intrigues me. The only woman who's made me even consider something like this. *Does that say something?*

"But you have to help me do dishes," I say, hopping over the rail.

Gabrielle's smile could light up the sky. Carter's emphatic attempt at negotiating dishes echoes across the lawn. And the beating of my heart is so hard that I'm sure Gabrielle can hear it as she gets in a quick hug once Carter's back is to us.

I brace myself, but I'm not sure why. Am I nervous this is going to go terribly wrong?

Or am I excited it might go terribly right?

CHAPTER TWENTY-TWO

Gabrielle

I hope you aren't expecting anything fancy," I say, turning on the tap. "We're having burgers and potato chips for dinner. And before you come for me that there isn't a vegetable on the plate—I know, and I don't care tonight."

"Are we eating now?" Carter asks.

"Go wash your hands and face. And change your shirt," I say. "Then get Dylan and tell him he can come down to eat."

Carter screws up his face. "Sure. Make *me* tell him."

"Go."

He stomps up the stairs, expressing his frustration in every step.

I wait for him to disappear before I turn to Jay. I'm about to steal a kiss when I'm reminded of his black eye.

"Do you want some ice for that?" I touch the side of his face gently. "It's going to bruise."

He glances at the stairs before grabbing my hips and pulling me to him. "Are you sure about this?"

"I wouldn't have asked you if I wasn't sure." I stand on my tiptoes and press a soft kiss against his lips. "It's just a meal, and Carter invited you. Not me."

"Carter said Dylan was being a jerk face to you."

I grin. "The day ends with a *y*, so yeah, that's true."

"I don't want to make things worse by being here."

My heart stills. "Do you not want to be here?"

His crooked smile melts me. My heart starts beating again.

"Strangely, I want to be here," he says, his voice just above a whisper. "But I'm not sure how you want this to go, and I don't want to fuck this up."

Footsteps sound from the floor above us. I swipe another kiss.

"This thing between us . . . I like it, Jay," I say, watching his eyes lighten. "It makes me feel good. You make me feel good."

"Sneak by tonight, and I'll make sure you feel *very good*."

I laugh. "It might be good for them to see me be happy."

"And I make you happy?"

"You make me very happy." I press my palms against his chest. "And it's time they see that."

If we were alone, I would explain all the things rolling around in my head—like how safe I feel with him. And how I notice the kindness he shows my children. I would tell him that I can't wrap my head around how easily our lives have intertwined and how he's proven to be everything I want in a man. *Even when I wasn't looking for someone.*

He's good and thoughtful. Smart and funny, in a grumpy kind of way. He's a hard worker and a good role model for my boys.

And he's so handsome, so sexy, I can barely keep my hands to myself.

But what I like most about Jay is how he makes me feel. Interesting. Beautiful. Important. And, although he hasn't said it, maybe even loved.

I might mention, too, that if given time for things to grow, I might be able to love him with my whole damn heart.

"You make me happy," he says, kissing my forehead.

The boys race down the steps, and we part. I immediately miss his body against mine and his hands around my waist. We share a smile before I turn to the stove.

"What's he doing here?" Dylan asks.

I glance over my shoulder and take in his scowl pointed directly at Jay. *Great. Freaking great.*

"I invited him for dinner since I hit him in the face with a ball," Carter says, climbing into his chair at the table. "I told him I have an arm on me."

"How are you tonight, Dylan?" Jay asks.

"I've been better." He sits across from his brother, keeping an eye on Jay. "So you're here because my brother hit you with a ball? Do you not know how to catch?"

"He does," Carter says, oblivious to the tension in the room. "He just took his eye off the ball. He'll learn."

I set a platter of hamburgers on the table next to the chips. I grab an extra plate, utensils, and a glass.

"Sit here, Jay," I say, putting the items at the seat across the table from me.

"Thank you, Gabrielle. This looks delicious," he says, sitting between the boys.

I get situated on my chair. "Carter, do you want to say grace?"

Jay swipes his hat off and bows his head. Dylan's chin tucks against his chest, but he keeps an eye on Jay. I close my eyes and say a silent prayer that this goes well.

"Thank you, God, for this food. Thanks for everything," Carter says. "Thanks for my mom and Dylan, most of the time. And thanks for Jay. And please help him learn how to play baseball."

I peek up and find Jay watching me. He grins.

"And thanks for our old cat, Meow Mix. And please tell Daddy we said hi and that we miss him. Okay? Thanks. Amen."

"Amen," I say, releasing a breath. "That was nice, Carter. Good job."

"I'm the family pray-er," he tells Jay. "It used to be Dylan, but one time he said a bad word during the prayer, and Mom said, '*That's it! Carter is the new pray-er.*'"

He shrugs, taking a bun from the package and adding a burger.

"How are you guys liking school?" Jay asks, making his sandwich.

"I love it," Carter says. "I love my teacher and have lots of friends, and I get two recesses, which is the best thing ever."

"Nice. What about you, Dylan?"

"Well, I'm flunking woodshop, which I didn't want to take in the first place. They're doing the math I did last year, so that's boring as fuck."

"Dylan, *watch your mouth*," I say, firing him a warning glare that he completely ignores.

"And the cafeteria food sucks," he says without missing a beat. "It's just peachy. Thanks for asking."

Jay lifts a brow and takes a bite of his burger.

Carter goes on a tangent and leads us through his day, hour by hour. Jay listens, asking questions and nodding along. Dylan looks like he could spit nails. I want to go to bed and not wake up until morning.

I knew this wasn't going to go without hiccups. I knew Dylan was going to resist Jay joining us for dinner. But I didn't expect my son to be *so* prickly.

Still, if I block out Dylan's attitude problem—which isn't exclusive to Jay being here—and focus instead on the dynamic between me, Carter, and Jay, it makes my heart sing. It's so nice having someone else here. It's so nice having a man here. It's so nice having *Jay* here.

And I think Carter agrees.

I glance at Dylan and catch him fuming quietly at me. *I don't think he's on the same page as me and Carter.*

"Hey, Dylan," Jay says, setting his drink on the table. "If it doesn't rain tomorrow evening, I will come by and hang the new light your mom bought for the front porch. Think you'll be around to lend me a hand?"

"Nope," Dylan says without looking at him.

"Oh. All right. Not a problem," Jay says. He catches my eye and winces. "Do you need any help with your woodworking class?"

Dylan slams his hamburger down on his plate. "No. I don't need any help with my woodworking class. I don't want to help you hang anything. I don't even want you here, but I don't have a say in that, I guess, huh, Mom?"

"You are going to stop that right now," I say.

What on earth is going on here? I'm bamboozled. Sure, Dylan can be a jerk face, as Carter says, but the last time he interacted with Jay, it was much calmer. Respectful, even. *What changed?*

"Why? Or what?" He rolls his eyes. "This is my house, too, you know. I think expressing my thoughts on unwelcome guests in our house is perfectly acceptable."

"Well, I like him here," Carter says, holding a chip in the air. "And I invited him, so shut up, Dylan."

"Don't say *shut up*, Carter," I say, the back of my neck pinching. "And you, Dylan, can express your thoughts on anything you want as long as you're respectful." I wait until his eyes meet mine. "Knock it off. I mean it."

He sits up taller in his seat. "I'm not a little kid like you think I am. I know what's going on. I know this jackass—"

"Go to your room, now," I say, fury and embarrassment filling my words.

"—is your new boyfriend—"

"Jay is your boyfriend?" Carter says, his jaw falling to the floor. "So cool!"

"—and you're happily forgetting that our dad just died. And you moved us from our home, where Dad is, and now you're trying to throw a pathetic replacement on us," Dylan says, his voice rising.

"You're my mom's boyfriend?" Carter asks Jay.

I don't dare to even look across the table at Jay. I can imagine what he must be thinking. Knowing his soft spot for situations involving single mothers and kids, I bet he's ready to get up and bolt for the door.

And I can't blame him. A part of me would like to join him.

"Do you want to talk outside, man to man?" Jay asks, his tone steady. "I'd be happy to do that."

"*No*, I don't want to talk to you," Dylan says, scooting his chair back. It squeaks across the floor. "I don't even want you here."

"Well, guess what. It's not your choice," I say, less cool than Jay. I'm racked with guilt, and logic, humiliation, and determination not to let my son ruin something good. "I'm not trying to replace your father, Dylan. But I am trying to live my life."

"Do you even care about us? Or are you leaving us behind too?"

"Why are you being so mean, Dyl?" Carter asks.

My eyes fill with tears.

I don't want to have this conversation in front of Jay. And I hate that we're having it to begin with. I have avoided this for the last year, but this is what I need. I'm desperate for a life that's mine—a reason to get up that's *for me*.

The last couple of weeks have been the happiest I've been in a long time. Despite the mom guilt that comes along with every choice I make as a parent, I know, down deep, there's nothing wrong with moving on.

"Do I even care about you? I love you and your brother more than the entire universe," I say, the tears flowing down my cheeks. "But it's time we start trying to move on, Dylan."

"Are you serious?" he snaps back.

"Yes. It's what your father would want," I say.

"Convenient that you can speak for him since he's not here to defend himself. What do you even know about what he would want? He divorced you."

"He was my best friend for many years, Dylan. I knew him better than anyone, and the last thing I'd *ever* want to do is disrespect his memory. I'm not getting into our divorce because that's none of your business. But your father and I loved each other, and I know he'd kick my ass if he knew I was letting you and Carter—and me, for that matter—sit around and stop living." I wipe my face with a napkin. "You can believe that or not. But it's the truth."

"I choose not."

Dylan stands and storms out of the kitchen, leaving the three of us sitting in his wake.

"He's big mad," Carter says. "Like, big, *big* mad."

I need a moment to gather myself. But all I feel is Jay's and Carter's eyes on me.

Jay. He saw and heard all that. Damn it.

I look across the table. He smiles softly at me.

"Hey, Carter," he says. "Does your mom ever let you eat in your room?"

"Sometimes. Not very often."

"Does that sound like fun?" Jay asks.

"Yeah. Duh. I can play my game and eat my burger."

I nod, then look at my plate.

"Why don't you go ahead and eat up there tonight?" Jay says. "I'll take it up with your mom."

"Yeah!" Carter grabs his plate and flies to the steps. "Don't yell at me, Mom! It's Jay's fault."

The sound of his voice makes me smile, despite my aching heart.

"Well, that went worse than I imagined," I say, my temple throbbing. "I'm so sorry you had to see and hear that."

Jay sits back and sighs. "You know that none of that has anything to do with me or you, right?"

"Right." I snort. "That has everything to do with me and a little bit with you, probably."

"He's in a bad spot. He's a teenage boy with raging hormones who's missing his dad. And he wants to do everything he can to protect his family. He sees me as a threat—like I'm going to be the guy that takes you, his last person on earth, away from him."

Oh, damn. "I didn't even recognize that."

"I was a teenage boy once." He rolls his eyes. "One that played varsity baseball and lettered for four years, despite what your youngest might say."

That makes me smile.

We sit quietly for a while, listening to Carter's footsteps above us. Finally, Jay sighs.

"Do you want me to go?" he asks. "I don't want to leave you alone if you need me. But I also imagine you might want to talk to Dylan."

"I do need to go up and talk to him. But, gosh, I don't want to."

Jay stands. "You go upstairs and wash your face. Take a second to calm down. Then go talk to him and remind him you aren't going anywhere." He stops beside me and kisses the top of my head. "I'll put the plates in the dishwasher and the leftovers in the fridge. Then I'll head home."

I put my arms around his waist and nuzzle against his stomach. "Thank you."

"It's no problem."

And then I think of Dylan's words. *"Convenient that you can speak for him since he's not here to defend himself. What do you even know about what he would want? He divorced you."*

A million thoughts flood my brain. *Is Jay right? Is Dylan saying all those horrible things because he's trying to protect his family? Trying to make sure he doesn't lose me?*

The thought breaks my heart into pieces. I've never once considered that Dylan, or Carter, would be fearful of losing me too—especially not to another man.

But how can he consider Jay a threat? Jay has been nothing but kind and supportive to both of them. Dylan can't seriously consider that I'd betray Chris's memory . . . *can he?*

With a heavy heart, I get to my feet and wish this night had gone differently. I have no idea what to say to Dylan. Not a clue. If Jay walked away from me now, I wouldn't be surprised. Hell, I kind of want to walk away from me right now too.

Instead, Jay pulls me in for a hug. In his typical way, it exudes comfort and strength. It makes me believe that we'll all get through this . . . somehow.

"I'll see you tomorrow," I say.

"I hope so."

We share a smile before I head for the stairs.

CHAPTER TWENTY-THREE

Gabrielle

"Dylan, can I come in?" I ask.

"No."

I crack open the door anyway and find him lying on his bed with his back to me.

"You don't have to say anything," I say. "But I want to talk to you."

"Whatever."

I step into his room and close the door behind me, then pad across the room to sit on the edge of his bed.

His room is decorated in blues and blacks, his father's favorite colors. I used to tease Christopher that his whole wardrobe was blue and black. I've often wondered whether Dylan likes those colors or whether they remind him of Chris.

"Seeing you lying like this reminds me of when you were a baby," I say gently. "I used to come to your room and check on you every thirty minutes. Your dad used to say I wasn't leaving you room to grow. But if I didn't get up and check on you in the middle of the night, he'd say he needed a snack. Then I'd catch him watching you from the doorway just like I did."

I place my hand on his back and sigh.

"I miss him, Dylan. Not a day goes by that I don't think of your dad a hundred times. We might've been divorced, but I talked to him every day. He knew things about me that no one else knew—not even Cricket. We shared so many things together. Every big, important moment until this point in my life was with your dad."

My voice flows smoothly through the room.

"He was so excited when he learned he was having boys both times," I say, smiling at the memory. "He literally leaped up and shouted in the ultrasound room. The technician laughed so hard she almost peed her pants."

Dylan's back shifts, and I wonder whether he's smiling too.

"That man loved you more than anyone has ever loved another person," I say, my voice thick with emotion. "It absolutely kills me that he isn't here to watch you grow up. It can't be him in the yard playing catch with Carter. He's not teaching you how to fix things around the house. Neither of you will go sledding with him or hear his stories from high school or learn to drive a car with him in the passenger's seat."

Tears trickle down my cheeks as I remember my ex-husband.

"He worked so hard, Dylan—sometimes twelve, fourteen hours a day when you were a baby, to save money so he could enjoy you as a teenager." I laugh. "Oh, the irony in that."

My son rolls over and faces me. His eyes are red. The front of his shirt is damp.

I want to cover him with a hug and try to glue him back together by sheer willpower. But I can't. It won't work. And the helplessness in that is the most angering thing in my life.

"No one in the world could replace Christopher Solomon," I say, squeezing Dylan's leg. "Anyone who tried would be a cheap replica."

"I miss him so much, Mom."

I reach for him, but he pulls away. It breaks my heart.

"It's not fair that we move on like he didn't exist," Dylan says. "What if he's watching us from heaven right now and sees Jay in our kitchen? What if Dad's feelings are hurt? What if he thinks we forget or don't love him?"

There's no way to stop the pain ricocheting in my chest, nor can I stop the flow of tears dripping onto my shirt. But I would move heaven and hell to take the pain out of my child's eyes.

"Do you know what worries me at night?" I ask.

He shakes his head, his T-shirt pulled up and over his nose.

"I lie at night and worry myself sick that your dad is watching us from heaven and is mad at me," I say.

"For what?"

"Oh, for failing as a mother. For letting you and Carter be sad for too long. For not figuring out how to make you guys happy. For not knowing how to handle you when you get angry and forgetting vegetables at dinner." I laugh through the tears. "He always wanted you to have vegetables."

Dylan almost smiles.

"You and Carter were the apples of his eye," I say. "And even though we were divorced, he wanted me to be happy. Hell, Dylan, that's why we divorced. We divorced so we could be happier. We were best friends, but there was room for a different kind of love in our hearts. I wanted him to have that. And your dad wanted me to have that. He told me so."

He sits up and scoots against the headboard. He watches me warily, unconvinced—but closer to accepting reality than before.

"I would never try to bring someone into your lives that I thought was unhealthy or dangerous. And I would never introduce you to anyone that I didn't believe, without a doubt, that your father would approve of. Because he might not be here with us, Dylan, but he's still your dad. And I will honor his wishes and make choices for you boys that I know he would want me to make." I smile at him. "So no one is going to Ohio State—not even if it's your life's dream and you'll pay for it yourself. I can't let that happen. Dad was a big Michigan fan."

Dylan's shoulders fall, and he breathes deeply. The corners of his lips tip upward.

"I know seeing Jay here shocked you," I say. "And maybe I underestimated you. I should've told you first or at least not assumed you wouldn't notice that he and I are . . ."

"Is he your boyfriend?"

My gaze falls to the blankets, and I think about it. "Honestly, Dylan, I don't know. He and I enjoy spending time together. I think he's a good man. I think, *I hope*, it has the potential to be something that lasts a long time. But it's still too early to start slapping labels on it."

He sighs, staring at the wall across the room. The wheels are turning inside his head. He's thinking deeply; his bottom lip is between his teeth. It's a quirk of Christopher's, but I don't mention it now. I'll save that for another day.

"Well, what do you want me to do?" He pulls his gaze to mine. "What am I supposed to think about this?"

"I'm not telling you what to think. I'm asking that you respect Jay when he's here and don't act like a child. He's done nothing to you and doesn't deserve you acting like you did tonight. You're better than that, Dylan."

My son pulls in a long, deep breath. "I'll try."

Thank God. "Thank you. Sometimes, we have to respect people even when we don't like them. Even if we don't like who they are in our lives. And sadly, this is a part of life, Dylan. Showing respect even when it's hard. And that's the man your father would want you to be. So yes, please try. That's all I want you to do, buddy. Try."

He leans up and wraps his arms around my neck. His hug is quick and tight, before he drops to the bed and rolls away from me.

"Will you leave me alone now?" he asks, his voice muffled by the blankets.

I pat his leg and stand. "I will. Thank you for listening to me. And thank you for trying."

"Go."

Teenagers, man. "Good night. I love you."

"Bye."

I leave his room, shutting the door behind me.

CHAPTER TWENTY-FOUR

JAY

I swallow the last gulp of tea in my glass, then rinse it out and place it in the sink.

The sun hovers above the horizon, promising an hour or two of sunlight before it sets for the evening. I wanted to be home an hour ago. But thanks to the pop-up showers that hit the jobsite all afternoon, we didn't get out of there on time.

My irritation can't be blamed solely on the weather, though. It has more to do with the kink in my stomach after last night's dinner than anything else. That's what kept me awake until a brief nap at dawn. That ordeal is what ran through my mind all day.

Dylan's pain has haunted me for the last twenty-four hours.

My heart hurts for all of them. Suffering a loss like they have is brutal. Gabrielle's ability to keep everything going in the midst of the tragedy is a testament to her strength.

She's an amazing woman.

What's bothered me since I left their house is that I can't help. This isn't something I can get involved with, because to Dylan, I'm the enemy. Or, at least, that's what he wants us to believe.

The problem is that I'm not the enemy, and we both know that.

My phone rings on the counter. I pick it up when I see it's Gabrielle.

"Hey," I say.

"Hi. How was work today?"

"Wet."

"Now you know how I feel every day."

I grin. "Funny. How was your day?"

"Hard."

"Now you know how *I* feel every day."

She laughs. "Look, I know we talked about this last night. But if you don't feel comfortable coming over here tonight, I understand."

"Do you not want me to come?"

"I didn't say that. It's just that you aren't here yet, and I know you got home about twenty-seven minutes ago because Carter yelled the moment you pulled into your driveway about wanting to go get you to play catch."

I touch my still-swollen eye. "Do you think you could get him interested in something less painful? What about . . . piano lessons?"

Gabrielle bursts out laughing. The sound settles in my gut, unwinding one of the knots that's been plaguing me all day.

"No to the piano," she says. "Your eye might feel better, but your ears would not."

"Damn it." I lean against the counter. "We're hanging the light on the porch, right?"

"Yup. I about killed myself trying to get in the other night in the dark. It's a matter of life and death at this point. I mean, I'd do it myself but—"

"It's electrical," we say in unison.

I can't wipe the smile off my face. "I'll be there in a few."

"Okay."

"See ya."

"Bye, handsome."

I slide my phone down the counter until it crashes into the bananas. *This woman is going to be the death of me.*

My boots are by the door. I slip them on and then head across the lawn. Carter sees me coming when I'm three steps into the grass and hauls ass across the yard. His hair flows behind him, and his smile is as wide as Texas. It does something to my insides that concerns me.

"Okay," he says, stopping on a dime at my side. Then he walks beside me, no worse for wear. "I've been thinking. Some guys are field guys. Some guys are batters. Maybe you're a batter."

This child. "Carter, buddy, I have some old videotapes of me playing baseball that my mother took when I was in high school."

"Really? They had videotapes back then?" His face contorts. "Wait. What's a videotape?"

I sigh. "Anyway, maybe we can sit down and watch some of it before we practice again. Just so you know that I know what I'm talking about." *And that I was recruited by colleges my senior year.*

"Okay."

He has no idea what I'm talking about.

"Hey, Jay?"

"Yeah?"

"My brother might hate your guts, but I don't. I like you."

Whoa. I clear my throat. "Did Dylan say he hated my guts?"

"No. But it sure sounded like it."

Fair enough.

Still, my hated guts twist as we reach the front porch. Carter babbles on about how to hold a baseball, but my mind is elsewhere.

I wonder if I could talk to Dylan. Would that be overstepping? Would that make it worse?

I take a deep breath. *Easy, Stetson. That's sounding an awful lot like being involved on a deeper level.*

Fuck. But isn't that what I'm supposed to be wanting now? To become involved?

My heart hurts for the boy. I want to help because I know I can. But helping always winds up biting me in the ass.

Gabrielle comes out wearing shorts and a genuine smile.

Maybe it won't bite me in the ass this time. This is different from my situation with Melody and Izzy. I feel it in my soul.

"Hey," Gabrielle says, running her hand through Carter's hair. She grins at me. "Do you think it's safe to work on this since it's so damp out here from the rain?"

"As long as the electrical parts are dry, it shouldn't be a problem."

She yawns and sits on the porch swing. "Is it just me, or has this been the longest day ever?"

"It's been the longest day ever for me," Carter says. "We had music class today. Do you know how long that takes? Forever."

Guess no piano, after all.

"It was pretty long for me too," I say. "I had a lot on my mind."

"What's that mean?" Carter asks.

I chuckle. "It means I was distracted, which is never a good thing at work."

"Oh." He squints at me. "Your eye is still black, you know."

"I'm aware."

"Okay." He turns to Gabrielle. "Can I have a snack? An itty-bitty one? It's a long time before dinner, so it won't spoil anything."

She holds out a hand. "Yes. You may. Only one, though."

I'm not sure Carter hears anything past the *yes* over his shouts of victory and the door shutting behind him.

"Can I sit by you?" I ask, making my way to her.

"Please do."

I lower myself onto the swing, and then Gabrielle snuggles up next to me. Instantly, the stress of the day fades into thin air. *How does she do that? Make everything just feel . . . right?*

"Do you know what's weird?" she asks.

"What's that?"

"Having you here makes things just . . . better." She looks up at me and grins. "I don't want to sound clingy, but it's true."

I kiss the top of her head.

Her admission doesn't sound clingy. It sounds like I'm a lucky man. But I don't want to tell her that—not here. Not after last night's debacle with Dylan and at a moment when Carter could run outside jabbering away about baseball. But I do want to tell her how I feel. I want Gabrielle to know that this isn't even the situation I thought it would be when I warned her the first night we had sex.

This is something more.

It's real.

And as scared as I was to fall for anyone—a single mom, no less—being with Gabrielle and Carter and Dylan, eventually, is the easiest, most *right* thing in the world. I don't know where in the hell it's going, but I know where I hope it leads eventually. I think we can get there.

That's what I want Gabrielle to know. She's not alone. I'm here and I want to make their lives richer, safer. And in some way, in the earliest form, I might even be falling in love with her. I might also care a lot more than I want to admit about those boys.

"Do you think we can figure out how to get the evening to ourselves tomorrow?" I ask.

"Probably. Why?"

I smile at her. "I just want to have you to myself and talk to you about some things without keeping one eye open for a baseball coming at me."

"Only one eye because that's all you have?"

I shake my head, making her laugh.

"All right," Carter says, bursting out the door with the energy of a child hyped on chocolate. "I forgot to tell you something."

"Who? Me?" Gabrielle asks.

"Nope." He turns to me. *"You."*

"Why does that feel like a threat?" I ask.

He bends over laughing, even though I'm not sure he understood the joke. Gabrielle, on the other hand, elbows me in the ribs.

"Okay," I say. "What did you forget to tell me? I know my eye is black. So if it's that, I got it."

"*No.* It's not that. It's that at school, they're having a Boat Box Derby."

"A what?" Gabrielle asks.

"A Boat Box Derby."

I lean forward, resting my elbows on my knees. "Do you mean a Soap Box Derby?"

"Yes. That. I didn't know what it was, but all the kids were talking about it. They do it every year in our grade and the principal comes and *there's cake.*" He pauses to make a face, as if that's a hook enough. He puts his hands on my forearms and leans so close that I can smell the chocolate on his breath. "I signed us up for it."

He stares holes in my eyes. And for the first time since I met Carter Solomon, he's as serious as a heart attack.

I'm not sure what to say. Sure, I'm happy to help him with whatever he needs. But this feels very . . . parental. That's what fucks me up a little bit.

"Carter, honey," Gabrielle says, scrambling to pull his attention away from me. "You can't just sign Jay up for stuff. Why would you do that? I'm happy to help you build a . . . soap box?"

He sighs animatedly. "It's a derby car, *Mom*, and that's why you can't help. You don't even know what it is. And Jay is good at building stuff. Have you even been in his garage?"

"I have," she says, her cheeks pink. "But just because he can build things doesn't mean he has time to build you a derby car."

"He does," Carter says happily. "All the kids are having their dads help them. And I told them Jay was practically my dad—"

Dylan bursts through the door, making us all jump. His face is beet red as he stares us all down. "Fuck that. He's *not* your dad."

I want to step in and say something. *But what do I say? Do I tell Carter that I'm not his dad? Or that I'm happy to help? Do I tell Dylan no one is trying to replace his dad, or do I stay out of it so I don't make this worse?*

"Okay, Dylan, calm down," Gabrielle says, standing up.

"*I'm not calming down.* You lied to me."

Gabrielle flinches. "What did I lie to you about?"

"All that stuff you said last night in my room. About how no one is trying to make Jay our dad. And how great my dad was and how much you want to do what's right by him. And now I come out here and hear Carter tell him"—Dylan glares at me—"that he's practically our dad. *I don't fucking think so.*"

"Dylan, can I talk to you privately for a moment?" I ask.

"No." He looks at me like I've grown three heads. "I'm not talking to you. I hate you. I wish we had never met you."

"Dylan!" Gabrielle says.

"Why are you being a jerk face to Jay?" Carter asks, reaching for his brother's arm.

Dylan shoves his hand away. "Because you don't understand what this means, Carter. This man is not your dad. He's not *like your dad.* He's nothing to you. Do you hear me?"

Carter's eyes fill with tears.

"I just want to hear you out," I say.

"Don't. Care," Dylan says, scowling at me. "There isn't an open spot in our family for you. We had a dad and now he's gone and the last thing we need is to have another guy step in just so he can leave us too."

"I've heard enough," Gabrielle says.

Dylan turns his scowl to her. "Good, me too." He reaches for Carter. "Come on, buddy. It's me and you. This guy is nothing to us. All right?"

"Dylan . . ." Gabrielle says, but her words are cut off by the look Carter gives us over his shoulder as he goes inside with his brother.

I exhale, running my hands down my face. *How did this turn upside down so fast?*

The boy's words cut through me, sobering me out of my daydream. *Am I delusional to think that I can fit into this family the way I want to? Is it possible to join them at their ages and expect to be accepted into the fold?*

My face heats as reality slams into me.

Gabrielle's sadness is palpable. "I'm sorry, Jay. I need to go in and deal with this mess."

"I'll go with you."

She frowns. "Thank you, but that's probably not a good idea."

What?

"Look, Jay. These are my kids. This is my problem. Not yours."

It's not the words that bother me. It's the tone she uses that cuts me to the quick.

"These are my kids. This is my problem. Not yours."

It's reminiscent of the last argument that Melody and I had the day before I came home and she and Izzy were gone. We had argued the night before over the fact that I hadn't proposed to her. The next day, the school called because Izzy was sick and needed to be picked up. That was the day I discovered that I had been removed from my daughter's emergency contacts list.

"She's my child, Jay. If you wanted her to be yours, you'd do what you need to do."

A tightness spreads through my body, nearly strangling me in the process. It's too close to déjà vu to be comfortable. It's too similar to the worst day of my life for me to live it again.

How did I get here? How did I get to a place where I fucking care? How did I put myself in this position to be kicked out of the lives of people I care about, like I don't matter at all?

This is crushing me.

Do I like this woman? Hell yes. *Do I want to try for more?* Absolutely. I can't deny it. But if this is what it feels like after being with her for a few weeks, then I don't think I can take the risk of waiting for a few years to pass before she says something like that again.

"These are my kids. This is my problem. Not yours." How apt. How fucking true. *You gotta move on from this now, Stetson. Do it before it's too late for everyone involved.*

Whether she knows it or not, Gabrielle Solomon just drew the final line in the sand.

"You know what? You're right. They are your kids, and it is your problem," I say, my heart pounding in my ears. "I hope you guys figure it out."

"What are you saying, Jay?"

I shrug. "I'm not saying anything other than . . ." My shoulders fall. "Tell Dylan I'm sorry. I'm sorry to you too."

I plant a kiss on her head, avoid her eyes, and walk down the steps toward home.

CHAPTER TWENTY-FIVE

Gabrielle

The door is locked.

I ring the doorbell and wait.

The moon is bright and high in the sky. The air is warm, hinting of summer, and scented like flowers. Sitting on the back porch with a glass of wine would be a lovely night. *God knows I need the wine.* But I also need to check on Jay.

I'm not sure what happened earlier this evening. All I know is that a boulder has been in my stomach since I watched him walk home. It was the way his eyes didn't sparkle when he spoke to me. The hollowness in his voice when he said goodbye. His lips lingered a moment too long against my head, almost in a silent farewell, before he marched off.

It does not sit right with me, but I've been too preoccupied to deal with it. Until now.

It takes longer than expected for him to answer the door.

My heart skips a beat as the lock clicks free. Slowly, he comes into view.

A pair of plaid sleep pants. Shirtless. Messy hair like he's been running his hands through it all evening.

Is that true? Has he? Has he been as confused and frustrated by this whole thing as me?

"Hey," I say, expecting him to move so I can go inside. But he doesn't.

"How did things go?"

"They went. Dylan is calmer than he was, but he's still pissed. I talked to him until I was blue in the face and finally decided to give him space to cool off."

Jay nods. "Probably a good idea."

I shiver, and it has nothing to do with the temperature. It has everything to do with his chilly reception.

"Are you going to let me in?" I ask.

He takes so long to step to the side that I think it won't happen. Finally, he moves and lets me pass.

My heart pounds as I step into his house like I've done most nights for weeks. It might be for a quick kiss, and it might be for more. But I've been invited to come by, begged to show up, and welcomed in when I do . . . except tonight.

Everything in me panics.

"What's going on, Jay?"

He stands out of arm's reach—a very un-Jay-like thing to do.

"I think," he says slowly and steadily, "that we got ahead of ourselves."

What? My eyes grow wide. "What are you talking about?"

"Tonight was a wake-up call, Gabrielle. We live in a fantasy world if we think things will work out between us."

My blood runs cold. *"Jay."*

"It's not even us. It's the situation. It's . . . No, I guess it is us." He sighs, watching me closely. "We both need to face reality."

I'm speechless. Even if I could form words, I couldn't say them. I'm clobbered, completely blindsided, by this, and it's all I can do to keep my head from spinning.

"This was a bad idea to start with," he says. "I should've heeded my better judgment and saved us the trouble."

A cord is snapped, and I'm a live wire.

"What do you mean you could've saved us the trouble?" I ask louder than necessary. "Is that what this has been to you? Trouble?"

How can this be happening? Oh, my goodness. *What do I do?*

My jaw hangs open, and every breath is audible. The air is hot, going in and out of my mouth rapidly.

"It doesn't matter, Gabrielle."

"The hell it doesn't."

He groans, exhaling. "Look, I'm not interested in getting involved in a situation that will only tear us apart."

"Go on. Explain that."

"What do you mean?"

"I mean, explain how getting involved with me will tear us apart." My nostrils flare. "You pushed for this. *You* came to my house and worked on my deck. *You* insisted on helping me with my project. *You* engaged with Dylan, and you humored Carter. And now *you* want to back out? What the fuck, Jay?"

He scrubs his hands down his face.

My disbelief turns to a hot, sharp fury. This isn't right, and it isn't fair. And if he thinks I will just be rejected into the night, he's wrong.

"If we get involved any deeper than we are, I'm going to tear your family apart," he says.

"So you're pushing me out because my teenager is having a meltdown? Is that what this is?" I almost laugh. "I thought you were more of a man than that."

"Dylan hates me, Gabrielle. Or he thinks he does. And you refuse to let me talk to him and try to help him, even though I have insight that could help him."

"I—"

"And Carter is signing me up for father-and-son projects. I'm left wondering if I've overstepped my bounds somewhere and led him to believe I was trying to be his dad. Because I've been careful, so careful, Gabrielle, not to do that. For his good and mine."

His jaw sets, and the mood between us shifts. I take a deep breath and try to focus—to calm down. Something I've been trying to do for hours. *Why are men so fucking complicated?*

I don't want to be rational and listen to what he's really saying, because a part of me doesn't want to bother with someone who gives in so quickly. My life seems to be a constant struggle, a permanent battle with different enemies. If he doesn't want to fight with me through this, there's no hope for the future.

But as I think about who Jay is, he's not a quitter. He held on with Melody for a long time for Izzy. He's been patient and caring toward the boys, even when Dylan has been not so lovable. And he didn't give up on me at the beginning, even when his fear told him to pull away. He didn't. He followed his heart and kept coming around.

I'm fairly positive I'm in love with him. And I think this is more than him just backing away because he's afraid he's going to tear our family apart. That he feels like it's too hard. It's not rejection I'm seeing in his eyes.

Jay is terrified.

A part of our conversation the night after Murray's runs through my head. *"That's why you're scared of getting involved with me. Because I'm a single mom just like Melody."*

Fear swims in Jay's eyes. The browns swirl with the golds, creating a beautiful but murky hazel hue that is as confusing as this situation. I only know that I hate seeing him like this. I hate seeing him scared—scared of me.

"They're your kids, Gabrielle. You were right. I don't belong in the nitty-gritty shit. It's not my place."

My voice from earlier echoes in my head. *"Look, Jay. These are my kids. This is my problem. Not yours."*

I pass a swallow and step toward him. He stiffens, silently telling me to stop.

"I didn't mean it like that," I say softly, his fear eating away at my heartstrings. "I was upset and frustrated and angry and worried. All I wanted to do was to get to my kids and try to fix this. I didn't mean to hurt you."

"You didn't."

Oh, but I think I did. "You wanted to talk to me tomorrow night. What did you want to talk about?"

"Doesn't matter."

"Yes, it does."

He paces to the other side of the living room. "We need to stop this."

"This argument?" I ask, even though I know that's not what he means. He means we need to stop this—*us*. "I'm happy to stop arguing with you."

He places his hands on the back of a chair, keeping it between us like a barricade.

"I don't want to do this anymore," he says. "We can't."

Anger bubbles from the depths of my soul. *Well, maybe I was wrong. Maybe he really doesn't want us.* "You don't mean that."

"I do."

"Why?" I glare at him. "Why did you go through all the trouble to make this happen, only to back out? Is this a game to you? Are you bored?"

"You know that's not true."

"Then what is it, Jay?" I refuse to let him look away. "Tell me why we suddenly aren't a good match. Is it because you aren't into me anymore?"

"Gabrielle . . ."

"Because I know the answer. It's because things got hard, you got scared, and now you want to quit."

He doesn't refute it. Probably because he can't.

I give him time to come around and admit I'm right so we can work through it.

But he doesn't.

Tears fill my eyes as I realize what's happening—that he answered the question I asked myself at Scottie's a while back.

When things get hard, he won't fight for me.

Why did I expect differently?

A swell of emotion rises from deep inside my soul—from a place that I've been harboring it for years. This is the theme of my life. Aside from something happening to my children, it's my biggest fear too.

I'm not worth fighting for.

Tears flood my eyes, making it a danger to blink. My heart pounds in a silent wail of pain. I tremble in my struggle to remain composed, so Jay doesn't see my heart break at his feet.

His blank stare scalds me, burning me with the truth.

When Christopher asked for a divorce, his words were soft. He wanted more for me. He still loved me. We'd still do life together, just from different houses. But the truth is that our love wasn't worth fighting for.

Hell, Levi and I weren't in love in elementary school, but even he didn't find me worth fighting for. It seems like a ridiculous thing to think about now, but the similarity can't be denied.

The differences in Levi, Christopher, and Jay can't be dismissed either. Levi and I weren't destined to be an item. We were children. And as much as it hurt when Christopher walked away, I knew it was the right answer. It was painful to my heart, but it was right in my soul.

There is nothing, abso-fucking-lutely nothing, right about losing Jay . . . except pining after him would be a giant waste of my time.

That's a lesson better learned too soon than too late.

"It doesn't matter how much I like you," I say, backing toward the door. I will the tears to stay away until I get outside. "It doesn't even matter that I was considering that there could come a time when I could even love you."

His face falls.

"None of that matters because you're right," I say, my hand on the doorknob. "We need to stop this. Because I won't fight for a man that won't bother to fight for me."

"Gabrielle . . ."

I open the door and step outside, jogging across the lawn before I can hear him call after me.

Because I won't stop.

If he's willing to give up on me so easily, then it's best he gives up on me now, before things get serious . . . and I admit that I think I'm already in love with him.

Jay

I growl into the air, flexing every muscle in my body until it screams to be released. "Damn it!"

My feet dance, wanting to run after Gabrielle and sweep her up in my arms. I'm certain my heart is bleeding. But my brain, the only part of me that I can still trust, reminds me of self-preservation.

I cannot go after her.

The look in her eyes pierces my soul every time it flashes through my mind.

"Because I won't fight for a man that won't bother to fight for me."

Can't she see that's not what's happening? Doesn't she realize that this relationship is only going to hurt all of us?

I knew better than to do this. Damn it, *I knew better*.

"No single moms, Jay. Don't get in a situation where you fall for a woman and her fucking kids. Be smarter than that," I say, mocking myself. "Jay, you're a fucking fool."

I turn all the lights out and lock the door again.

"You can't risk it. You can't keep falling for them," I say to the empty house. "You can't be the problem for Dylan and be banned from trying to help him. You can't be the poison."

I still.

Fixing things with Dylan won't fix things with Izzy.

My stomach clenches, and the distinct taste of bile coats my tongue.

I pace the floor, my brain suddenly clear.

My desire to help Dylan stems from a fear that I didn't do enough to help Izzy. I know down deep that isn't fair—that I did all I could for her. But knowing that Dylan is struggling and sitting back and watching him hurt and not doing a damn thing about it feels a lot like I'm failing someone again.

Did I overstep? Maybe.

"But was walking away overstepping too?" I ask, my voice falling flat in the empty house.

Even as I ask the question, I know the answer.

I took the easy way out, even if it was inevitable.

I stand in the dark and look out the kitchen window at Gabrielle's house. The lights are off there too. I wonder if she's awake in her bed or in the kitchen with a cup of tea. Is she talking to Dylan or helping Carter get back to sleep?

Is she crying?

Does she hate me?

"I could never hate you, Gabrielle. Not when I think I love you."

The shadows cover me as I turn and head for bed.

CHAPTER TWENTY-SIX

Gabrielle

I hate to be the one to admit this," Cricket says, breezing into Scottie's kitchen. "But Della—you're a genius."

Della bows as if she's a princess.

Scottie and I laugh from behind the island.

Cricket drops her bag on Scottie's kitchen table. The sun shines on her through the window, highlighting the blond streaks in her red hair. There's a glow about her that I used to know personally. I used to have it too. Cricket beams practically as brightly as the new tennis bracelet around her wrist.

"Thank you for moving the monthly cocktail date up so I can fill you all in," she says, accepting a peachy drink from Della. "It's so fun to be the one with news."

"I want you to know it's been killing me not to ask how things are going with Peter," Della says, side-eyeing Cricket. "But since his car has been home every night over the last two weeks, and you've been missing in action, I'm hoping that means you're getting some action."

"Ladies . . ." She presses her lips together until they break into a squeal. "I'm having fun sex!"

Della laughs as Cricket bounces on her toes.

"I take it the trench coat worked," I say, wondering whether it's too soon to ask for another drink.

Cricket sashays across the room. "Oh, it worked, all right. He was shocked at first. I thought I had overplayed my hand and he was going to wrap me back up in the coat and send me to a priest for confession. I didn't need confession until after he"—she gives Della a devilish grin—"*fucked me* on his desk."

"My little girl is growing up," Della says, earning a swat from Cricket.

"I've spent the last fifteen days either being ravaged by my husband or trying to prepare for the next round," Cricket says. "I have no idea what's going on with you girls. Fill me in. What's been happening?"

Scottie looks at me to see whether I want to go first. I look away, making it clear I do not.

Every morning, I wake up and think it will be the day that things get easier. I won't miss Jay as much as I did the day before. I'll stop looking at his driveway to see when he gets home and stop being disappointed when he doesn't arrive until well after dark. Maybe I'll also stop wondering whether the delay is to avoid me and the kids.

How can I miss him this much? How is it possible to have grown that attached to one person in such a short amount of time?

"I'll go," Della says, pouring me another drink. "I met this couple last weekend randomly. I was in a store buying a hammer, of all things, and we just started talking. Anyway, it turns out that those two were into some funky shit, and the wife asked me if I would be her husband's birthday present."

My jaw drops. *"What?"*

She shrugs. "He was hot as hell. Six two, six three, and all muscle."

"Did you do it?" Scottie asks.

"Of course she did it," Cricket says, snorting. "Do you even have to ask?"

"Of course I did it." Della winks at Cricket, earning an eye roll. "I went home with them, and the guy fucked my brains out while the wife

watched from a chair across the room. She loved every minute of it." She looks at us. "What? It's a fetish some people have. I might as well take the orgasms, because someone was going to."

"This only happens to you," Cricket says.

"*Thank God.* That man had a tongue that could do things I've never seen done before—and that's saying something." Della laughs. "So that's my news. Scottie, you're up."

Scottie hops on a barstool and grins. "So Della worked her magic and slipped the vet my number and he called."

"Let me chime in and say the vet is *very* good looking." Della tips her glass toward Scottie. "And he was a complete gentleman while he looked over Lark's dog. Nice catch, babe."

"I can't believe you actually took Lark's dog to the vet to give him Scottie's number," I say.

"If a girl won't help you snag a guy, what kind of a friend is she?" Della asks.

Then help me snag Jay.

The thought alone makes my heart crack a little more, because I don't want to want him. I wish I didn't want to snag him. If only I could hold on to the anger and the hurt and stop replaying the pain in his eyes when he ended things between us.

"We're going to a play on Monday night," Scottie says. "And he made reservations at a fancy restaurant in Columbus. I'm so excited."

"I'm happy for you," I say.

"Thanks." Her smile slowly fades. "Do you wanna go or . . ."

"Yes, Gabby. What's been going on with you and that hunk of a neighbor of yours?" Cricket asks. The room grows still, and she sets her glass down. "What? Why are you all looking at me like that?"

I take a breath. "It's fine. Jay and I aren't seeing each other anymore."

Cricket brings a hand to her chest. "What? Why?"

The thought of going into it blow by blow is exhausting. I've watched it in my head like a bad movie a million times. I've analyzed it, tried to make it make sense—tried to figure out how to punch holes in his arguments so I can march over there and demand *he* make it make sense. But every replay of the night Jay broke up with me ends the same way.

He doesn't want to be a part of my life. Plain and simple. And you can't argue that.

I take a long drink and will the vodka to kick in.

"It's a long story," I say, realizing Cricket isn't moving on until I give her a satisfactory answer. "Basically, he doesn't want to get wrapped up in the kids' lives, and I can't blame him."

Cricket takes a moment to digest this. "That's surprising. It's not like he didn't know you have kids."

"I just think it was a lot different when he had to engage with them, you know? When things got real." I sigh. "And when Dylan turned into a shithead."

"Oh, Gabby," Cricket says. "I'm sorry."

"It's okay. Truly." *Liar.* "The kids obviously come first, and if he can't accept them, then he can't have me."

"I'm just so surprised," Cricket says. "I didn't get that vibe from him."

Scottie puts her arm around me and pulls me into her side. The human contact from someone other than Carter crawling over me, asking me why he can't go to Jay's, is nice.

"Della, give her advice," Cricket says. "You saved my marriage. Save hers."

I lean off Scottie and laugh. "We were *barely* boyfriend and girlfriend. This isn't a marriage to be fixed. It's probably not even something that will work in anyone's imagination—even Della's." *I know. I've tried.*

"Try the trench coat. It works." Cricket shrugs. "Here's a tip: use lingerie that can be torn off your body easily. But don't use the expensive stuff because it just gets obliterated."

"Look at you," Della says. "You're slowly turning into me."

Cricket points at her. "I will never do such a thing. Don't even joke about that."

We all laugh.

Everyone busies themselves getting our meal together. Scottie takes a platter of sandwiches from the refrigerator, lamenting that she had to order them because we didn't give her time to plan an actual meal. Della whips up another pitcher of the peach drinks, and Cricket sets the table. I take the potato salad and sandwich toppings to the table and set them next to the chips.

We chat about nothing as we work, keeping the conversation lighthearted. I weigh in occasionally, but my mind is mostly on Jay.

Once again, I consider writing him a letter. *But what good will it do?* Until he changes his view of dating a single mom, nothing I can do or say will help. And that's what sucks.

Scottie peeks out the window as a truck goes by. "Was that Kyle?"

"Ah, yes." Cricket sighs happily. "Kyle got a new girlfriend, an adorable little thing named Matilda. Well, it turns out that Matilda loathes the sound of his truck as much as I do. And Kyle quickly took it to the shop and had it fixed."

"You didn't pay her off, did you?" Della asks.

"No. But I'm not above it."

"How are your boys doing, Gabby?" Scottie asks. "Are they getting settled in at school and everything?"

We all take a seat around the table and begin making our plates.

"Carter loves it," I say, taking a small turkey sandwich from the tray. "He has three birthday party invitations next week. His popularity is starting to get expensive."

Everyone laughs.

"Dylan is . . ." I scoop a bit of potato salad next to my fork. "Dylan is doing okay. His grades are very mediocre. He's not enthused to go to school in the morning. But I must admit that I haven't gotten a call from the principal in over a week, so that's a plus."

"What on earth could he do to warrant a call every week?" Della asks.

"Oh, having gum in class when you're not supposed to. Not having your computer charged. Not having a writing utensil. Throwing an apple across the lunchroom to see if you can make a basket but hitting a kid in the side of the head instead."

"Ouch," Scottie says.

I sigh. "There's a list. And at some point, they stop just handing out detentions and call the parent every time. I suppose they think we'll get tired of hearing it and will do something about it. But I try. I ground him. Take his phone. Have long talks until I'm out of breath." I shrug. "I don't know what else I can do."

Della holds a forkful of potatoes in front of her mouth. "If a week has passed since the last call, maybe he's starting to pull himself together."

"Let's hope."

Despite Dylan's attitude toward Jay, he hasn't been nicer since Jay left. I thought he'd be relieved, that he might even gloat in his perceived victory. But nothing has shifted. If anything, Dylan seems more upset. More withdrawn. Sadder. I even found Carter in Dylan's room, sitting on his bed and talking to him, this morning. If that's where we are, it might be worse than I thought.

There are times I feel like I'm failing on all fronts with that boy. This is one of them.

The conversation shifts to Taylor from Betty Lou's. She won a beauty pageant at the state level, representing Alden as Miss Coal Festival. My friends brainstorm ways they can donate to the fundraiser to help her attend the national contest. I smile and nod when necessary or prompted. I try to engage myself in what they're saying. But my mind keeps fading back to my neighbor.

My heart pulls, and I wish I could find him and tell him we'll figure it out. I wish I could turn back time and erase our fight from existence. But neither is an option. I'm left with only one.

Try to forget the man next door.

And hope I get my heart back.

After all, it's not the first time I've lost it, so I know I can do it again.

Eventually.

CHAPTER TWENTY-SEVEN

Jay

"Maybe I need to consider Alaska, after all," I say to the empty house.

I sit on the edge of my bed with a load of despair weighing me down. I've done the unthinkable for more than two fucking weeks. For seventeen days, I have come home late and left early—completely making myself unavailable to Gabrielle and Carter. There's no worry that Dylan will try to talk to me.

But even as the word *Alaska* comes out of my mouth, I know it's another impossibility.

I still feel a deep connection to Gabrielle.

If I weren't absolutely certain that my presence in their lives would create a fissure between them, I would be pounding on the door and pleading my case. *I'd fight for them.* I would tell Gabrielle I'm sorry for walking away and telling her we would never work out. I'd apologize to the boys for giving up on them so easily when they deserve a man on their side—not to replace Christopher, but to help them navigate their lives. I would explain that I allowed my past failures and wounds to show up in the worst of times—and they didn't deserve that.

But maybe I don't deserve them either.

"How am I going to do this?" I ask, standing up and meandering around the dark house. "I can't keep living like this. But I can't stand in the shadows, stare at their house at night, and try to send my love to Gabrielle telepathically."

I'm a damn fool.

A sound makes me jump. I stand alert in the bathroom doorway, listening closely for another sound. Again, it rings through the house. Harder this time.

Someone is knocking.

I glance at my watch. *Who would be knocking at my door after midnight?*

I move quietly through the living room and peer out the peephole.

What the hell?

My blood pressure screams as I yank the door open. "Dylan, what's going on? Is everything all right?"

His hair is mussy, like he's been sleeping. He has slumped shoulders, wrinkled clothes, and a frown that touches the ground on both sides. Despite it all, he lifts his chin and looks me in the eye.

"Can I come in, Jay?" he asks.

I step to the side and motion for him to enter. "Of course. What's wrong?" The door closes with a snap.

I turn on a lamp by the couch. The air around us stills. The house is so quiet that it doesn't quite feel real. But the kid in front of me, the one watching me with a silent plea, is as real as it gets.

"Are you okay?" I ask as smoothly as I can manage. "Are your mom and Carter okay? Just answer that for me, please."

He nods. "Yeah. Everyone is fine. I guess."

"You guess?"

He nods again.

You're going to have to talk to me, kid. I scratch the top of my head and think. *How do I get him to open up to me?* "Does your mom know you're here?"

"No. And I don't want her to know."

"Okay. But it's late, Dylan. She will freak out if she can't find you in the house. You know that, right?"

"She's not going to know."

"How are you so sure?"

He looks at the ground, and then back up at me. "Because she's crying in her room."

Oh, God. I grip the back of the couch and try to catch my breath.

"That's why I'm here," he says warily. "I don't want to be here."

I clear my throat. "Of course. But do you know why she's crying? Is everything okay?"

He waits so long to answer me that I'm not sure he will reply. A myriad of emotions sweep across his features so quickly that it's hard to keep up. The one thing I can glean is that Dylan is tired.

"Do you wanna sit down?" I ask.

He doesn't answer but slides into the chair beside him. I sit on the couch, too, so that he doesn't feel threatened by me standing.

"I'm assuming you came here to talk," I say. "I'm listening."

"Mom is sad, Jay."

"Why?"

"Because you're gone."

I inhale a long, deep breath, hoping it keeps my heart from splintering. But there's no amount of oxygen or time or conversation that can stop it from happening. Inside, I fall apart.

"It reminds me of after Dad died," he says sadly. "She would smile and act like it was fine during the day. But as soon as Carter and I were in bed, if I listened closely enough, I could hear her cry. And she's doing that again now."

My head hangs in defeat.

"It's my fault," he says.

"No." I jerk my eyes to his. "This isn't your fault."

"It is. I was pretty shitty to you, and I wasn't very nice to her either." He swallows, shifting his weight from one foot to the other. "I wasn't respectful to either of you and it's my fault you had a fight and it's my fault you left and it's my fault she's crying."

He struggles not to cry. I struggle not to march across the room and pull him into a hug. That's probably what he needs, but that's also likely to make him feel like a child when he's very much trying to be a man.

"Let's get a few things straight," I say. "None of this is your fault. If it was, I'd tell you. I'd talk to you man-to-man."

"Even though I've been acting like a baby?"

I smile at him.

I'm uncertain of how much to tell him. How deep do I go in explaining this complicated situation to a child? As I mull over the question, he sits stoically before me. He's ready to take the blame as long as it fixes his mother.

And that's pretty damn mature.

"You think you're acting like a baby?" I ask. "Because I think you're acting more like a man than I've seen anyone behave in a long time."

His brows lift. "Really?"

"Don't get me wrong. The shit you pulled at your house the other night was childish."

Dylan's face falls.

"But that's the thing about men, and about people in general," I say. "We don't have it together all the time. And when we go through things that are painful or hard, like losing your dad, it can make it really hard to always do the right thing."

He nods, watching me closely.

"Look, the fact that you came over here tonight—even though I wish you would've told your mother or left a note or something—because you have a problem and need help is mature. And being able to take responsibility for your mistakes is as mature as it comes, Dylan. I respect the hell out of you for that."

His lips twist, and I think he might cry.

My heart goes into my throat. "What happened between your mother and me isn't your fault." I swallow. "Actually, it's my fault, if you want to know the truth."

"Why? What did you do?"

I can't sit. I stand and move enough to try to dispel some of the energy building inside me.

"Do you know how the loss of your father makes you scared that you could lose your mother?" I ask.

"Yeah."

"Well, I know that feeling. And do you know how that feeling made you angry? It made you feel like everything was your enemy. Your dad died unexpectedly in a car crash in the middle of the night, so you can't trust anything. At any time, something might steal someone else you love from right under your nose."

He nods. This time, tears well up in his eyes.

I stop and face him. "That pain is indescribable, and it puts you in panic mode. You push everyone away because you know you wouldn't survive that twice . . ."

"Yes. That's right." Tears flow down his cheeks. "No one gets it. No one understands. It's like everyone else can go on like they're not worried that another one of us is going to be plucked away. Carter is too little to understand it, I guess. But I feel like I'm the only one worrying about it—the only one trying to keep us safe."

"I get it."

"How?" He wipes his nose with the back of his hand. "How do you get it?"

I exhale and sit down on the couch again.

I don't want to go here with Dylan—I don't want to go here at all. But it's the only way for him to understand that I get it. And that I'm not the enemy.

"Years ago, I met a woman with a little baby girl. We fell in love, and she moved in with me. And I raised that little girl like my own child for many years."

Dylan's tears slow as he listens.

"Izzy, that was the little girl's name, wasn't my blood daughter, but damn it if I didn't love her like she was. She couldn't have been more mine. I would've done anything for her—I would've died for her."

"What happened to her?"

I sigh. "Things didn't work out between me and her mother. And her mom moved her across the country and refused to let me talk to her again. Because I'm not her biological dad, I don't have any rights. If I pressured her to let me see Izzy, it would've made things a lot worse for all of us—most of all for Izzy."

"So, what? You never see her again? That's bullshit, Jay."

"I know." I smile at him. "It is bullshit, and it hurt me like no pain I've ever felt. And for years, I felt like I couldn't survive that again. I walled myself off, steaming with anger, and refused to let anyone close to me. It felt safer to keep everyone at arm's length rather than to let them in and risk that kind of devastation."

"How did you get over it?"

I laugh softly. "Your mom fell off your deck. Your little brother kept coming by to use my pumper."

He cocks his head to the side, absorbing my words. And for the first time, I think Dylan is listening.

And for the first time, I think I'm listening to myself.

I didn't just get over it from Gabrielle and Carter. I got over it because of Dylan too.

My heart tightens as I look at him. "Do you know what else helped me?"

"What's that?"

"You." I grin. "I didn't realize it until this moment, but you are like looking in the mirror in a lot of ways."

"We don't look anything alike."

I chuckle. "No, we don't. But your anger and defiance and . . ." I scoot to the edge of the couch. "Do you know how you use being pissed off to keep everyone away from you? No one will approach a guy who looks like he wants to bite their head off. Right?"

His face sobers, and I know I've hit the nail on the head.

I talk faster. "That's me, Dylan. Or it's been me, anyway. You've been through some shit and have every right to be mad at the world. When I look at you, I see that pain and I hate it for you. I want you to let some of it go and enjoy your life. You're just a kid. There's so much more to life for you, and I know your dad would want you to enjoy it. Your mom would do anything for you to be happy. Hell, Dylan—*I* want you to enjoy it."

"You don't think that Izzy would want you to enjoy your life?"

Fucking kid. Wetness dots the corners of my eyes. "I do. And it wasn't until I met you that I could see that perspective. You've helped me whether you know it or not, and I want to be there for you."

"So how do I get through being pissed off all the time?" he asks. "How do I stop feeling like I want to punch everyone? I don't want to fight with my mom all the time. I want to be another kid at school and not be the one that everyone expects to screw up. And I don't want to live with this . . . this twisted-up pain in my stomach every day either. But I don't know what to do."

I rest my elbows on my knees and smile at the kid who just taught me a lesson without meaning to.

"The only way to get through it, Dylan, is to look around at what you still have. Your mom would do anything in the world for you. Every decision she makes is done after she analyzes from ten directions to make sure it won't hurt you and Carter."

He grins.

"And you have Carter, who thinks you're a jerk face sometimes but also pretty cool," I say.

Dylan laughs.

"And," I say, holding my breath, "if you'll accept my apology for walking away from your family, maybe you can have me."

His smile wobbles.

"I don't want to replace your dad, Dylan. He sounds like an amazing guy. I hope, although I doubt that it's true, that someone out there is reminding Izzy of how much I love her. And that's what I want to do for you and Carter." I sigh. "Christopher built a hell of a good man in you and Carter. I want to have a chance to have the honor of being a part of your lives."

Dylan sits taller in his chair. "Let me ask you a question."

"Sure."

"If I have all of that, what all do you have?"

The smirk on his lips lifts my spirits, and I realize I'm not dealing with a little boy. I'm dealing with a young man—one who understands a lot more than people give him credit for.

"You want to be there for me and my brother, but what about my mom?" he asks.

"I'm pretty sure I'll have to grovel, but I'm hoping she'll accept my apology."

"Does this mean you'll make my mom stop crying?"

Together, our lips part into a grin.

The silence in the room isn't so deafening now.

I stand, and Dylan follows me to his feet. The air between us isn't so tense. I think we're both a lot lighter than before.

"No pressure," I say, leading him to the door. "But you can talk to me anytime. I'm not trying to be your dad—"

"Jay." He turns to me and stops by the doorway. "I know."

"I'm glad."

He sighs. "I better get home before Mom does check on me. I wouldn't put it past her to call the police and have everyone in Alden looking for me."

"It's just because she loves you."

He smiles the first real, wide smile I've seen on him. "I know."

I open the door, and he steps into the darkness.

"You are going to fix this, right?" he asks over his shoulder.

"Let me get a plan together. Your mom deserves more than a simple *I'm sorry*."

"Well, don't take forever."

I laugh as he jogs across the lawn.

I wait until he's safely back inside his house before I close the door. Then I walk to the kitchen window and gaze across the yard.

My heart is warm, almost full, as I watch the light turn on in Gabrielle's bedroom. There's one final piece that I need to click everything in place. I need her. My girl. *The love of my fucking life.*

No matter what it takes, I'm going to fix this. I'm going to convince Gabrielle to take me back. It might have taken me a long time to get here, but I'm not going back.

They are mine—all three of them. And I won't let them go again.

CHAPTER TWENTY-EIGHT

Gabrielle

"Feelin' a little froggy today," I say, eyeing the outlet covers that need to be changed in the kitchen. "But do I feel froggy enough to leap?"

I clean up the boys' breakfast mess and try to keep myself distracted so I don't open the curtains and look at Jay's house. I thought it would get easier as each day passed, but it hasn't. Even when Della asked me to go to Murray's last weekend, I turned her down. Whereas I was so eager to go out and live again just a few weeks ago, I have no use for it now.

It's almost as if I found what I was looking for.

Too bad I can't have it.

My eyes are a little puffy from crying last night. I told the boys I have allergies. They were only too happy to take my explanation and continue their lives. I'm happy they don't know how wrecked I am over Jay. It would disassemble the progress I've made with Dylan over the last few days. *Let's hope that lasts.*

I rummage around beneath the sink and find my pink tool bag.

How could Jay walk away from me like that? Was I misreading the situation? Or is he truly just that nervous to get involved again?

"To hell with Jay," I say, finding my screwdriver. "If he can just toss me aside and not realize that I am afraid, too—that it's hard for me to consider losing another man I love—then fuck him."

I wipe my face with the end of my shirt.

"Let's roll the dice today and try a little electrical work," I say. "What's the worst that can happen? I know how to find the breaker box."

My eyes instantly fill with tears as I remember the only time I've been down there. *With him.*

I'm reaching for the outlet when my doorbell sounds, filling the house with the melody of a dying fox.

"Gotta get that changed too," I say, reaching the front door. I pull it open, and all the air vacates my lungs.

Jay.

"Hey," he says carefully.

"What are you doing here?"

I steel myself against his smile, leaning into how uncertain it is instead of how handsome he looks first thing in the morning. I don't flinch and barely blink. I'm not sure what to make of this.

"Can I come in?" he asks.

"I'd rather you didn't."

He runs a hand through his hair. "I committed the biggest mistake I've ever made and walked away from you."

What? My hand slides down the side of the door until it falls limp at my side.

"I've barely been able to breathe, Gabrielle. I've avoided being home so I didn't have to watch you living without me. Not a second has passed that I haven't thought of you and your boys and wished that I was welcome here with everything in me."

I force a swallow. My head spins, unsure what to make of this. I want to jump in his arms, have him wrap me up against him, and breathe in his cologne. I want what I thought we had.

But if I do that, if I give in without knowing why he's suddenly pivoting back to me, it will be a mistake. I hate that it's true. It's just too bad that I'm wise enough to know that unless he's truly had an epiphany and isn't acting out of loneliness, this will all play out again.

That's not an option.

There can't be Band-Aids when it comes to my family. Either he gets it, or he doesn't. He's in, or he's out. And that's his choice to make.

"Believe it or not, my reaction was based out of fear . . . but also out of wanting what's best for you and your boys," he says.

My sight blurs and I will myself not to cry. *Stay strong, Gabby. Get through this.*

"Dylan came by last night," he says.

"*What?* Dylan came by your house? When?"

"It was late."

I groan. *What did Dylan do now?*

"We had a long talk," Jay says, shoving his hands in his pockets. "Well, as long as a teenage boy is willing to talk."

I smile at that.

"And when he left, we had cleared the air and come to an understanding." He chuckles. "He didn't mean to, but he made me think a lot last night."

"I'm sorry. I had no idea he left the house, which probably makes me a bad mother. But I'll talk to him. I'll tell him not to bother you."

"You see, I hope that's impossible."

I balk. "Excuse me?"

He runs a hand down his jaw, his eyes searching mine. I have no idea what's happening, what they talked about, or why Dylan felt it necessary to talk to Jay without talking to me first. Especially considering his outburst sparked this fallout. I also don't know why Jay is here, and that's eating a hole in my gut.

"Jay, I'm sorry for—"

"Stop."

"Stop what?" His tone slices through me. "Did you come over here wanting a fight? Because I'll give you a fight."

He smirks, and I see red.

"Let me tell you something," I say, poking his chest. "You don't get to do this. You don't get to leave me and break my fucking heart." My voice cracks, but I keep going. "Then come over here and stand on my porch and tell me my son was bothering you, and it made you think, and now you want to . . . I don't know what you want. But I want you to leave just like you did before."

Tears gather in my eyes, and it takes everything I have not to break out into a sob.

"Gabrielle, please. Let me finish."

"You already finished us. You walked away. You told me it can never happen between us. *I* didn't do that. *You did.*"

Tears trickle down my face despite my anger. Crying in front of him only makes me madder. It's just new material for me to obsess over tonight when I go to bed, and God knows I don't need more things to ponder.

"Please leave, Jay," I say, looking at his handsome face for the last time. "And don't come back."

He doesn't move. Not a single muscle in his body twitches. He stands in place and looks at me like he's trying to decide what to make of this situation.

"I have to go," I say, turning to the house. "I have outlets to change."

"That's electrical."

I smile, knowing he can't see it. "So it is."

"Damn it, Gabrielle."

He steps in front of me, blocking the doorway.

I commit every line in his face to memory. The way the corners of his eyes crinkle in the morning light. How his lips are shaped, and how his brows pull together when he's thinking.

Just as I finish my inspection, my vision clouds over again. I don't try to hide it from him. *Why bother?* Let him remember that he broke my heart.

"Gabrielle," he says, his voice clear and warm. "I'm sorry for hurting you. I let another woman's actions affect my relationship with you, and that's wrong. There's really no excuse."

I blink, trying to keep the tears from falling, and shove the screwdriver in my back pocket.

He reaches for me but stops short of making contact. Instead, he smiles. "I came here to tell you that I will never walk away from you again and I'm a fucking fool for doing it the first time. I'm fighting for us and I won't stop."

I gasp, sucking in a breath that isn't discreet. It earns a twitch of his lips.

"My respect for you runs deep," he says. "If you don't trust me, if you want to protect your boys, that's fine. I understand. But I will work every fucking day to show you that I'm committed. *I'm here.* I will fight for us, even if you think it's over." He takes a step toward me. "Because it's not over for me. *It can never be over.* Because I love the hell out of you."

"Jay . . ."

His name breaks across my lips, and tears flood my cheeks. I consider that I'm dreaming—that I tried to change the outlet and finally got electrocuted. But when he slides his arms around me and brings his lips to mine, it's real. *He's real.*

This is real.

He rests his forehead against mine. "You're in control. You call the shots. I'll play by your rules as long as you let me play."

"I didn't expect this. I'm kinda unprepared."

"Will you let me love you?" he asks. "Can I have another chance?"

He pulls back and searches my face, undoubtedly looking for a sign of hope.

"Before I agree to anything," I say, having already decided what I will do, "what kind of a chance do you want?"

"All of it. The whole chance. As much of a chance as you'll give me." He flashes me his crooked grin. "I have Dylan's blessing, in case that helps."

"What?" I laugh. "How much did you guys talk last night?"

His grin grows wider. “Long enough for him to not hear you cry in bed.”

My stomach drops. “He heard me?”

“Yeah. And he came over and asked me to make you stop.”

My sweet, sweet boy.

The tears come again, but for a different reason this time. It feels better to cry out of happiness and relief than sadness.

“Well, I’m glad you listened to him,” I say.

“You have no idea.”

I don’t know what that means, but I don’t ask. Something tells me the two of them share a secret. It’s more than I could have hoped for.

Jay takes both my hands. “I love you. I thought I might, and that’s partially why I bailed. But I realized last night I love you so much that I can’t walk away. All I could do was hide from it—or try to, anyway.” He strokes the back of my hand with his thumb. “But I also care about your boys, Gabrielle. That’s a stickier situation, but I want to be here for them. As much as I missed you, I missed Carter needing my pumper and knowing Dylan was okay.”

The stress and weight on my shoulders evaporates into the warm air. Suddenly, everything is as it’s supposed to be.

“I love you,” I say, watching his face light up. “That’s why it hurt so bad when you broke things off. Because I had already trusted you with my heart. I just didn’t realize it.”

He plants another kiss on my lips. This time, he lingers a little longer.

“One more thing,” he says, his hands roaming down my back. “No more electrical.”

He jerks the screwdriver out of my pocket and shoves it in his.

“Hey,” I protest, laughing.

Jay scoops me up, my legs going over one arm and my back supported by his other. I wrap my arms around his neck as he carries me inside.

“How long until the boys are home?” he asks.

"Why aren't you at work?"

"Because I had to fix things with my girl. Priorities."

I sigh happily. "The kids will be gone for another six hours."

"I know a way we can pass the time."

"Me too." I kiss him again. "Let's change the outlets."

His eyes twinkle. "Well, since you need my help, you'll have to buy my time. And I'm not cheap."

My stomach clenches. "And how do you suggest I do that? What kind of currency do you trade in, Mr. Stetson?"

"Let's go upstairs. I have *lots* of ideas."

I giggle as he carries me to my bedroom.

EPILOGUE

Gabrielle

Boys! Time for dinner!" I shout into the backyard.

My heart sings as I wait for a reply. Happiness bubbles out of me so freely that I annoy myself. *Life is damn good.*

"Mom! Come here!" Carter's voice finds me before I can find him. "You gotta see this."

I toss the hand towel I was carrying onto the kitchen counter and make my way onto the deck. Carter and Jay are in the field between our houses, playing catch. Dylan is in Jay's driveway with the derby car and a pint of paint.

"I finally taught Jay how to throw," Carter says. "Watch this!" He punches a hand in his glove and focuses on the man across from him. "You ready, big guy?"

Jay gives me a look, making me giggle.

"Okay," Carter says, holding up his glove. "Right here. You can do it. Step and throw."

Jay barely tosses the ball, and it sails through the air and hits the middle of Carter's glove. He doesn't squeeze it fast enough, and the ball falls unceremoniously to the grass.

"Ugh. You'll get it. Keep working on it," Carter says.

Jay shrugs, holding his arms out to the sides.

"Yeah, Jay," Dylan says. "Keep working on it, and one day, you might not suck."

Jay turns his back to me. I can't hear what he says to Dylan, but it gets a full belly laugh out of my older son.

It's hard to believe that two months have passed since Jay showed back up on my porch. Carter and Dylan weren't surprised to see Jay at the house that afternoon, leading me to believe that they plotted together to fix things.

God love them.

"Wanna see the derby car, Mom?" Dylan asks, getting to his feet.

I step outside into the bright evening sun and cross the yard. Jay hasn't stayed at his house more than once or twice since our reunion. Whenever he tells the boys he must go after dinner, they give him hell until he agrees to stay.

I'm not complaining.

Jay reaches for me as I walk by. I stop, letting him pull me in for a kiss.

"They wanted this thing red," Dylan says, motioning to the car. "I told them every derby car is red."

"And I didn't want to do the painting," Jay says, walking with his arm around my waist.

"And I'm not a very good painter," Carter says. He tucks himself under my other side. "So Dylan said he'd paint if I let him pick the color."

Dylan looks at me and smiles.

Black and blue. Of course.

"It looks good, guys," I say, checking out the car the three of them have been working on for two weeks. I'm not sure what a derby car is supposed to look like. But even if this is all wrong, my guys made it. It's perfect. "You guys are a good team."

Dylan and Jay exchange a grin. I think my heart might burst.

Carter bounces up and down like a pogo stick. "*Jay . . .*"

Dylan nods.

Jay smiles.

What's going on here?

"Mom," Dylan says, "I have to tell you something."

"What?"

My curiosity is piqued—and not in a good way. I stare at Dylan, waiting for the ball to drop.

"I know we still fight sometimes, and I can still be a—"

"Jerk face," Carter cuts in.

"Be nice," I tell my youngest.

"Whatever," he says.

Dylan laughs. "Dad would like this. And it makes me happy to see you so happy."

"Aw," I say. "That's so sweet, Dylan."

Carter shoves off me and stands by his brother. "And I want everyone to know I'm *very* happy. Like, very, very happy. I like watching movies with you guys, teaching Jay to play baseball."

Jay sighs, making me grin.

"I like going for hot chocolate at Betty Lou's with Jay in the morning before school," Carter says. "I like when you tuck me in at night, Mom. I like when you cook us dinner and we all sit at the table. I like it when—"

"That's enough," Dylan says under his breath.

Carter covers his mouth with his hand. "Oops. Sorry. That's all."

Jay kisses the side of my head and then stands next to Carter.

The hairs on the back of my neck stand on end, and butterflies take flight in my belly. My three guys all look at me with anticipation. *What the heck is going on?*

"I've already talked to the boys about this," Jay says as the boys beam at his side. "I love you, Gabrielle. You gave me another chance at life. You welcomed me into your family, and—"

"And we want Jay to be a part of our family," Carter says.

What? My heart thunders so hard in my chest that I think I might pass out.

Dylan looks at the sky. "We practiced this. How do you not remember when you're supposed to go?"

"Because I'm a kid." Carter throws up his hands, almost hitting his brother in the face. "I'm doing my best here, okay?"

Jay watches me, not a bit flustered by their antics. I might find them funny if I weren't waiting for him to speak.

My hands start to shake as I anticipate what's taking place. Surely I'm wrong. I don't want to be wrong. But how am I not?

"Gabrielle Solomon," Jay says, lowering himself to one knee.

I gasp, covering my mouth with my hands. Tears fill my eyes as I try to stay focused on this moment.

He pulls a small black box from his pocket and opens it. The diamond inside catches the sunlight.

"Will you do me the biggest honor in the world, and be my wife?" Jay asks.

"Say yes, Mom," Carter says. "I mean it."

I laugh, falling into Jay's arms. He holds me tight as the boys chatter away beside us.

I'm reminded, unfortunately, of what he said about Melody. She left him because he wouldn't marry her. A streak of panic rips through me, and I squeeze my eyes shut.

"You don't feel pressured into this, do you?" I whisper into his ear. "Because this—"

He pulls back and looks me in the eye. "We're already together forever. This shows you, and the boys, that I'm not going anywhere. Ever. And that's important to me."

"Did you say yes, Mom?" Carter asks.

I step away and give Jay my hand. "Yes, Jay Stetson. I will marry you."

"Yay!" Carter shouts, jumping up and down.

Dylan pats Jay on the shoulder as he stands up.

"Now let's go eat dinner," Carter says. "I'm so hungry."

Jay slips the ring on my finger and kisses me.

"I can't believe you did this," I say, taking in the beautiful ring. "I . . . I'm so damn happy, Jay."

"There's no way you're any happier than me, Gabrielle."

"Hey, Mom!" Carter says from halfway across the yard. "How long do marriages last?"

I look up at Jay and laugh.

"A long time," Dylan says. "Leave them alone. Let them have a moment, Carter."

"But how long is a long time?" Carter asks.

"We will be married our whole lives," Jay says, squeezing my hand. "Between now and forever."

ACKNOWLEDGMENTS

There are so many people to thank and acknowledge for helping get this book into your hands.

First and foremost, I would like to thank my Creator. Always.

My husband and four sons are my biggest cheerleaders. They pick up the slack when I'm on a deadline and bring me dinner to my desk. I literally could not do this without their love and support. Also, my extended family is so wonderful about the oddities of my job. I'm grateful for them, as well.

I want to thank my editors, Anh Schluep and Alison Dasho, for believing in this story. A huge thank you to Lindsey Faber for working with me again. Everyone at Montlake—Kellie, Lauren, Lindsey, Ashley, Karen, and the team—is so encouraging and supportive. I'm blessed to work with such an amazing group of people.

Thank you to my agent, Georgana Grinstead at the Seymour Agency, for always being at the ready to tackle a project or an idea. Big hugs to Kim Cermak, Christine Miller, Ratula Roy, Meagan Reynoso, Sarah Norris, and Kelley Beckham at Valentine PR for being one of the hardest-working teams in the business. I'm blessed to work with you all.

I'm grateful to my assistant, Tiffany Remy, for her help in keeping the ball rolling. Thank you to Marion Archer, Jenny Sims, and Michele Ficht for being not only valuable pieces in my book puzzles but also great friends. I'm lucky to be able to work with Brittni Van (the Running Bookworm)—especially when I hit a brain block. Stephanie

Gibson, Kaitie Reister, Jordan Fazzini, and Sue Maturo are key pieces in the Locke worlds online. I'm so blessed to have you all on my side.

I have so many peers whom I look up to and lean on. I appreciate all of you more than you'll ever know: Mandi Beck, S.L. Scott, Jessica Prince, Dylan Allen, Anjelica Grace, Kenna Rey, and Chelle Sloan.

To Books by Adriana Locke on Facebook—your support and encouragement are overwhelming in the very best ways. Thank you for being my happy space and for loving my stories. I love you.

And to every reader and listener reading or listening to this—thank you for taking a chance on this story. I know you have a million choices, and I'm honored you chose to spend a little of your time in one of my worlds.

Addy xo

ABOUT THE AUTHOR

Adriana Locke is the *USA Today* bestselling author of *Nothing But It All*, *The Sweet Spot*, the Landry Family series, and the Exception novels, among many others. She writes contemporary romances about the two things she knows best: big families and small towns. Her stories are about ordinary people finding extraordinary love with the perfect combination of heart, heat, and humor. Hailing from a tiny town in the Midwest, Adriana spends her free time with her high school sweetheart (whom she married more than twenty years ago) and their four sons (who truly are her best work). Her kitchen may be a perpetual disaster, but if all else fails, there's always pizza. She loves fall weather, football, reading about alpha heroes, everything pumpkin, pretending to garden, and connecting with readers. For more information, visit www.adrianalocke.com.